A n

BEATRICE BRADSHAW

Love in the Scottish Winter Highlands

Part 1 in the 'Escape to Scotland'-Series

One wintry castle in Scotland, two frozen hearts on the line...

Londoner Marla inherits a crumbling castle in Scotland and is determined to restore it. Her handsome, grumpy neighbour Niall is still haunted by the memories of his wife's fatal accident. He's desperate to leave the Highlands and his past behind.

Sparks fly when they meet. But their instant attraction sours when Niall learns that Marla stands in his way. He wants to sell his land, which he can only do if she gives up her castle. And that's never going to happen.

Wherever they meet, they clash. But a Christmas party stirs unexpected feelings. And what begun as a rivalry turns into an irresistible attraction. Until during a snowstorm, their guards come down—and they share a night of deep desire.

Can Marla thaw Niall's frozen heart or will his secret agenda tear them apart?

Content Note

Please be aware: this story contains two explicit open door scenes and some profanity. It also references topics that could trigger certain audiences, such as abandonment, cancer, a suicide attempt, alcoholism, and burnout. Mostly rooted in the backstories of the characters, but it's best to be prepared.

For my grandparents

Chapter One

Pale morning light pierced through the clouds. The cold air smelled like peat fire and rain, like smoke, like frost, like everything that she loved about winter. The hills around this small town were almost as chalky as the sky. From a distance, they looked like folds of a wool blanket. It was still early. Marla flipped up the collar of her peacoat and walked along the cobblestoned street. Despite the November chill, her face was glowing.

This place, half-snuggled in a valley, was a far cry from the busy, tiring city of London she had called home for fourteen years and left behind yesterday morning.

Yet here she was. In Scotland.

Marla swallowed, unsure of what lay ahead. The past few weeks had been a whirlwind. A swirl of conflicting emotions surged in her chest. There was a rush of anticipation, yes, but also a warning that nagged at her mind, reminding her of the risks. It was the glimmer of possibility, too hard to ignore, that made her cheeks flush.

I'm really doing this, aren't I?

As she sauntered to her appointment with the solicitor, she took in the sights and sounds of Kilcranach's old core. Side roads led up the hill and wound their way through the village like a gemstone necklace that someone had carelessly dropped. In contrast, the high street was built in a straight line and flanked by quaint shops with whitewashed facades. With their slate roofs and pointed gables, the houses looked like they had been there since the time of Mary, Queen of Scots. Or at least since some enlightened, eighteenth-century landowner had stuffed his crofters into efficient lodgings so they could collect kelp while sheep grazed on what used to be their land. The sea, as the screeching chorus of gulls in the background announced, wasn't very far away.

Behind a bend, Marla noticed the small castle looming in the distance. A structure with blonde sandstone walls, overgrown with ivy. Even from afar, it appeared as sad as in the photos. And calling it a castle was a stretch. It looked more defeated than defensive. Although it must once have been an inviting eighteenth-century country house. Marla imagined glamorous balls and hunting parties with people wearing tweed. In truth, she had no concept of what the Scottish nobility used to do in their extensive spare time two hundred years ago. Even two years ago, for that matter.

Today, the former grand house was a neglected three-storey building with dull panes in its many large mullion windows. It seemed tired, forgotten, and lonely. This house had the weight of well over two hundred years pressing down on it—and it appeared as if it was done pushing back.

Her house now. Her weight.

Marla snorted in disbelief, and a frosty cloud of breath formed in front of her nose. What the hell had happened? Four weeks ago, she had been living her life in London, working as an oncology nurse for the National Health Service NHS. Often reading books while curled up on her couch. Completely unspectacular and utterly intentional. After everything, Marla had designed her life to be as stable and safe as possible. A solid wooden drawer with cosy velvet lining.

Until one phone call changed it all.

She had just returned from running errands when her mobile rang. At first, she thought it was a prank. Who wouldn't?

'Good afternoon! Marla Wilson? You will not have heard of me, but I have something important to tell you,' said the male voice on the other end.

'Not at all a bizarre thing to say. Bye.'

'Wait! There is something you must know,' the unknown caller cut in.

'Oh, really? Must I?' Marla's day off had been unpleasant so far. She was in a *mood*. 'Let me guess: you're calling in the name of Prince Harry and need cash for a charity? Or better still, you're a Nigerian prince and need my help with wiring four million dollars to my account? Guess what, I don't believe in princes and—'

'Miss Wilson, there seems to be a misunderstanding. My name is William Collins. I work with Arniston Solicitors, and the reason I'm calling you today is to inform you of an inheritance.'

'Ha! I knew it. No thanks,' she scoffed.

'Does the name Gordon Wilson ring a bell?'

Marla gasped. That was her grandda's name.

How does he… What…?

Anger welled up inside her. 'What do you know of my grandfather? Is this a cruel joke? My grandda died two years ago. Don't you feel ashamed using dead people's names in a scam?'

'No, no! Of course not, Miss Wilson. It is just… How do I put this delicately? It seems that in his youth, Gordon Wilson had made an acquaintance of some… emotional significance. Let us leave it at that.'

'Pardon me?' She noticed a trace of shrillness in her voice.

'I would much prefer to discuss the details with you in person. But as far as we know, he knew the young Lady Hamilton, and it appears that Gordon Wilson… made a lasting impression on her.'

'Lady who?'

'Lady Helena Cecilia Hamilton,' he said.

'Never heard of her.'

'I see. Well, that is not at all surprising. She lived a secluded life. Lady Hamilton passed away six months ago.'

'I don't know what to say. Eh… I'm sorry for your loss?'

'Thank you for your sympathy,' Mr Collins said. There was something in his voice that resonated with Marla. She recognised the incorruptible truth of grief. He must have held that lady in great esteem. Marla paced up and down her hallway, the shopping bags still by the door.

'She was our client for many decades,' he continued. 'A good person, an amiable woman. One of a kind. She died without an heir, but her will—here the entire affair becomes more than a little unorthodox—unmistakably states that in these circumstances, the castle and estate should pass to the living descendants of Gordon Wilson.'

'What? Okay. That's… mental,' Marla said. 'My grandfather mentioned no lady. Ever. And I'm sure my gran wouldn't have approved of other women in his life. If you know what I mean.'

'Certainly, Miss Wilson. I did not intend to insinuate—'

'Right. So, wait. You're telling me that a complete stranger left a castle—an entire castle—to my grandda and his offspring? You can't be serious.'

'I assure you, this is not a joke to me, Miss Wilson.'

'Oh, I don't think this is funny either. And I have a lot of questions. Like why didn't he tell anyone about any of this? Ever? What on earth is going on?' Her voice rose. 'How am I supposed to even know who my grandda was dating in his youth? That's wrong,' she huffed. 'And who in their right mind doesn't give their godforsaken castle to the National Trust instead of leaving it to a stranger? Doesn't that sound suspiciously wrong to you?'

'To you.'

'Who?'

'To you. She left Hazelbrae House to you. We have done some digging, you see. Since he passed two years ago and your mother in 1992, you are the only living blood relative of Gordon Wilson. Unless you have children, of course, but we could not find any records,' he explained. 'Hence, it follows—according to Lady Hamilton's will—that it is you who inherits her estate.'

Marla flopped onto a chair, ungracefully landing on the cupcake she had bought herself as a treat and placed there when her phone rang. She didn't notice it. All she noticed was a tingling numbness ascending from her legs, along with an uncomfortable ringing in her ears. After a pause, she said, 'No siblings. No children. Neither existent nor planned.'

'I apologise if this sounds intrusive. But you certainly see that we—'

'Estate,' Marla mumbled. 'What does that even mean?'

'I would much rather discuss everything in person,' he said. 'But for now, I can tell you that the inheritance encompasses a large, listed house with a few acres here in Scotland. Although the building is in a state, most unfortunately, and the land is a fraction of what it once used to be.'

'Sorry, I have to ask, for the record—are you for real? Do you have any proof of whatever you're saying, like… right now?' Not that any serious, self-respecting scammer would answer that question with anything close to the truth. Nonetheless, she had to ask.

'I guarantee that this is a most serious and lawful matter.'

She let out a breath. 'You understand that I can't simply believe everything a random stranger tells me on the phone?

That's one thing my grandda taught me,' Marla said, mostly to herself, feeling the comforting weight of Gordon's small knife in the side pocket of her jeans. Along with the all-too-familiar twinge of loss.

'Yes, Miss Wilson. That is sensible. I would expect nothing less. I can send you all the relevant information and preliminary legal documents, the title, photographs, et cetera. And then, if you're interested, Arniston Solicitors would love to welcome you to Kilcranach.'

That had been one month ago. The town hall clock towered above Marla. Its long, thin hands showed a quarter past nine. Almost time for her meeting with William Collins to finalise the particulars of this odd inheritance. She was a few minutes early. But her mind was racing, and she couldn't sit in the car for one more second. *I can't believe it,* Marla thought. *What if it's too much for me?* Initially, she'd been less than thrilled at the thought of inheriting a castle from a stranger—everybody knew those houses were bottomless money pits—let alone the mystery surrounding her grandda's dubious ex-lady-friend or whatever position Helena *Whatshername* Hamilton had once held in his life.

It was Marla's pal Trish who had encouraged her to take the leap of faith, stuff her car with her favourite clothes and books, and move to Kilcranach to take on her inheritance—a property she hadn't even set foot in.

'Marl, what are you talking about? A flipping castle in Scotland, for fuck's sake. That's an amazing opportunity. Think what you could do with that!' Trish had squealed from beneath her cloud of brown curls. 'That's how all those Mills & Boon novels start! And if it's shit, you can sell it for a few million pounds to a Danish billionaire and bam! No more worrying about pensions or any of that. That's you, sorted for life!'

Marla couldn't help but smile at the memory of Trish's innate enthusiasm and unwavering faith in the world. Most of the time, it was unfounded. But it somehow still made things better. Inexplicably. Or maybe even magically.

She moved past the bookshop. A narrow, three-storey, timber-framed building with a small café on the ground floor. A few people were grabbing a coffee to go. There was a pair of American tourists in trainers, hunched over their phones. Probably a lot fewer of them in the Highlands in November than during summer. The faint aroma of roasted beans and the scent of yellowed books wafted into the cold air. A young woman wearing a pointy hat and a black coat was peering into a shop window. Her long, emerald-green hair was fashioned into a braid and flowing down her shoulders on top of a woollen tartan shawl. She looked like a witch. Maybe, just maybe, this tiny town had more edge than Marla had imagined.

Whatever her doubts, and there were plenty, she was here now. After having drained a reassuring bottle of Bordeaux with Trish, Marla had made a promise to herself. Come rain or shine—and considering that this was Scotland, rain was the much more likely scenario—she would find a way to make it work. This wasn't just an unexpected inheritance. It was a once-in-a-lifetime opportunity to give back to her colleagues in the NHS, who worked so hard to save their patients' lives. Create a retreat for tired doctors and nurses. Like herself. Like the ones that tried to save her mum twenty-five years ago or the ones who took care of her grandparents at the end. Renovating Hazelbrae was also a way to be connected to her grandda. To honour his memory, to find out who he had really been and where he was from.

And to start over after all the loss and sorrow.

The solicitor's office was in one of the historic buildings just off the town square. The heavy door creaked as Marla opened it, revealing a claustrophobically small lobby. It wasn't even large enough to contain a gathering of five people. Two timeworn oak chairs and an equally ancient wooden reception desk testified to the age of the office. The darkly panelled walls were adorned with antique paintings of ships conquering raging waves. It smelled of dust and varnish, with a slight salty tang. The entire room seemed like the wooden sea chest of a nineteenth-century naval officer. Behind the panelled desk sat a woman with white streaks in her flaming red bob, knitting what looked like a Fair Isle jumper. She didn't so much as lift her head when the door creaked.

'Hi. Good morning,' Marla said, plastering on a polite smile.

Now the woman looked up. She gave a nod and put down her needles. 'Morning. Welcome to Arniston Solicitors. How can I help you?'

Marla explained who she was and why she was there. The receptionist nodded again. This time, with squinted eyes. As if she couldn't believe it. Neither could Marla.

'Of course. Mr Collins is expecting you, Miss Wilson,' she said, rising from her chair. 'Please follow me. And watch your step. It's a wee bit uneven.'

Marla walked behind her up a narrow spiral staircase with ornate cast iron steps and rails that were cold and coarse under her fingers.

'Ah, Miss Wilson,' Mr Collins called from the back room. 'Welcome to Arniston Solicitors! Glad you made it. How was the journey? Not entirely unpleasant, I hope?' Mr Collins emerged from his office wearing a tweed suit with a waistcoat and a pocket watch, round glasses perched at the end of his pointed nose. He looked like an obscure side character in an unpublished Sherlock Holmes story, scholarly and anachronistic to the point of eccentricity. Much more interesting in person than on the phone. Marla liked him right away.

Mr Collins ushered her into his tiny office, where several

stacks of documents were scattered around the room. The slope of the roof was low and crooked, Marla could hardly stand upright. A square window let in a few resilient rays of winter morning sunlight, illuminating several shelves of books lined up like soldiers at attention.

Over a cup of tea, Mr Collins explained the legal details of the inheritance. There was no family dispute, since this was a minor branch of the Hamiltons without relatives. The property had been surveyed and valued, the inventory and other forms completed, taxes and debts paid. So was the basic upkeep for a year, excluding insurance. Now was the time for the title transfer. Marla understood all of it, or so she hoped. Dealing with small print had never been her core strength. She would inherit Hazelbrae House with about ten acres of surrounding land. Apparently, Helena Hamilton had declared that the house was not to be turned into a museum. 'Hazelbrae is neither a shrine nor a zoo, it is a home,' were her words, as related by Mr Collins. Miraculously, there was no remaining debt on the estate, but there had been no renovations since the 1980s. Good bones, neglected state. The estimated renovation and conservation costs were… astronomical didn't even begin to describe it.

And yet… Marla had felt drawn to Hazelbrae since she had first seen the pictures in Mr Collins' e-mail.

It was still baffling, though. 'What about their relationship? Were they—' Marla trailed off.

'Lady Hamilton and your grandfather?'

'Yes, those two. Who else would I be talking about?' she said, narrowing her eyes at him.

'Sadly, there is not much more that I can tell you.' Mr Collins adjusted his glasses. 'She changed her will shortly before her serious health problems started, and I never had the opportunity to ask her personally. It is all a mystery. Or simply private.' He dug out a document and followed the lines with his index finger. 'According to Lady Hamilton's will, in which she bequeathed her estate to his family, Gordon Wilson was, and I quote, "the truest, dearest friend I ever had. I owe him my life and more than I could ever repay." End of quote.'

'What's that supposed to mean? Did he give her a kidney or something?'

'I could not tell you. Lady Hamilton was a private and fascinating woman.' Shifting his glasses again, he continued. 'My guess? Since your grandfather was from this area and moved away when he was twenty, if our research is correct, they most likely knew each other in their youth. Mr Wilson must have been a friend or confidant to Lady Hamilton. Class difference aside.' Mr Collins leaned back in his squeaking swivel chair and folded his hands in his lap. 'We could try to investigate further. Although I have not the slightest idea how. We looked at her correspondence, but it didn't include any significant private letters or documents, unfortunately.'

Marla shrugged. 'I'm just so curious. I mean, who wouldn't be? There must be more to this story, but it seems we're not getting anywhere right now. So be it.' She straightened her shoulders. 'All right then, Mr Solicitor. Let's do this.'

With the legal details outlined, explained, and mostly understood, Marla picked up Mr Collins' pen in her right hand, her left hand on the document. She felt the tight weave of the paper fibres under her fingertips. The pen had an old-fashioned shape and a black, lacquered finish that had been worn smooth by generations of signers. Marla took a deep breath.

A few circles and scratches later, Mr Collins announced, 'Congratulations, Miss Wilson. You are now the proud owner of Hazelbrae House. Good luck.'

Marla left the solicitor's office exhilarated, bordering on terrified. To calm her jittery limbs, she decided to walk from the village to the castle and explore the area. It was eleven. Plenty of time in the day.

Time to make plans.

She would restore Hazelbrae House and, with a bit of luck and lots of work, turn it into a retreat for NHS staff. Marla would find a new purpose and her roots here. She had rented out her tiny flat in London and pressed pause on her job. Indefinitely most likely. It dawned on her how much she had been longing for a new beginning.

There was no way back. A half-ruined castle in this remote Scottish village was her home now, which left only one possible conclusion… she must be insane.

Chapter Two

Niall trudged along the churned-up dirt path through the forest on his inspection rounds, his boots squelching in patches of moss and mud. Winter had stripped the trees of their foliage, leaving behind brittle branches outlined against the hazy sky, like a charcoal sketch.

A heaviness crept into the air. He knew the Highland weather and these woods like the back of his hand. This was his land, after all. It had been his father's and his grandfather's before that. But Niall didn't feel a sense of connection. Not anymore. Only obligation, to an extent.

Besides his own forestry, he had been an estate manager on the Hamilton land for thirteen years now. Close to a third of his life. It was a job that needed to be done, and he happened to be the one doing it. There was nothing more to it.

'Barclay? Barclay!' Niall called out for his dog. He paused and listened. Nothing but the long, rolling sigh of the breeze as it rustled through the branches. Niall turned around to survey the territory, to reassure himself that everything here was fine, that nothing was out of place. There were only familiar sights, like the old, gnarled ash tree with its branches twisted into shapes resembling faces. He called again, and this time he heard a bark in the distance.

That silly bugger can't help himself, he thought affectionately.

Thirty seconds later, the black and white border collie came shooting out of the thicket towards him. Niall smiled and scratched Barclay behind his ears. 'You sure love to run off on your own, don't you, boy?' At this time of year, there was nothing to be wary of on this part of the estate, and he allowed his faithful companion these independent excursions. At least Barclay always returned to him, no matter how far he had run off. It was some comfort that there was one thing he could always rely on—the unconditional love of his dog. 'Let's get going, eh?' And the two of them plodded along the same trail they always followed, Barclay alongside his owner and friend. It was in fleeting moments like these when Niall was almost at peace.

Almost.

As they walked, Niall noticed the ambassadors of winter, like a stray snowflake settling on his shoulder, the chill in the air, the flurries of fallen leaves being tousled by the breeze. Out here, in the middle of the forest behind Hazelbrae House, there was always an air of peace, a serene atmosphere that he had come to cherish.

Hazelbrae.

It had been over half a year since old Lady Hamilton had died in the care home where she had spent the last months of her life. A heart attack, they said. Niall still didn't know what was going to happen to that place. That unsettled him. He didn't like loose ends.

But, more importantly, it had brought his plans to an indefinite halt.

He had mulled over it for much longer than anybody in Kilcranach would ever have suspected, but when the developer had approached him with an offer to buy his land about a year and a half ago, Niall had been ripe and ready to make a deal. He wanted to move on. There was no spark of excitement or new beginning about it. This wasn't about opening a new chapter.

No. It was about finally closing an old one.

Because, more often than not, Niall felt trapped—like a solitary wanderer in the frame of a gloomy landscape painting. Forever doomed to roam the moors.

Or forest, in his case.

With the money from selling his acreage, he would likely never have to work again. At least if he lived sensibly. He could buy a boat and live on it. Go sailing. It used to be his favourite hobby when he was a student, his soul unbent, his heart unbroken, his light undimmed.

Before… everything.

He hadn't done it in ages. But he rather wanted to be at the mercy of the elements than at the mercy of the memories that surrounded him here at every turn.

Niall stopped and zipped up his lined wax jacket. The air was getting frostier. He emitted a cloud of white breath and resumed the walk while his thoughts wandered in their own direction. He couldn't say that he had been pleased with the plans the developer had for the area—a huge luxury hunting, shooting, and fishing destination hotel with a spa for wealthy clients with helicopters and such—but it could bring a few jobs to Kilcranach. To people who needed it. Frankly, he cared little about the details. Times were changing. That was a fact. Better to change with them and make the most of it. He had been looking forward to it.

But just when he had started to feel something akin to hope, Niall had learned that Hazelbrae, sitting in the middle of it all, was a crucial part of the deal. They wanted the entire bloody thing. Not just his land. No, the crumbling mansion on the hill was the cherry on top of their billionaire-playground property cake.

Niall had tried to convince them otherwise. In vain. He

had also made several attempts to persuade old Lady Hamilton to sell. To no avail.

A part of him knew she would never be willing to cut ties to her home of over seventy years, the place where she had been born.

Still, he had to try.

Not that he didn't understand her. Hazelbrae was not just her home, but the place where her family's memories lived. Their presence was tangible in every nook of the house, starting with the faded pictures and paintings that spoke volumes about family roots that ran generations deep within this forgotten corner of the world.

No matter how eloquently Niall argued when they discussed estate matters, neither facts nor feelings made any difference. Lady Hamilton's friendly but firm response was always the same. 'My dear, dear boy,' she would say in her commanding voice, only a little frail. 'Don't you know that all of Hazelbrae is part of me? And I wouldn't sell my own arm now, would I? And what would your father think of that?' she had asked, patting his hand and shaking her head.

The last time they had spoken about it was a month before she suffered a second stroke and had to move away into care. A good six months before her death. She had finally left this place for good. He was still stuck here.

Niall had even tried to sell his land discreetly to other candidates. Unsuccessfully. Unless it was an absurdly large acreage with a romantic castle, a potential nature reserve, or one of those tiny symbolic bits of land with a fantasy title, no one seemed prepared to buy land in the Scottish Highlands.

The canopy of wiry branches parted to reveal the decaying grandeur of Hazelbrae in the distance, a splendid house in a state of forgotten glory. Grass, moss, and birch saplings sprouting from the black rain gutters. All giving silent testament to its neglect. *Only a few harsh winters away from falling into utter disrepair,* Niall reckoned. Astonishingly, the roof still held up, withstanding the years, the wind, and the intense rain here in the West. He hadn't set foot inside of Hazelbrae since… not in a long time. There was a quick sting of pain and loss. A feeling as familiar to him as these ancient woodlands. Relentless murmurs of his unforgivable mistake. Niall shook his head in an attempt to shake off his memories.

He didn't know how Lady Hamilton had spent her last time there or what the inside of Hazelbrae might look like. All he knew was this half-ruined grand house stood between him and his ticket out of Kilcranach. Between him and his hope of lifting the crushing weight that had been suffocating him for six years. Whether he liked it or not, Hazelbrae was the key to his freedom and peace.

Barclay dashed towards a babbling brook beneath a small slope. Following the path to the left would lead them past the gates of the grand old house. *Och, why the heck not? Let's see how deep those cracks really are,* he thought and whistled. Barclay obeyed and came back as fast as an arrow. Niall and his dog walked side by side through the woods.

Suddenly, he heard a voice from somewhere in the nearer distance.

'You treacherous damn shitty shit tree!'

Barclay pricked up his ears. Niall frowned.

What—

'I hate you! I hate you from the bottom of my heart! Stupid fucking tree!'

Yes, that sounded like a woman. An angry woman, Niall noted. The only problem was that her voice seemed to come from… above? Barclay jolted towards a mature oak tree and barked.

'Well, hello there! Awww, look at you. Such a good boy,' the voice said to Barclay, all anger vanished. Niall took a few steps closer to the tree. He squinted in disbelief as he peered up at the top.

A woman in a dark blue pea coat was clinging to one of the oak's branches. Her jeans were splattered with mud, and her complexion was bright red. She stared at him with a mix of surprise and suspicion. Niall blinked in bewilderment. He had no inkling who this woman was or what she was doing here.

In a tree, no less.

One of his trees, by the way.

'Hi,' she called out. 'Hello! Oh, thank God. Do you think you could help me down? I can't seem to do it on my own. Not that I would normally admit that to anyone,' she laughed nervously. The warm sound of her voice tingled in his ears. Niall furrowed his eyebrows in puzzlement. Why would a normal grown-up person climb a tree? He scoured his brain for explanations, but there were none that made any sense to him.

'What are you doing up there, if you don't mind me asking?'

'Good question. Might I suggest I tell the tale once I've returned to Planet Earth, Major Tom?'

'What's it you want me to do? Afraid I sold any space-ships or flying tin cans to the charity shop ages ago,' Niall replied.

'Ah, so you're a funny one. But I'm about ten seconds away from a proper panic attack, so if you don't mind.'

'*You* started with Major Tom.' Niall noticed he was smiling. Barclay wagged his tail in excitement. That there on the tree was not the usual squirrel.

'Get me down. Now!' she insisted. 'I mean… please?'

'All right, all right. Let's see.' Niall examined the situation. It seemed that the crucial branch about halfway down had broken, preventing her from descending the same way she must have got up. He would have been irked by the sight of damage done to the trees under his care and supervision. But he knew the inhabitants of his forest well. This particular tree was a bit of a troublemaker that had been worrying him for a while. 'Can you turn around?' he asked.

'Are you joking?' She sounded slightly angry again.

'You know, I could continue my walk and pretend this never happened,' he said, oddly enjoying this bizarre encounter.

'You would not.'

'Try me.'

'Okay, I guess I could make a quarter turn.'

'Brave,' Niall said. 'If you turn and slowly try to sit down on the branch that you're standing on right now, you could jump.'

'And break my ankle? Not a fat chance,' she said resolutely.

'I could catch you, you know.'

'You? But you're a stranger! How do I know you won't take a step to the side and let me land face-first in the mud?'

'Guess you won't know for sure until you try.'

'Honestly.' She looked dispirited. 'This is not a good way to encourage someone with trust issues.'

He folded his arms. 'Sometimes you have to take a leap of faith.'

'Really? Okay, as soon as I'm on firm ground again, we'll go into town and get matching "Live, Laugh, Love" tattoos.'

And Niall laughed. A sound so rare that Barclay barked twice in confusion. The woman in the tree shifted her feet awkwardly, still clinging to the higher branch. Gradually, and with wobbly knees, she lowered herself into a sitting position, while holding onto the bark of the thick tree trunk.

'Okay, I'm sitting.' She looked relieved.

'I can see that,' he said.

'And now I jump?'

Niall positioned himself underneath her. It was less than six feet, not too terrible. He spread his arms out. 'And now you jump.'

She landed in his arms like a hundred sacks of flour. The momentum pushed Niall backwards, staggering. She wasn't a fairy, this was a woman of substance. He lost his balance, and with a thud, they both landed on the mossy, leafy forest ground. Barclay ran circles around them, while Niall lay flat on his back. Judging by the pain, his coccyx must have hit a thick pinecone or something.

'Ouch.'

'Sorry,' she replied, sitting astride him.

Niall stared into a pair of grey eyes with a silver glint under long, dark lashes. Tiny beads of sweat had formed a tiara at her hairline. There was a dab of dirt on the tip of her nose. She bit her lower lip. 'I'm Marla, by the way,' she said. 'Thank you for being my mattress, Major Tom.'

Barclay licked her cheek and she let out a low, contented giggle.

Deep inside, Niall had always suspected that there must be some magical creatures living in these woods.

He just never thought they would be so gorgeous.

Chapter Three

'Are you hurt?' Marla asked the man that she was straddling after jumping off a tree right into his arms, like a human tree frog. *Oh God, I'm sitting on him as if we were...* She stood up, her heart racing. Marla could feel that her face was on fire, which somehow seemed to be the theme of the day.

'No,' he said and grinned. 'I'm okay. I'm Scottish. Takes a lot more to knock me out.'

His accent reminded her of her grandda. A surge of nostalgia welled up in her heart, into which droplets of grief flowed like watercolour. She let the wave subside and reached out her hand to help him up. As he took it, Marla felt his rough, warm skin against her icy fingers. So, he works with his hands, she thought and wondered why she even noticed.

'I'm Niall. And this is my dog and partner in crime, Barclay,' he said with a serious look.

His eyes were light brown and warm, like pine resin. His chestnut-coloured hair was thick, a little wavy, and untamed, as if his last haircut simply had grown out. Recklessly tousled for a man his age. He must be in his late thirties or early forties. *A bit older than me.* There were fine lines around the corners of his eyes, a sprinkle of grey at his temples and in his stubble. A galaxy of freckles spread out over his straight, domineering nose. He was over six feet, it wasn't often that she encountered men taller than herself, with broad shoulders. Unbending, exuding a quiet gravity. *A man like a tree,* Marla thought and felt a strange rush of flittering heat inside her belly.

'Hi, Niall. Nice to meet you.'

'I would say the same. But playing catcher in the rye is not one of my usual daily tasks.' He brushed some wet leaves off his jeans. 'Pretty sure I'm bruised in impractical places. If you don't mind telling me, what were you doing in that tree? Hiding? Are you on the run?'

'It's really silly.' Marla sighed and put her hands on her hips.

His mouth showed the suggestion of a smile.

'Okay, so I was going for a walk to clear my head when I heard a sound. A squeak or something. And another one. At the time, I thought it was a kitten.'

His smile got wider, and she noticed it.

'I can tell you all about the rats in my tenement, but I know nothing about forest animals and wildlife. I thought I saw a baby cat running up the tree. It was white and fluffy and squeaky. I thought it needed help,' Marla explained. 'Long story short: I climbed the tree to save a kitten that was possibly something else all along. And when I couldn't find it and tried to climb down in shame, the stupid branch broke off. End of story. Happy now?' Her silvery eyes glinted in defiance.

'Why would I be?' Niall's mouth quirked up in amusement.

'You don't think it's embarrassing?'

'Oh, no. It's absolutely embarrassing,' he said. 'But in the best way. You likely met a stoat.'

And for some reason, Marla wasn't embarrassed. On the

contrary, she was at ease. And she liked this feeling, this unexpected sense of comfort. 'I guess I must have thought, since I used to climb trees all the time as a kid, I could still pull it off in my thirties. You know how it is. When you get older, but your mind doesn't follow,' Marla said, stroking Barclay's head. 'I didn't take my adult form into account.' She wasn't sure whether she felt his gaze linger on her for a beat and quickly stuffed her hands into her coat pockets. He was far too hunky for harmless flirting. Especially up close. Even more especially because flirting of any kind was the last thing on her mile-long to-do list. Barclay lost interest in their conversation and nuzzled his nose through moss and leaves.

'Anyway, thanks again for saving me at a great personal cost. I would have frozen to death on that tree. What an unglamorous way to go,' she laughed.

'Right. You're shivering,' Niall noted. 'Let's get moving. Where do you have to go?'

'Down this road, I think,' she said.

'Great, I was heading in the same direction.'

They set out along the woodland path, matching each other's steps, Barclay in slow pursuit. 'By the way, kudos for getting my Bowie reference,' she said.

'Naw, that was an easy one. Although I'm more of an Oasis guy.'

'Ah, the nineties! Good aulden days of yore. I was merely a teenager then,' she said and added, 'Oasis is, well, a bit of a Beatles rip-off. Don't you think?'

'Hey, all musicians are inspired by someone.'

'Oh, is *that* what you call it?'

He shook his head. 'And here I was thinking what a nice lady you were.'

'Okay, okay,' she said, 'if I had to pick one Oasis song because my life depended on it—and only then—it would be Champagne Supernova.'

'Interesting choice.' He scratched his chin.

'I didn't grow up in a tree, you know?' she said and smiled broadly.

'Clearly not. You certainly don't seem to feel at home in them. Now, about that tattoo—'

'Unfortunately, I don't believe there's such a wild thing as a tattoo shop anywhere near Kilcranach.'

'So, your proposal was a fib all along?' Niall asked with feigned indignation.

'Don't sound too disappointed. As if you'd ever get a tattoo.'

'You underestimate me,' he said. 'Huge mistake.'

'Oh, now I expect nothing less than a frisky butterfly right above your bum.' She smirked. 'I wouldn't have taken you for tramp stamp material.'

Niall laughed again. It sounded full and cordial. *Wholesome*, Marla thought.

The heaviness had faded from the air, and the canvas of clouds in the winter sky had dissolved. Splashes of sunshine dappled the forest floor, glittering off frosty trunks and branches with small patches of snow still clinging to the shadowed parts of the woods. Ahead of them, where Barclay was exploring, the forest thinned out. Knee-high bushes of heather and birch trees lined the path.

'And if you don't mind me asking, what are you doing here? Just walking your cute and friendly dog?' she asked.

'I live here, I walk here, that's part of my job.'

'Don't tell me you're a professional dog walker,' she said. 'That would be too cool to bear. Oh, the envy!'

'No, I'm an estate manager for my own land and for others in the area. Taking care of the land and the forest. Broadly speaking.' Niall quickly added, 'What about you? Never seen you around before, and this is a small town. I would have noticed you. Are you here on holiday?'

'I'm not sure,' she said.

'An unusual thing to be unsure about,' he said. 'I'm intrigued.'

'It's complicated.' Marla gave a nervous laugh. 'Actually, it's completely bonkers. You wouldn't believe me. Hell, I can't even believe it myself.'

As each step inched them forward, there was a gradual incline in the terrain, ever so slowly rising beneath their feet. Marla spotted a solitary magpie hopping along the fringe of the path. A little gentleman looking for a shiny trinket. Or, more likely, for food.

'Good luck,' Niall said. 'Magpies are a sign of good luck, I mean. So the Scottish saying goes.'

Marla smiled. There was a sudden glow in her chest, as if she had taken a generous sip of whisky. They walked in comfortable silence along the grey dry-stone wall that rose to shoulder height beside the path. Moss, lichen, and ferns were growing out of its cracks and joints. She let her fingertips glide over the rough stone while they walked. The wall followed a smooth curve until it ended in a pillar.

They stood at the gates of Hazelbrae.

Two sandstone pillars carved with a detailed bas-relief of a stag and hound stood to each side of heavy, wrought-iron gates, patterned with intertwining thistles. The finish had once been a glossy black. Now it was coated with a patina of rust. Even in its neglected condition, enough of Hazelbrae's former grandeur still shone through to capture the eye of any beholder and warrant a pause.

'It's stunning, isn't it?' said Marla, her eyes fixed on the house behind the gate.

'Practically a ruin. But it wasn't always like this,' Niall said. 'In the Middle Ages, there was a proper fortress on this hill. Robert Bruce razed it to the ground during the First War of Scottish Independence. After that, there was a smaller castle for a few hundred years, before the grand house—Hazelbrae—was built in the late eighteenth century on the site of the old castle.' He briefly squeezed the tip of his nose. 'For ages, all the land that you can see here belonged to the local branch of the Hamilton family. Used to be part of the grand estate,' he explained and made a sweeping hand gesture. 'Like so many of the old families in the twentieth century, their land was parcelled out over time. To pay for the upkeep of the house.'

'I watched *Downton Abbey*. I get the gist,' she said.

'The land was sold off bit by bit. To my grandfather and others. Part is now a national reserve. Another part is two big farms, or crofts, as they're called here. I own the rest of the land, except for the house itself and the ten acres surrounding it,' he continued. 'About a year ago, the owner—Lady Hamilton—had a second stroke and couldn't live on her own anymore. She moved to a care home. They couldn't find a nurse in the area. Since then, Hazelbrae has been empty. But it had been in decline for decades before that. Although it was… still used for celebrations occasionally.' His glance drifted far away, as if he was somewhere in the past.

'So, we are neighbours then,' Marla stated and smiled. She pulled a small key from her pocket and twisted it between her fingertips. 'I always assumed opening the gates to a castle would require a huge, ancient, and possibly golden key,' she said half to herself. 'This isn't a fairy tale, I suppose.' She slid the key into the padlock hanging on an iron chain around the metal bars and turned it. There was a barely perceptible click, and the lock opened. With a clinking rattle, Marla let the iron chain slide free of the gate.

'What do you mean by neighbours, and why do you have the keys to Hazelbrae?' Niall asked. There was something akin to clouds in his voice.

'Because I think I live here now,' Marla said. 'I know how

absurd it sounds, but I inherited it from Lady Hamilton. Apparently, she had a thing for my grandda. Don't ask. I still have to get to the bottom of it. At first, I didn't want to accept. As you said, these houses are insanely high maintenance and crazy expensive.' She grimaced. 'But then I had a change of heart. I'll try to restore it. Turn it into a retreat for people who need some peace and calm. Medical staff who are burnt out and exhausted.' She blew out a breath. 'Am I in way over my head? You bet. But I mean, how often do you get the chance to do something like that? Never. I think if one day I'm living in a nursing home like Lady Hamilton and I look back on my life, I'd regret saying no much more than I'd do the other way around.' Her voice ebbed as she saw how his face was changing. His expression hardened, his jaw clenched.

'You own Hazelbrae? *You*? And you want to keep it?' he asked.

'Yes, I own it, and I'm going to keep it. Or at least try.'

He looked puzzled and dark. 'But why?'

'Why not? I can sense in my bones that it's the right move, that's all. I'd regret it forever if I didn't at least try to restore it and do something meaningful with it. And this is part of my grandda's legacy.'

'To be clear, you plan on living here?' he asked with a peculiar tone in his voice.

Marla nodded, edging towards unease. 'Yes, as I said.' It felt as though anything else she might have wanted to say was blocked by an invisible wall as soon as it was about to leave her lips.

'I see.' Niall rubbed the back of his neck.

Marla smiled, trying to bridge over the obvious rift that had opened between them. But when he looked at her with hard eyes, her smile faded. What was she missing? His silence was heavy, and disapproval emanated from him. It was baffling to her what she could have said or done wrong. A few heartbeats ago, he had made her feel comfortable and at ease. Now he couldn't be colder and more distant if he were in Antarctica.

'Fine then. I wish you all the best,' he said tersely. 'See you around.' He turned on his heel without another word and walked away with angry steps, Barclay hesitantly following.

And with that, something wilted.

Chapter Four

She walked through the gate, letting it fall into place behind her with a clunk. The coarse, mossy gravel crunched under Marla's boots with every step along the curved path toward the grand entrance of Hazelbrae House. She had no explanation for what had brought about this mood swing in Niall. Marla couldn't escape the nagging feeling that perhaps she had done or said something too silly, and yet she couldn't think of anything that would have prompted such a harsh reaction.

Then again, he was a stranger. She didn't know him. Unpredictability, the sudden switching between hot and cold, on the other hand … that sort of thing she knew all too well. It used to be exactly her type. At least before she managed to work on her unhealthy relationship patterns.

Mostly by not having any relationships.

With instinctive accuracy, her heart always seemed to pick the untrustworthy ones. Guys with problems and secrets, who couldn't commit. Subconsciously, she always went for the non-stick fellas, the Teflon-types. The ones who would eventually, inevitably leave her. And since her heart reliably chose the unreliable, she had decided a long time ago not to rely on it anymore. Her heart needed protection. Mainly from itself.

Marla reached the three curved steps leading up to Hazelbrae's double entry door. She paused and looked up at the building. This was her first time seeing the property up close, not in pictures. The house lay in stillness, awaiting her. Despite the obvious signs of decay, she was moved by the beauty of the structure. An ivy blanket covered the tall sandstone walls, and the sound of rustling vines was both calming and eerie. Marla hesitated. Her stomach fluttered in a mixture of anticipation and dread. What would she find inside? Spiders? Rats? Pickled pumpkin from 1986? Probably all of those things.

She closed her eyes and took a breath. Then she reached for the large, ancient door handle. When she pushed it down, it creaked. But that was all. *Ah right, I forgot something*. She fumbled another unassuming Yale key out of her coat pocket and slipped it into the small steel lock that was as good as hidden beneath the shadow of the giant handle. This time, the door swung open, almost of its own accord.

Marla took another breath and stepped inside.

'Hello there!' she called out. Not because she expected a welcoming committee, servants, a butler, or anyone—but because that's what she did. An old house, in Marla's view, was an entity and deserved to be treated with respect. Whenever she came home to her shoebox flat in London, she used to say 'Hi!' each time. And so far, Marla and her home had got on very well. At least before she had to sublet it to move to Scotland into this ginormous place.

After another step, Marla stood in a large foyer, hushed and dim. The first thing she noticed was the broad staircase wrapping itself around a massive, carved wooden column. A threadbare runner undulated down the steps, most likely burgundy red a few decades ago, now faded salmon pink. The walls were half-clad in brown panels.

Along the turned banister was a stair lift for people who couldn't conquer all those steps anymore. This first tangible sign of Lady Hamilton stirred something in Marla. She was just not sure what.

The stairs led up toward a stained-glass window that radiated coloured light. A myriad of dust flakes danced on the transient rays, like fairies on moonbeams in the tales of her childhood. Beneath her feet, the marble floor stretched out in a chessboard pattern, forest green and white, thin cracks spreading out like rivers on the tiles.

Looming large on the wall, behind the colossal column, was the cracked oil painting of an eighteenth-century nobleman on an enormous canvas in a gilded frame. A tall, dignified figure at the zenith of his life with a powdered wig and a gold-buttoned waistcoat. His posture was upright, his hand resting on top of a silver-tipped cane. He had a strong and stern face with commanding eyes. Confident and unperturbed, expecting the world to follow his rules and bend to his will. Which, considering his wealth and privilege, had probably been the case for him from cradle to grave.

Marla turned her head. On the opposite side, in a similarly opulent frame, hung the portrait of a woman. Clearly his equal in terms of wealth, privilege, and portrait size. Her face was both delicate and strong, with an air of intelligence and grace. She had black, mysterious eyes. Her dark brown hair was pinned up in an intricate arrangement of curls and adorned with glistening beads. The silk damask of her dress shimmered in the contrast of light and shadow. She looked like she was about to attend a ball, yet she was holding a book. Whoever she was, she reminded Marla of timeless elegance and strength—and the fact that not having to work or worry slows down the ageing process considerably. She didn't know who those two people were, but they belonged to this place.

It comforted Marla to be in the presence of those who had

been here before her. She felt a sense of peace, mixed with a certain loneliness. Namely, the loneliness of being the only human in a large, old house that had seen so much life, so much history. At some point, they had all stood here, in the same space. Only separated from her by the veil of time. It was a humbling and heavy sentiment. Hazelbrae's past seemed to murmur to her. She meandered around the main hall, taking in her surroundings. Then, with careful steps, she headed up to the upper floor.

Hazelbrae had twelve bedrooms and three storeys: the ground floor, the first floor, and the attic or servant area. Because, as she knew from several documentaries and shows, all the people who kept those grand houses running back in the day, the ones who were really in charge, were supposed to be invisible. Neither to be heard nor seen. Keep up appearances and disappear. And then there was, as Marla knew from the floor plans Mr Collins had mailed her, also a souterrain or basement with a large old kitchen.

After climbing the stairs, Marla made her way along the gallery. Everywhere she looked, she found signs of evanescent grandeur. A few remaining pieces of antique furniture beneath grey sheets. Most had been sold decades ago. There were veiled mirrors; heavy, moth-eaten silk and velvet curtains; high ceilings adorned with detailed carvings; paintings of exuberant classical motifs—battle and nature scenes, gods and goddesses, nymphs and satyrs. Tales of love, lust, and loss, all captured in wood, stone, and flaking paint. There was peeling chinoiserie wallpaper with peacocks and cherry blossoms. A corner with tromp l'œil murals, framing faux views out into fake Roman gardens. Historic houses had always fascinated Marla, and Hazelbrae far exceeded anything she could ever have imagined. Despite the positively morbid state of disrepair and disturbing number of dead wasps on the windowsills, Marla was in awe.

As she turned into one of the bedrooms, she noticed a

faded scent of lavender and rose hanging in the air. The large room seemed as good as bare, aside from a writing desk with a chair and an antique four-poster bed. On one side of the bed stood a nightstand holding an empty medication dispenser, on the other a pair of crutches. She could almost feel Lady Hamilton's presence lingering in this room as if she had never left, as if she was still living here amongst these old walls. Sadness fell leaden on Marla's shoulders, and she tried to shake it off. She wandered towards the elegant Victorian ladies' desk facing the large the window. With a swift move, she peeled back the curtain—and her heart skipped a beat.

What she saw was nothing short of stunning. The winter sun was beginning to set and dipped the sky in a thousand shades of pastel pink and orange. The landscape stretching out below was majestic and untamed. Rolling hills and fissured, snow-covered mountains further behind them. Clouds sticking to their jagged edges like wool on a nail. *If you could run your fingertip over the horizon, you'd cut yourself on it,* she thought. Narrow brooks ran along the curves of the hills like silver ribbons, wintry pastures spread out forever. She saw clusters of white sheep grazing in fields connected by a stone bridge that crossed a glistening river. A scene that transcended time. More marvellous and idyllic than even William Turner's brush could have captured on canvas. Her heart widened, and Marla felt overwhelmed by a sense of eternity, longing, and belonging.

This was the country her grandda called home. This was what his heart could never forget. This was part of his legacy. Was it a part of her?

She stood there for a while, taking it all in.

No wonder Lady Hamilton chose this room, Marla thought, before she pulled herself away and descended the stairs to the foyer. Lady Hamilton's bedroom was certainly the most beautiful in all of Hazelbrae.

Now it would become hers.

Marla felt like she had been in some kind of dream, a vision of long ago and far away, and she was slowly waking up. She had to remind herself that she was the caretaker and guardian of Hazelbrae and had to fix it up.

Her initial, and admittedly severely naïve, plan had been to stay here for the night. She even had a sleeping bag and camping gear in her car, just in case. But after her tour of the house, she realised that wasn't workable yet. Not for quite some time. The thought made her heart sink. For one, she didn't know how the heating worked—whether it was functioning at all—or if the pipes were okay and clear. She also had to figure out if there was clean running water and safe electricity, if there were vermin infestations of any kind, and whether the rooms were safe to stay in. Who knew what else? The report had mentioned no major damage, but better safe than sorry.

Marla returned to Hazelbrae's entrance and exhaled. She was willing to make this her home, but there was a long road ahead of her. She had bitten off more than she could chew. But bitten it off, she had. So now came the chewing part.

Before she could revel in existential panic, however, she had to find a place to sleep. She cursed herself for not planning ahead enough. But then again, this had been a life-altering event. It was only natural that some details had slipped her mind. Since it was low season, she speculated on finding a room in one of the B&Bs or hotels in the area, maybe an Airbnb, with someone from the village. A knot of apprehension rose in her chest. She was also not sure how the locals would respond to the fact that an outsider was the new owner and resident of the castle. These things tended to be sore subjects, for good reason. And if Niall's reaction had been any indication, she could be in for a rough and lonely ride.

Business as usual then, she thought. It had been her grandparents, Rose and Gordon, and Marla against the rest of the world for most of her life. Now it was only Marla.

With a heavy heart and a queasy stomach, she remembered her car was still parked in Kilcranach. Also, she hadn't had a bite to eat since breakfast and it was long past three in the afternoon. Marla made the executive decision to postpone exploring Hazelbrae's gardens and making a thorough inventory of the repairs until tomorrow.

Food first, crazy castle renovation second.

Chapter Five

Marla descended from Hazelbrae back to Kilcranach. The small road down from the castle towards the village was winding, and she felt the strain of all the walking and climbing and jumping from earlier today. But her fatigue wasn't purely physical. This tumultuous day was taking its toll on her mind as well.

The sun succumbed to the twilight, suffusing the air with the luminous hues of dusk. In Scotland's latitudes, dark came early in winter. Marla loved the blue hour when the dwindling sky glinted like a candlelit silk veil and tree silhouettes stood out in contrast to the azure. This mystical space between day and night when everything seemed possible.

Even insane plans like renovating a huge, half-ruined, eighteenth-century castle.

She took her time strolling to Kilcranach, a million thoughts raving behind her forehead. The reality of the situation was sinking in. She had come to Scotland with the little savings she had accumulated working as a nurse and the money from selling her grandparents' tiny terraced house in Birmingham. That was enough to cover the necessities, but not all the renovation work.

Marla loved her profession. She had chosen it in memory of her late mum. But after years and years of watching too many of her patients die and working in an ineffective, bureaucratic system, she was exhausted. Ready for something positive. Something less draining. A new calling.

She had zero experience in renovating listed buildings, and she knew next to nothing about requesting funding from governmental or private agencies. Where to even start on something like this? Restoring an old house was anything but cheap and simple. It would require vast amounts of labour, expertise, and money. More than Marla could gather without some help. Stopping in her tracks, she turned and stared up at Hazelbrae. Her heart ached at the sight of the dilapidated structure, standing tall despite its state.

Marla remembered something her Gran Rose always said, 'You don't need to know everything, sweet pea. You only need to know who to ask.' The thought of her wee gran, who tried her best to fill Marla's mother's shoes, flooded Marla with love and gratitude. It must be unspeakably hard to raise another child when you just buried your only one. *Fucking cancer.* And her gran had given it everything she had. And so had her Grandda Gordon.

Marla's father hadn't known what to do on his own with his little daughter. Being a single parent wasn't part of his plan. So, after her mum had passed, he abandoned her and never looked back. No postcard, no phone call, nothing. The last thing that Marla remembered of him was the sound of a closing door and then roaring silence. She didn't know where he went or what he did. His parents hadn't been in the picture, as far as Marla knew. She didn't hear a single word from her father ever again.

Not that she wanted to.

Her hand clasped her grandda's pocket knife. He had always carried it with him and taught her how to whittle with it. Marla was aware of how lucky she was to have had Rose and Gordon Wilson in her life. Her father was just as dead to Marla as her mother, of whom she had distant, foggy memories.

Further down from the ridge, the village of Kilcranach opened up in front of her, nestled right between the hills. With its cottages scattered along the uneven streets and up the slopes, the village looked like someone had tipped out a box of toys. Honey-golden light poured from the windows into the cobalt-blue air. A low rumble broke the peaceful silence. Marla's stomach growled, and the thought of a proper, cooked meal in the village pub filled her with anticipation.

She found her car in the car park where she had left it this morning, grabbed her purse, and walked across the town square towards the Blue Bonnet.

As she swung the door open, a waft of toasty air embraced her, straight away lifting her spirits. *Ah, the undervalued joys of central heating*. Marla stood in the doorway, letting her eyes adjust to the light. It was a typical pub—thick tartan-checked carpeting in four different shades of blue with a gauzy red. A net of thin branches intertwined with fairy lights covered the low, white-washed ceiling. The Blue Bonnet must have been a farm cottage or something similar, because a string of adjoining rooms led off from this first room, merging into one another, forming one long tube. All exterior walls were made of massive, uneven natural stone. The smoother interior walls were painted, their lower halves panelled with pine slats that had aged to an amber hue. Absolutely nothing fit together.

Marla felt cosy at once.

The centrepiece, the heart of every pub up and down the country, was without a doubt the bar. Built from rectangular rough-hewn stones and topped with heavy, glossy redwood. In front stood six modern, rectangular pine stools with footrests. Empty.

Behind the bar, however, Marla saw an interesting surprise —the woman with the pointy hat and green hair from earlier today. She was young-ish, likely in her mid-20s, Marla guessed. And petite. But there was something indomitable about her. Apart from looking like a textbook witch, she seemed like someone the wind would consider easy to blow over. Only to be unpleasantly surprised by her tenacity and steadfastness.

'Hello!' Marla announced with a grin.

'Afternoon,' the pointy-hat-woman replied with a cheery smile. Her front tooth was missing a corner, giving her an audacious appearance. On top of the green hair and unusual hat.

'I'm famished,' Marla said. 'I could gobble up an entire bonnet, blue or otherwise. Can I see a menu?'

The woman shook her head. 'I'm afraid not, love. The kitchen is closed between two and five.'

'No food at all? Not even bread and butter? Soup? A granola bar? I had a long, long day and very, very little food. Please?' Marla's stomach felt hollow, and her hands were unsteady from the lack of sustenance.

'Oh, I'm awfy sorry. Not even a bite an' a soup.' The woman looked genuinely sympathetic under the brim of her hat. 'I can offer you crisps, if you're interested?'

Marla must have looked like someone had doused her with a bucket of ice water because the green-haired woman stopped polishing pint glasses and said: 'There's one supermarket in the area, but it's a thirty-minute drive.'

'I'm afraid I won't make it. Save me and hand me the crisps! And throw in a flat white, please.'

'I can make you a coffee with a lot of milk, if you like,' she said, grinning.

'Fab. I'll take two of those in a pint glass!'

Whimsical customs in those rural Highlands, Marla thought and sat down on one of the stools. *Better get used to it.*

While munching on her salt-and-vinegar crisps a few

minutes later, she asked the woman behind the bar, 'Do you have a room where I can stay for a few nights?'

'Sorry again, love. We're booked until next week.'

'Booked up? In November? Here?' Marla said in complete disbelief.

'Aye, there's a Gaelic folk music festival nearby. Popular with a certain group of people.'

Marla let out a defeated whimper and put her forehead down on the counter. It was sticky, but that was to be expected. 'Today is so not my lucky day.'

'Or,' the pointy-hat-girl said slowly, 'you could stay at my place, if you don't mind. It's nicer than this old joint, if I might say so.'

Marla lifted her head again. 'Don't toy with my feelings. I'm a desperate woman.'

'No, really. I got a spare room that I rent out on Airbnb,' she said. 'It's free right now. You can have it.'

'You'd be the second person today who's saved me,' Marla said as she thought back to that guy, Niall, and the tree. It seemed like forever ago.

As if on cue, the door opened, and a chilly breeze blew into the room, causing the curtains to billow. And it had someone in tow: Niall.

Of course, it's him, Marla thought and rolled her eyes. *Must be the claustrophobic awkwardness of small-town living everybody was always going on about.*

'Hi, Niall. I hope you're well?' the woman said. 'You're here for your parcel?'

'Aye, Gwen. I am.' It came out like a gruff order.

'All right then. Let me get it for you, it's somewhere in the back.' She disappeared into a cupboard.

Silence ensued. Marla sat motionless on a chair, he stood a good four feet away. His scent of leather, linen, and pine wafted to her and made her heart beat faster. Marla wished he'd say something—anything—to break the awkward tension. But all he did was look at his feet, his hands in his pockets. She felt like she was going to burst from the questions she wanted to ask him. *What's wrong with you? Did I say something weird? I thought you were nice. What happened? Are you a narcissistic psychopath?* She pulled herself together and simply said, 'Well, hello again.'

'Hello,' he replied politely.

'You didn't bring your partner in crime this time.'

'He's in the car.'

'I see.'

Once more, silence filled the space between them. Marla, aware of every breath and movement, shifted in her seat and glanced at the wall before her. The more she thought about the situation, the more annoyed she became. Her mind spun in circles. Despite her efforts to stay composed, a wave of frustration built up inside her. No, she was certain. She had done absolutely nothing wrong, and she wouldn't let anyone manipulate her emotions and gaslight her into believing otherwise. Not anymore.

Anger bubbled up inside her and boiled over. 'So, are you Jekyll or Hyde right now? I can't tell. You look pretty much the same in both forms,' she quipped.

'What's that supposed to mean?'

'Oh, nothing,' she said. 'But you seem to experience severe mood swings. Have you ever thought about therapy?'

'And you must suffer from pathological reality distortion,' he countered.

'Excuse me?' Her voice sounded half an octave higher than usual.

Niall snorted, shaking his head in sheer annoyance. 'Seriously, what do you know about this place?'

She narrowed her eyes. 'What do you mean?'

He sighed exasperatedly. 'I mean, you come in here with your lofty plans and naïve dreams of renovating a big, listed building and dealing with an estate in Scotland. Do you even have the slightest concept of what you're getting into? Do you really?'

Marla paused for a beat before responding. 'I know enough.' Her voice was dangerously measured and calm.

He turned to her, his eyebrows furrowed. 'You really think you can do it? Oh, please! You don't even know a single thing about the people here. How it all works. What's your vision of life in the Highlands—men in kilts? Jacobite risings? James Fraser? Bagpipes for breakfast?' He grunted. 'That's a far cry from reality, love. Life here is not idyllic. It's not a fairy tale. It's difficult. You think anyone gives a fuck about us outside tourist season? Or besides hunting, fishing, and whisky?' His amber eyes were blazing. 'Your ideas are absurd and ridiculous. You'll be broke in weeks. Running home with your tail between your legs. Do all of us and yourself a favour. Let it be and get back to where you belong!'

Marla's expression changed from surprise to anger in an instant. His astonishing arrogance and blatant dismissiveness took her aback. A part of her sensed he wasn't talking about her. There clearly was another issue at play. Yet her cheeks were burning with rage as she faced him squarely. 'And you know nothing about me! Who I am. What I can do. Just because I'm an outsider and new here doesn't mean that I'm not capable of understanding this place and making something out of it!'

'Reality distortion, as I said.' His voice dripped with sarcasm, and it made her furious.

'You have no right to be so fucking condescending!' Marla spat out the words, her fists balled up on the bar as she glared at Niall. The tension was crackling between them.

'And you have no right to waltz in here and play princess in the enchanted castle!' he yelled.

Marla was about to respond with unhinged fervour. But Gwen, reappearing from the back with a brown cardboard box, interrupted them. Calmly, she handed the parcel to Niall. 'Awrite, that's you.'

'Thanks, Gwen. And bye.' Niall gave Marla one last piercing glance before turning and storming out of the pub.

'Rude, mean, and moody!' Marla grumbled under her breath.

'Who? Niall McCarron?'

'Indeed. What a prick.'

'He's a bit of a grump sometimes. More of a reclusive type, that Niall,' she explained. 'But he's usually friendly.'

'Not to me, he's not.' Marla closed her eyes and tried to calm herself as her face flushed with rage and embarrassment. How could he get her so raving mad within mere seconds?

'I'm Gwen, by the way. I'm the inn and pub owner.'

'Wait. You own this place?'

'Aye, my parents moved to Alicante last year, and I took over. Didn't know what else to do. I like it here,' Gwen smiled and exposed her charming, chipped tooth again.

'Hi, Gwen. Nice to meet you. I'm Marla. I own the fucking castle,' Marla said, and giggled. 'Shit. I own a castle! On top of the hill. The castle!' She couldn't stop giggling. Her giggles swelled into a gale of laughter. It was as if all the tension of the past weeks had broken like a dam, erupting in one extended release of senseless, breathless guffaws. Tears squeezed from the corners of her eyes.

'So, it's you then,' Gwen said and tried to suppress a giggle herself. 'We all wondered what would happen to the place after old Lady Hamilton kicked the bucket.'

'Oh, I can tell you. The next crazy cat lady moves in!' Marla laughed and Gwen joined in. Her laugh sounded like a hundred bells in a jar. She wiped the tears from her eyes.

'Oh my. You really own Hazelbrae House?'

'Yep, I'm afraid so,' Marla said, her cheeks hurting. Gwen reached for two glasses behind the counter, pouring whisky for both of them.

'To your new life, then. Welcome to Kilcranach,' she said and clinked her glass against Marla's. The two women savoured their drams.

'I have to ask,' Marla said after a while. 'And I hope I'm not offending you. But… are you a witch? I mean, the pointy hat and so on.'

'Naw, not in the typical sense. I get why some people want to reclaim that label. But I believe most of the thousands who were executed for witchcraft—in Scotland and elsewhere—didn't voluntarily claim to be witches,' Gwen explained. 'That being said, I love folklore and herbal remedies and stuff. And I like to wear costumes and dress up. Makes life here less dull. Some people think I don't have all my marbles.' She lifted one shoulder. 'That's fine by me. They can think whatever they like. They do anyway. But because I own the pub, they still have to be nice to me,' she said and grinned cheekily.

'I like you,' said Marla. 'Another round?'

That night, when Marla lay in Gwen's spare room—after many a dram, interesting conversations with Gwen, and meeting some other Kilcranach locals—her head and heart were spinning in sync. And it wasn't just the whisky.

Slightly dizzy, Marla reviewed the day. She had inherited a castle because her grandda might have had a thing with a gentry chick, she had met a ridiculously attractive guy who turned out to be a jerk, she had toured Hazelbrae, and met a costume-loving pub owner with a pointy hat. It was all profoundly perplexing, but it still felt right. She might have been daunted and on the fence about keeping the grand old house initially, but now she knew that this was the right challenge for her.

If only this unnecessary man-person hadn't appeared, pushing all sorts of buttons. Marla still couldn't believe how quickly he had infuriated her. But he had. With mortifying ease. His words were still gnawing at her. 'Princess,' he had called her. What an insult. If anything, Marla was the anti-princess. She was proud of doing things on her own. Also, would a princess always carry a pocket knife? Or climb trees?

She knew her thoughts were childish and embarrassing. But she was unable to suppress them. Fury was swirling inside her belly, along with the whisky. 'Your ideas are naïve and ridiculous,' he had said. And Marla couldn't get the echo in her head to stop.

Because… if she was honest with herself, as much as she didn't want to hear it, he might have a teeny, tiny point.

But now she was hell-bent on proving him wrong.

Chapter Six

Niall slammed the door of his old jeep so hard that Barclay jumped. 'What a silly cow,' he grumbled in the direction of his dog and stuffed the package into the footwell of the passenger seat.

Immediately, a hint of regret crept up on him. Niall slumped into the driver's seat. It wasn't her fault she didn't know any better. Most people didn't. To many, Scotland was an exciting, ancient country where slivers of fairy tales and folk magic endured to this day. A hotbed for all sorts of revolutionary ideas. Or a great place for deer stalking and oil rigging. Niall understood the appeal of Walter Scott's romanticised version of Scotland, with clans and bagpipes and tartan and all that. He really did. And it was partly real, of course.

But people didn't see, know, or care much about the mundanities of life. The non-existent supermarkets or post offices. The buses that never came. The closure of doctor's surgeries and schools. The difficulties of managing the land and farms. The second homes driving the prices up and locals away. The party-houses to rent online for a weekend. The piles of tourist shite on the sides of the awful, dangerous roads. Didn't matter as long as they had their fill of romance. They only saw the beauty, not the rest of it. A one-dimensional view. To them, Scotland was a commodity, a sort of real-life Disneyland. They wanted the *Outlander* bits, but not *Trainspotting*. Which to him was like only eating the filling of a custard cream, not the actual biscuit. Nostalgia or destitution were the two common perceptions of his country. For many reasons. Neither of those versions of Scotland was the whole truth. But both existed.

No, being tempted by the romance of inheriting a castle—why and how still eluded him—wasn't her fault.

Her stubbornness and insistence on keeping Hazelbrae, however, on deciding to stay rather than selling it, against all better judgment, the choice to stand in his way—now, that was *definitely* her fault. He only needed to secure Hazelbrae and the rest of the land for his plan to come to fruition. But now this idealistic outsider had stepped in and complicated everything. He couldn't believe that she was the owner. Her. And what she wanted to do… burn out?

Bunch of crap.

She seemed determined to keep Hazelbrae, no matter what it cost her.

And him.

Niall had to admit that she had some courage, however misplaced, something he found both admirable and enraging. Because it meant that his plan was slipping away. Again. Of all the people in this cursed and forgotten town, of course he had to stumble upon the single person who stood in his way.

No, she wasn't bad looking. But he had been an idiot for letting himself get caught up in the moment. He leaned back in his seat as a torrid wave gushed through his core. This stranger seemed to have a way of bringing out his temper. Definitely not what he needed. Or wanted.

He had to get out of Kilcranach. Now and preferably forever.

Barclay, as if sensing his human buddy's feelings, nudged Niall's ear with his nose. 'You're right, pal. Let's go home. Time for supper.' With a flick of his wrist, Niall started the engine.

The sun had set, and darkness engulfed the countryside. An endless void of inky blue, with only a few stars glinting through the clouds. He drove down the road, his headlights barely illuminating the packed trees and scrubland on either side. He had been so lost in thought that he almost missed the turnoff onto the narrow country lane that led to his cottage, on the fringe of the forest. His hands gripped the steering wheel as the jeep briefly lurched.

You of all people should know to drive carefully.

He eased his foot off the gas. Tall trees that seemed to disappear in the vast black sky lined the road. It felt as though he was being swallowed up by the night. The vehicle creaked and groaned, and after a few more bends and turns, Niall spotted the outline of his cottage. It was as good as hidden in the shadowy depths of the forest. He pulled up the driveway in front of the house. When he stepped out of the car, a heavy cloak of silence enveloped him. People who weren't used to this utter absence of sound could find it deafening. But not Niall. This silence, along with the cool November night air, calmed him.

With the parcel under his arm and Barclay following on his heels, Niall carefully kicked the door open. No need to lock up. There was nothing to steal here. And nobody to do the stealing.

The cottage was cosy and small. A single-storey house made of rough stone with a moss-covered slate roof. Built as a crofter's home in the mid-1800s. One small bedroom, a large lounge with an open kitchen, a bathroom, and a cupboard. He didn't need much. It was more than spacious enough. And it was quiet. Niall had done most of the renovations himself. The insulation, the polished hardwood floors, the kitchen cabinets, and the small wood stove. Nothing fancy, but all done with care and craftsmanship. His home was minimalistic and tidy. He had allowed himself one indulgence, though. A single, large pane of glass that filled the short southeast wall of his home. The window fused the inside with the outside, creating a reflection of nature. Through the glass, he could contemplate the outdoors and feel as if he was among the trees. *Talk about taking work home,* he thought and kicked his boots off. Barclay's claws were clicking against the wooden floor as he made his way straight to his bowl. 'I gotcha, buddy,' said Niall and scratched Barclays's chin before setting the parcel on the kitchen island and filling his dog's bowl.

Then he packed the log burner with sticks and dry twigs to make a fire. When the flames crackled, Niall set about opening the package.

Suddenly, he felt like a fool.

Of course, he knew what was inside the box. He remembered the night he had ordered it, after way too much wine. Two weeks ago.

The anniversary.

The thought punched into his chest, and all the air escaped from his lungs.

Is it six years already, my darlin'?

Somewhere in the darkest corner of his soul, he could feel a dim echo of the old rupture rising, twitching, writhing. He had locked away his grief and guilt deep, deep down, under crusty slates of stone, where no one knew they existed.

Except himself.

The bottle of red hadn't been a great idea. *Neither,* Niall thought, *is this thing*. With a resolute movement, he ripped the cardboard and opened the box.

There it was.

A model kit for a sailboat.

He had intended it to be an inspiration, a motivation. A reminder of his dream and his ticket out of here. Something tangible to help him focus on what lay ahead, instead of being pulled back into the past. Here in front of him, it seemed childish and ridiculous. A weak moment and a brief lapse of judgment, fuelled by fermented grape juice. He exhaled and stuffed the box into the cupboard. *Happens to the best of us.*

Niall poured himself a dram before supper—he was in the mood—and slumped into the scuffed leather armchair beside the stove. By now, the logs were roaring and giving off a cosy heat. A hiss of sap could be heard now and then, lulling him into a quiet trance that allowed him to think about the situation. His life. Beside his feet on the jute rug lay a snoring Barclay, with a full belly and not a care in the world. *If only you knew how much I envy you, pal.*

Niall's mind wandered back to his two meetings with Marla. Along with the warmth of the whisky, a sizzling anger spread through his core again. *Impossible person.* He couldn't believe that she wanted to keep Hazelbrae, despite the warning he had tried to give her. Although, Niall admitted, he had not been particularly rational. But she must know on some level that this was insane. Flat-out madness. It was annoyingly obvious that she didn't understand the financial or any other implications of her plans. As far as he could tell, there was no plan. He noticed that he had been grinding his teeth.

And what was more, she wouldn't fail alone. No, she would drag others down with her. Like him, for example.

There was something infuriating about her and her recklessness.

Damn that woman.

Though his chest burned with anger, a different emotion streamed through his body. There was something else that lurked beneath his rage. A raw force, much more potent and powerful. Something he'd rather not think about. But it replayed in his mind anyway. He remembered the weight of her body pressing on his when she sat on his lap in the woods and the way her silver-grey eyes flickered when their thoughts were one and the same for a split second…

Niall leaned back in the chair, one hand rubbing the stubble on his chin, the other clutching his glass. He wasn't sure whether it was the whisky or the stove, but his face felt flushed and his mouth parched. A primitive longing surged through him that was beyond his control. An urge he thought to have buried with the grief and the guilt ages ago.

Damn that woman!

Something about her reached places in him that should not be reached. Ever again. He had taken great pains to construct his protective armour.

He hadn't done it for fun.

No, he had done it to survive.

This weird woman with her messy bun and muddy jeans and insane plans seemed to cut through it. And he didn't even know her. Neither did she know anything about him. He had met her twice in one day, briefly. *What's happening here?* Niall leaned forward, a hand on his forehead, trying to make sense of it all. He knew he shouldn't be feeling this way. He wasn't supposed to feel anything.

The last time he felt something, it had ripped him apart.

Sometimes he wondered how he was still alive. The last time had nearly killed him.

Because he had killed *her*.

It didn't matter that the police and the insurance both said it wasn't his fault. Or everyone else.

He knew better.

If he had driven Nathalie that night like she had asked him to, if he hadn't insisted that she take her car instead of his although it was raining, if he had taken her car to the shop as he was supposed to... If they hadn't fought... If he wouldn't have been... If...

And there it was. All of it.

The pain.

The guilt.

The shame.

The grief.

It shot to the surface like a jet flame scorching everything, leaving nothing but ash. It rushed through him, hot and sharp. With a growl, he bit his fist to make it go away. It suffocated him. He felt like his throat was closing. There was nothing but dizzy blackness behind his eyes.

Damn. That. Woman.

With heavy lids, he stared at the light strip of skin where his wedding ring had been until two weeks ago. He thought he had to take it off eventually. It still felt bare. Exposed. Cold.

It took him a long time, many slow breaths, and all of his strength to wrestle the demon back into its dungeon and shut the vault.

For now.

Eventually, Niall pushed down on the armrests of the leather chair and lifted himself up, his body feeling as if it was being weighed down with a dense fog. He dragged his feet toward the kitchen, poured the remaining whisky back into the bottle, and put the glass into the sink. He thought about making himself something to eat. But he was too tired, even for toast with butter and Marmite. This couldn't go on. It was too much for him. He had to get away from here and all those memories, beyond any shadow of a doubt. He couldn't risk it all coming up again. And again. He didn't have the strength. It was high time to bury the past and move on. Once and for all. And he refused to let a chance encounter with a random outsider throw him off course. Silver eyes or not.

As he saw it, there were two options: Marla sold the castle, or he would make her sell it. One way or another, he would get her signature. To include Hazelbrae in the deal was his only chance to sell his land to the developer, take the money, buy a boat, and finally—finally!—be free.

And he knew exactly what to do.

Chapter Seven

With a gaze unmoving, like a frozen Scottish loch, Marla stared at the screen of her notebook. It was as blank as her mind. For three and a half weeks she had tried to come up with a proper plan for comprehensively renovating, restoring, and reviving Hazelbrae. In vain. Everything that she could do herself, she had done already. She had sifted through heaps of paperwork. She had done an enormous amount of research on restoring listed buildings. She had sorted the remaining furniture and meticulously updated the inventory. She had ripped out some of the old eighties carpet. She had sealed draughty windows. She had touched up paint here and there. A few days ago, she bought a new mattress, sheets, and several toilet seats. She had mended and dusted and cleaned and scrubbed until her knees were blue and her knuckles raw. Not to speak of the crippling back pain and aching limbs.

Renovating Hazelbrae was both, exhausting and exhilarating. But nothing could change the fact that there was major work to be done and she simply couldn't do it. Not alone anyway.

Yet there didn't seem to be any contractor within a

sensible radius available and willing to work on Hazelbrae. No matter who she called or contacted, their answers were always the same. 'That old house in Kilcranach? Sorry, love. We're busy' or 'We don't do listed buildings.' As much as she didn't like admitting it, Marla was running out of options. She didn't care for it, not in the least. She had always done things on her own and somehow—some would say through sheer stubbornness—managed to do it all. This wasn't any different. Except it was much, much bigger.

So much bigger.

Not that it wasn't without its magical moments. She had discovered a yellowed piece of newspaper from 1970. AXE FALLS ON 3,400 JOBS sat above RINGO TO BE A FATHER. She had kept it. A bit of history and Beatles nostalgia. Along with his pocket knife, her grandda had passed on his love for the music of the four Liverpudlians to Marla.

And Hazelbrae, at least to her, began to look less defeated. As if the main thing that the house needed was someone to live in it. To believe in it. To love it.

Ha, don't we all?

With a thud, Gwen placed a steaming mug of coffee next to Marla's laptop. 'Here, darlin'. You look like you need it. Even more than usual,' she said with a sarcastic smile. Marla replied with a half-hearted grumble. It was still early, and the pub was not officially open yet. But Gwen, who had become a friend over the past weeks, let her sit and work while she prepared the Blue Bonnet for the day. Initially, Marla had set up shop here because, unlike Hazelbrae, the pub had Wi-Fi. But since then, it had become their little routine and Marla loved it here. It was cosy, quiet, and not dusty.

From the window next to her favourite seat in the corner, Marla had an excellent view of the town square. Watching people go about their daily business and running errands was as calming as it was inspiring. Kilcranach felt alive to her, even on a quiet day and with few people. She took a satisfying sip of coffee. 'Thanks, Gwen. You're a kind soul and a lifesaver.'

'I know. I also know that speaking to you before your first coffee is senseless. And dangerous. Consider it a form of self-preservation,' Gwen said as she emptied glasses from the dishwasher onto the shelves. 'So, what are your plans for today? Or is it still too early to ask?'

'I honestly don't know. Going for the messages at some point.'

'Look at you, sounding all Scottish!' There was only a tiny trace of teasing in Gwen's voice.

'Possibly. That's what my grandda always used to say. I suppose I must have absorbed it.' Marla smiled with a trace of sadness. She could feel the weight of Gordon's tiny knife. It wasn't just the coffee that both warmed and pierced her chest, sweet and bitter at the same time. 'I have someone from the Trust coming tomorrow to go through the process and analysis for listed building renovations and what not,' she said to Gwen, her smile fading. 'I hope they can help me with funding and regulations and such. Or at least point me in the right direction.'

'You know you'll find someone, right?' Gwen ran her towel around the rim of another pint glass. 'I already asked my cousin Craig, but they're backlogged until 2097.'

'If I didn't know better, I'd wonder whether there was a curse at play,' Marla said with a wink.

'No way,' Gwen replied with a straight face. 'I already cast a protection spell for you.'

'Ha, I knew it! Always a relief to have a witch on your side. Even though you're not officially one.' Marla grinned and reluctantly returned to her empty Excel sheet, watching the cursor blink.

What now?

She propped her chin on her hand and distracted herself by watching the hustle and bustle of the town square. A hustle and bustle that, here in Kilcranach on this winter morning, consisted of a few gulls circling the tall Christmas tree in the centre, Mrs Bellbottom walking and talking to her grumpy border terrier Muffin, and Jack, the postie, making his rounds in his red jacket and knee-length shorts, despite the biting chill of early December. It was one of those rare sunny days on the Scottish West coast. A biting pang of loneliness seized Marla. London lay behind her. But she hadn't fully arrived in Scotland yet. Yes, she had met a few villagers and made a lovely friend in Gwen. Working like a maniac on Hazelbrae all by herself, however, wasn't a particularly communal activity. She felt like a wanderer between worlds. Nothing half and nothing whole.

And without warning, there was… *him*.

He appeared out of nowhere. Most likely from the small parking lot behind the towering pine tree. Marla's heart pounded against the inside of her ribcage and then plunged into the depths of her stomach. There was the rage again. The sight of his thick hair, glowing like embers in the winter sun, his upright, resolute stride, the stern set of his jaw, and the serious drawl around his mouth—the mere glimpse of him—made her furious. She hadn't seen him in over three weeks. It was just as well. If it were up to her, he could crawl through the undergrowth forever, wood gnome that he was.

She still had no clue what was wrong with him. Such arrogance and self-assuredness, bias and stubbornness, all wrapped into this handsome lumberjack-ish package. She wanted to look away, but she couldn't seem to move her head. *How can anyone be such a smug ass?* More than anything, he was a walking—no, striding—reminder of her doubts. And she had decided to stuff them into the furthest corner of her consciousness.

No wonder the mere sight of him made her livid.

Niall paced towards the bookshop, hands in the pockets of his jeans, shoulders hunched. Barclay was trotting alongside him, not in any way impressed by Muffin's grumpy yapping. Before Marla could raise one of her stiff fingers in an obscene gesture, they were out of sight. But those ten seconds were enough to leave a stinging flame of defiance crackling in her centre. Something to keep her going, at least. To counter and overcome the tiredness within her bones. Something to be grateful for. Rage and coffee. That was all the fuel she needed now.

Hopefully it was enough.

'All right, Gwenny. I'm off,' Marla said and closed her notebook. 'There's only so much time I can spend staring into the abyss of my aimlessness. Better get going and do something. Anything.' She pushed herself up and shoved her laptop into her backpack.

'Okay. But don't overdo it. You're only human. And Hazelbrae is a lot,' Gwen said with obvious concern.

'I know, I know.' Marla blew a raspberry. 'Please don't rub it in. I'm doing that fine on my own.'

'Och, hen. I don't want you to collapse within these old walls, die of exhaustion, and become a ghost. Although ghosts *are* cool.' Gwen tilted her head, and the pointy tip of her hat tickled the chin of the plush Highland coo's head on the wall.

'There are at least thirty-seven worse visions of my future I can think of right now,' Marla said.

'Don't be daft! Will you be back at the pub for dinner tonight?'

'I might.' Marla shrugged into her pea coat. 'Depends on whether hunger or exhaustion wins this time.'

'If you don't show up tomorrow for your coffee, I'll form a search party and come rescue you.'

'Love you, Gwen.'

'Love you, too, Marla!'

When Marla stepped into the crisp air, she felt reinvigorated. There was still anger glimmering inside her, while a touch of frost bit her nose. Which made her aware that she didn't have a single bite to eat at home.

Home.

Hazelbrae.

How alien that sounded. It didn't quite fit yet, like a beautiful brand-new leather shoe. Although the water and electricity were working, Marla didn't dare to use the old stove before a professional had checked it. So, she had set up her camping cooker in the kitchen. Which meant that her diet consisted of toast, ramen, and canned soup. Alongside cheap cheese, chocolate, biscuits, and wine. A distant reminder of her youth and her first year at the School of Nursing and Midwifery in London.

Marla had eaten her last piece of toast with butter and Marmite last night, before collapsing onto her new mattress. Fully clothed and depleted. There was no way around it. Time to hit the grocery store.

As soon as Marla started driving and her phone connected, her radio blared *I'm So Tired* by the Beatles. She let out a short dry laugh as McCartney sang about not having slept a wink. She loved serendipity, even when the universe was taking the piss.

The thirty-minute drive to the supermarket took her through the bleak winter landscape, rugged and eerie. The sun, now dimmed by milky clouds, cast faint patches of light and shadow on the rolling moors and ragged hills. Slumbering, prehistoric beasts about to let out a rumbling growl. Covered with clumps of trees, crouching together against the relentless wind, and tufts of dry heather clinging to the steep slopes like castaways to driftwood. A harsh land, wild and untamed, desolate and deserted. Hauntingly beautiful.

Why is it so empty, where did all the people go?

She remembered the words of a historian in a documentary about the Highlands. 'This is not pretty. But by God, it's beautiful. And it prints itself on your soul, a place like this.' Marla couldn't agree more. She could feel the ancient, deep-rooted energy of the land resonating in her every cell.

Or she was simply dead tired.

Luckily, the shop wasn't too busy. This branch was on the smaller side in the grand scheme of supermarket chains. And it was the only one for miles. Mindful of her financial situation and considering her circumstances, kitchen and otherwise, Marla thought it best to stick strictly to the basics.

She headed directly for the wine section.

Since it was early December, the entire supermarket was in full Christmas swing. Large golden paper stars dangled from the ceiling. Three-foot thick and never-ending garlands, made of shiny, green plastic branches wrapped in gold and silver baubles, rested on top of the freezer section. Marla used to love Christmas. She'd been the one who always insisted on proper Christmas dinners at their house, including music, a pretty tree, and nice food. Her grandparents never cared that much, but they had played along. For Marla's sake. Her heart grew heavy in her chest.

Maybe it was because she was absentminded. Maybe it was because she was so exhausted that she couldn't see straight, and this was unknown terrain. Or maybe she was too keen to stock up on Merlot. But when Marla turned into the aisle with the drinks, her shopping trolley clattered into another one. 'Oh, my God! I'm so, so—' Her gaze met an uncomfortably familiar pair of scintillating amber eyes. 'Shit.'

'I see you're still here.' Niall's voice was irritatingly calm.

'You bet I am,' she replied. 'Where else would I be?'

He shrugged. 'Don't know. Mars?'

She decided to be the bigger person and not lower herself to his level. A decision that lasted all of two seconds. 'Running out of battery acid, I see?' she said with a deprecating look at the bottle of rosé on his trolley. She couldn't keep her tongue in check when he was near, apparently.

Instead of being goaded, he said, 'You look exhausted.'

Marla ignored the iota of concern in his comment. Because there couldn't be any. 'What a gifted observer you are!' sounding a lot more acerbic than intended.

'Life in the rural Highlands isn't for everyone, love,' he said and teasingly slowly lifted a second bottle of rosé onto his trolley. Then a third. 'Maybe you'd feel better in your natural habitat in the big city. You know, with soy lattes and vegan muffins.'

'And you thought *I* was full of prejudice. That's the pot calling the kettle black, don't you think?' This time, she sounded precisely as snarky as she wanted. Now it was she who turned on her heel and left him standing in the aisle.

... only to turn right back again to grab a bottle of red. She wouldn't let this rosé-slurping Scottish tree man rob her of her night's sleep. Not in a thousand years.

After Marla had stocked up on toilet paper, ramen, Vaseline and gloves for her hands, and all the other essentials, there was only one thing missing. As she stretched out and reached for the last jar of Marmite, she heard someone clearing their throat behind her.

'We have to stop meeting like this,' Niall said.

'We have to stop meeting, like, in general.'

'That's going to be a bit of a problem,' he noted. 'There are about five people living in this area.'

'And, if I understand you correctly, you would prefer it to be four.'

He didn't respond but pointed to the container in her hand. 'That's the last one.'

'Ah, the observer being observant again,' she scoffed.

'What if *I* wanted it?'

'Then I would tell you that you're too late, Captain Obvious. Small victory, but I'll take it.'

The air between them thickened with humming energy as if two magnets were stuck. It felt like an invisible force field that separated two dimensions, threatening to break any second. For a fleeting moment, there was a possibility of laughter. But there was also something else. Something melancholic and hollow.

'I'm fine, you know,' Marla said into the silence, hiding red chapped hands in the pockets of her jeans. She held on to the little knife. 'In case you wondered.'

'Good. I'm glad,' Niall said. He sounded earnest, but not convinced.

'See you around then, I guess.'

'I'm afraid that can't be avoided. Meanwhile, try not to climb any trees,' he said. 'Next time, I'll leave you there.'

Suddenly, Marla remembered their first encounter. And into her consuming anger towards him poured another kind of heat. She could feel her face tingling and turned around before her cheeks could betray her.

Safe in the driver's seat, Marla let out a sigh of relief. She turned on the ignition and pulled out of the parking lot. As she drove down the quiet road, her mind kept drifting back to Niall. How could he get under her skin like that? His rugged good looks couldn't cancel out his stubbornness and general ass-ness. 'Soy latte and vegan muffins'—what did he know about her life in London? Not a thing. Let alone anything about growing up in Birmingham as a child without a mother, being left by her father, working hard for a degree, taking care of the only two people she could call family, watching them wither away…

Not to wallow in self-pity, but shut up, tree man.

Marla clenched the steering wheel, the cracked skin over her knuckles so taut that a drop of blood oozed out.

He knew nothing of her. And she knew nothing of him.

Best to keep it that way. Even though his amber eyes made the blood in her veins fizz, and she had to blink back the hot pressure behind her eyes.

Besides, he was way too contradictory and unreliable. Hot and cold. Never a good idea. Ever. What did her Gran Rose always say? 'Don't fall for potential, sweet pea.' Marla shook her head and focused on the road ahead, determined to push any thoughts of Niall out of her mind. She had things to do, a place to be, and a castle to fix.

She could and she would get it done.

Fuck the knuckles.

Chapter Eight

Christmas was fast approaching. At least that's what the annual card from Niall's mother indicated. 'Joyeux Noël, E.'—red letters on white handmade paper. She sent it every year in the first week of December. He hadn't seen Eleanor in years, and it was just as well. She was living some sort of bohemian dream with her artist boyfriend and his extensive family somewhere in the Provence. *To each their own,* Niall thought and shrugged.

Perhaps it was indeed the season, but he had finally tried putting the sailboat model together. It was an ambitious project. A good distraction. He was working on the boat's hull at his reclaimed wood table, which served as both a dining space and a work area. Tools and instructions lay scattered on the planks. Niall looked up to wipe the sawdust from his forehead. Through the panoramic glass window, he could see a vast expanse of slim, majestic trees stretching up to the sky like sentinels keeping watch over the land. Their dusky brown needles swayed in the winter wind. Diffuse sunlight filtered through the branches, pouring onto a carpet of moss. Barclay lay snoring in front of the wood burner after running around outside all morning. Serenity and peace filled every corner of the cottage.

Yet a sense of emptiness was looming in the background, like a single black thread woven into a colourful tapestry.

Niall felt the urge to fill the silence. He wiped his hands before picking out a record. It had been a long time since he had consciously chosen to listen to music. Because music, like scent, was the closest humans could get to time travel. And he hadn't been ready for the trip.

Eventually, he pulled out Oasis' *(What's The Story) Morning Glory?* and placed the vinyl on the record player.

1995 was a good year, he thought and let the needle do its job.

He was finishing the hull when the first notes of the last song on the album started to play.

Champagne Supernova.

Marla's image appeared before his mind's eye. He'd noticed dark circles under her eyes when they bumped into each other at the supermarket. Well, *she* had bumped into *him.* Forcefully. But somehow… Niall wasn't sure, she had seemed drained. Somewhat dimmed. He shook his head, but he couldn't shake the thought of her. There was something else. A twinge of an unease gnawed at him.

Sure, he had good reasons for wanting her to leave and put Hazelbrae up for sale. There was a rationale for wanting her signature on a contract with the developer. Unfortunately, the fastest way to achieve that seemed to be letting her entire project crash. He didn't enjoy any of it. But *she* was the one who insisted on taking it all on despite everything and against all reason. He knew it was best for everyone if Marla abandoned Hazelbrae and sold it. The sooner, the better.

Still, doubts of his own actions crept in. Perhaps it had been a tad too Machiavellian to let every contractor in the area know that working on Hazelbrae was not a good thing to do.

Pretty much financial suicide. Which, to be honest, wasn't entirely false. Probably.

Lost in thought, Niall rubbed his chin while Noel Gallagher scrubbed his guitar. As he had heard from Gwen and a few others, Marla had done an impressive amount of work already. He had to acknowledge that maybe she wasn't the dainty London city dweller that he'd thought she was.

If he was honest, there was nothing dainty about her. On the contrary.

He couldn't prevent it. An image slid into his head. His thoughts wandered to the sight of her superbly round backside when she had stretched for that last glass of Marmite. He would have gladly given it up for that view. She didn't need to know that, though. And it meant nothing, of course. He was a man of taste who could appreciate a magnificent physique when he saw it. From a purely aesthetic perspective, so to speak. But it was strange. Since... then, he hadn't so much as looked at another woman that way. Any woman. Niall pushed aside the thought that there might be any interest in her on his part. That couldn't be. For thousands of reasons.

His glance fell upon the sailboat-in-the-making on his table. Longing washed over him. For the sea, the freedom of being one with the skies and the elements, peace, dissolving into a million pieces under the stars.

Hazelbrae had to go on the market so that the developer could buy it and his land along with it. Then Niall could bid Kilcranach farewell once and for all. The offer still stood. He had been in touch.

Two quick knocks on the door interrupted his thoughts. Barclay jumped up and shook his fur. 'Come on in,' Niall said. It was Jack the postie. Niall hadn't even heard his car on the gravel, thanks to Oasis and his distractedness.

'Mornin', Niall! Got a wee package for you. I was in the

area, so I thought I'd come out here and save you the trip,' he said and rubbed Barclay's chin.

'That's nice of you, Jack. How are you?'

'Ah, busy man. Less than three weeks until Christmas. Even in this forgotten place, some people send gifts and cards and all that.' His laugh sounded like a good twenty years ago when they were in school together. Before Niall had left for university.

'Wait, that's Oasis!' Jack said. 'I remember. That's one of the bands we covered with the Salmons of Knowledge.'

'Christ, don't remind me of that.' Niall snorted in nostalgic embarrassment. Teenagers with nose rings and questionable haircuts, they had tackled their desperate boredom by forming a band with an ironic name. Completely ignorant of the fact that this irony was lost on everyone else. Their band played cover songs at parties. Guns 'n' Roses, R.E.M, Pearl Jam, Oasis… whatever was popular in the early 1990s. They reinvested their meagre earnings in new vinyl, instruments, and beer.

'Are you still playing?' Jack asked.

'Naw, I don't. Been ages. Wouldn't be able to move my fingers at all. Do you? I mean, regularly?'

'Aye, I'm playing tonight, mate!'

'Tonight?'

'At the Ceilidh in the Bonnet. Like every first Friday in December. Why don't you come down for a pint?'

'Don't think so, Jack. Group dancing in shapes and circles isn't my thing.'

'Aye, I get it,' Jack said. 'But your house is pretty secluded. And it's Christmas time, you know. Don't want you to be lonely out here and all that.'

'Naw, I'll be fine. I'm used to it. Don't worry about me. Next time.'

'You know as well as I do that there's not much else going on here. If you change your mind…' Jack put his hand on

Niall's shoulder. 'People would be glad to see your stupid face, mate. Pop in anytime. I'm serious.'

'Thanks, Jack. Have fun tonight.'

'All right. Ta-ta!'

Niall clicked the door shut behind Jack and exhaled. His thoughts trailed off to carefree times when he still used to play acoustic guitar every day. The warm wood settling into his hands, the way he could get lost in the music, plucking chords for hours, forgetting about everything else. But he knew that nostalgia was a treacherous friend. He used to be a different man back then.

Sometimes he missed that guy.

Marla pulled her shawl around her shoulders as she stepped out of Hazelbrae. She had been working hard all day, and now she was done. Dividing all the tasks into smaller ones had helped her to make a little progress. Even though she had come to know unprecedented levels of mental and physical exhaustion.

Stop it, it's supposed to be a fun night out.

She walked down the road towards the pub, strolling past the old stone church with its spire reaching towards the sky. All of Kilcranach shone in Christmas splendour. The houses along the now familiar cobblestone streets were adorned with bright strings of twinkling lights and lush evergreen garlands above. Glittering decorations draped the shop windows, and every door had a holiday wreath with bows and shiny baubles. People had bundled up in heavy coats and scarves, with hats and gloves to keep warm. And, more importantly, dry. This used to be her favourite time of year, with hot toddies, chocolate oranges, and gingerbread galore. Marla could feel a sliver of the old Christmas sparkle quiver inside her heart. She smiled and waved at Bert McIntosh, the bookshop owner, from across the street.

It had taken a while, but they all knew her by now, and she knew them. At first, Marla hadn't thought that she could feel at home in such a small town, but she was beginning to. Maybe it was the tight-knit community or the rough beauty of the landscape. Or the way the locals had welcomed her, despite her being an outsider. It was a sense of community that she hadn't experienced before. In Birmingham and London, everyone had been too busy and self-absorbed to even make eye contact, let alone acknowledge each other's presence. Here in Kilcranach, people took the time to stop and chat, to ask how she was doing. It was a welcome change from the fast-paced city life. That was the main reason she had decided against visiting Trish and her family in London for Christmas. It was nicer here. More magical. One day, when—if—Hazelbrae was done, she would invite them all up here. Maybe to an enchanted Scottish castle Easter extravaganza or a grand opening of some sort.

The pub windows shone invitingly. Marla stomped her feet free of mud and entered the warmth. 'Hey there! All set for the Ceilidh?' she said into the festive-looking room. Gwen had gone all out and decorated the bar and tables with candles and holly. Tartan bows hung in fir garlands on the wall and the scent of mulled wine mingled with a whiff of the smoke that always laced Kilcranach's winter air. At the back of the pub was another door leading to a room with a dance floor. The band was about to play.

'Marla, meet my parents!' Gwen smiled and swept her hand toward the two tanned, freckled, and friendly-looking people next to her. Fascinatingly, Gwen's face resembled both of her parents to an equal degree. She had inherited her slender frame from her mother, who was just as petite and surrounded by the same resolute radiance as her daughter.

'I'm so glad to meet you both,' Marla said. 'Gwen has told me so many things about you.'

The couple chuckled and exchanged a knowing look. 'Oh, has she now?' Gary said and winked. 'We hope only good things.'

'Of course!' Marla said. 'She speaks highly of you both.'

They chatted for a while, swapping stories and sharing laughter. Gary and Linda had flown in from Alicante to spend Christmas with their daughter. 'And to stand behind this bar again for a night,' Linda said. 'First, I couldn't get far enough away from it. Now I miss it. Weird, isn't it?'

Marla took a sip of her mulled cider and smiled at the couple. They were kind-hearted and welcoming. She could see why Gwen loved them so much. Despite living far apart, they were a tight-knit unit. Just as Marla and her grandparents once had been.

'Hello young lady, how's our wee castle doing?' Marla turned around and saw Janet Bellbottom standing behind her, looking as fashionable as ever, with her signature leopard coat. Underneath it, she was wearing a flamboyant floral dress.

'It's starting to come along, slowly. It's difficult to get contractors, but I'll find a way,' Marla said with a wrought smile.

'I know you've been reluctant to ask for help, dearie. But I think you should ask Niall. He's good with tools, and he knows this town like the back of his hand. He might even have some connections in the region to help you with your project,' Mrs Bellbottom said. 'And he knows the estate like no other.'

'I appreciate the advice. But no.' Marla's mouth narrowed into a line. 'Thanks, but no thanks. I'd rather hammer a rusty nail into my eyeball.'

'Oh, I see. So, he's managed to annoy you already?'

'That's one way to phrase it.'

Mrs Bellbottom let out a snigger. 'Och, don't mind him, love. He's a bit grumpy these days. But he has a good heart.'

Marla rolled her eyes. 'I'm sure he has something tumbling around somewhere in that large chest cavity of his. But it doesn't change the fact that he's been nothing but difficult since I arrived. Don't know why.' She lifted one shoulder. 'I guess we rub each other the wrong way.'

Mrs Bellbottom gave Marla a shrewd look. 'I was his teacher. Did you know that?'

Marla shook her head.

'I've known that cute wooden head of his since he first walked into my classroom.' Mrs Bellbottom let out a sigh. 'He hasn't always had it easy.'

Marla furrowed her brows, intrigued by Mrs Bellbottom's words. 'What do you mean?'

'He used to be a quiet, artsy boy in school. Always drawing or doodling in his notebook. And when he was a teenager, he started a band with his friends. Something silly with salmons, I don't remember. But they were good, you know. Niall was their lead guitarist and singer,' Mrs Bellbottom said, her eyes nostalgic. 'But then, tragedy struck. First, his father passed away. The cancer took him within three months. It was terrible.'

Fucking cancer. Marla felt sympathy for Niall. And something new, an emerging form of kinship. *But I didn't have it easy, either, and I'm not an ass. I think.*

'When Niall went to St. Andrews to study, his mother packed up and moved away. To France. Their house here became a holiday let. Can you believe that? The boy didn't even have a proper home.'

'That must have been tough,' Marla said. 'Poor guy.'

'It was. But while he was in St. Andrews, he met his wife. Nathalie. Lovely girl. They eventually moved back to Kilcranach and got married here, at Hazelbrae. Ah, I remember it well! That was one fantastic garden wedding. Fairy lights and all that,' Mrs Bellbottom gushed.

'I didn't know he is married,' Marla said and felt a scathing, short sting.

'He isn't. Not anymore,' Mrs Bellbottom took a breath. 'She died in a car accident six years ago. Awful business, such a dreadful tragedy. How long were they married?' Mrs Bellbottom called out to Gary behind the bar.

'What are you on about now, Janet?'

'Niall and Nathalie.'

'That must have been about eight or nine years,' said Linda, as the shadow of memory darkened her face.

'That's so terribly heart-breaking,' Marla said softly.

'Yes, it was. You have no idea. After Nathalie's death, he withdrew from everything and everyone. Including us,' Mrs Bellbottom said, sadness in her voice. 'He used to be a pillar of this odd community, always happy to help. But then… for a long time, we hardly saw him. He still keeps mostly to himself nowadays. And he likes to pretend to be gruff and grumpy.' Mrs Bellbottom smiled. 'But let me tell you, there's still the kind-hearted, generous boy inside. Somewhere.'

Marla's throat tightened and her stomach lurched as the pieces of Niall's story fit together in her mind. It all made at least slightly more sense now. She stared at the floor, searching for a way to reconcile that fresh notion of guilt for judging him so harshly with her pride. But she wasn't sure if she could bring herself to ask for his help. Not after how arrogantly he had treated her. 'It all sounds devastating. But what does his story have to do with me asking him for help?' Marla asked.

'It means that he might surprise you. He might be the help you need to get things going with Hazelbrae. And who knows, you might be the one to help him in return. You never know. He has a good heart. He just needs someone to remind him of that,' Mrs Bellbottom said and finished her pint of Scottish lager in one go.

Marla wondered if Niall ever talked to anyone about what he had gone through. She knew all too well what it was like to lose someone. But still. 'I'll think about it,' she said and then quickly added, 'How's the other Mrs Bellbottom doing?'

The distraction worked.

'Ah, Sylvia's grand. She'll be coming in later for the dance.' Mrs Bellbottom's face lit up when she spoke of her wife. 'Still can't believe that such a catch agreed to marry little old me.' She giggled like a schoolgirl.

Marla smiled at the love and joy radiating from Mrs Bellbottom. It was comforting to see such pure happiness amid all the doom and gloom in the world. 'I'm so glad to hear that. And I'll keep your suggestion in mind.'

Mrs Bellbottom patted Marla's hand. 'Of course, dearie. Now go on, forget about the worries and enjoy yourself tonight. Don't let an old woman bore you with sad tales from the past.'

'Never! I could listen to your stories all night.'

She watched as Mrs Bellbottom made her way toward the dance floor, her leopard coat swishing behind her. Marla heard the music and laughter from the room at the back of the pub. The rhythm was infectious, her foot tapped along. She glanced at the dance floor where the Ceilidh had started and people were moving to the music of the band. Janet Bellbottom had wasted no time and was being whirled around in a terrifying tempo by William Collins, the solicitor. Marla was mesmerised by the scene. It looked like fun, like something else than the constant problem-solving that had been dominating her life recently. She had always wanted to experience a Ceilidh, a classic Scottish social dance, but she had never had the opportunity. And, well, she hadn't been looking for one. Perhaps because she wasn't the most gifted dancer, and the thought of making a fool of herself was daunting.

But then she remembered her grandda's stories about the wild fun of the Ceilidh, and she felt a surge of determination. Marla pushed off her stool and made her way toward the dancing crowd. The time had come to awaken her inner Scottish dancing fairy.

Chapter Nine

Niall's hand lingered over the handle. *What the hell am I doing here?*

Barclay looked up at him excitedly. He, at least, knew what awaited him inside. 'If only I had half the trust in myself that you do,' Niall said with a wry smile. 'But we're here now. Might as well see it through.'

With a valiant move, he opened the door and entered the Blue Bonnet. The warmth of the room hit him, along with the chatter and laughter of the guests. From the back room, the sound of lively traditional Scottish music wafted through the pub. That's where the action was. The bar at the front was as good as empty. Twinkling lights and garlands of fir and holly decorated the pub. Despite feeling out of place, the cosy ambience and music gave Niall a sense of being at home.

As he made his way to the bar, Niall felt self-conscious, but he reminded himself why he had come. If everything went according to plan, this time next year he would be lying on the deck of his sailboat somewhere at sea. Counting the stars. This was his last Christmas Ceilidh ever and, he told himself, something of a farewell to Kilcranach. Saying goodbye without making anybody sad or angry. He was being polite. That was all.

Gwen stood alone behind the bar. 'Niall?' Her mouth dropped open and her eyes widened before she frowned in confusion. 'What are you doing here? There's nae parcel for you or anything.'

'Believe it or not, I've been asking myself the same question,' he said, leaning his forearms on the wooden counter.

'Great to have you here. It really is. I haven't seen you out in ages,' Gwen said with a smile on her face that changed as quickly as the weather, darkening in a flash. There was a storm brewing. 'Let me ask you another question,' she said calmly, while throwing Barclay his usual treat from the glass on the counter. 'Why are you being such a massive, stupid arse?'

A cloud of fierceness and disapproval had gathered around her pointy hat, and Niall felt confounded and uncomfortable. 'Beg your pardon?'

'Haud yer tongue and listen,' she said. 'Don't think I wouldn't know that you're the one behind all the delays with Hazelbrae. You know, no one coming out to do any work and such.'

'Not sure I know what you mean.'

'Cousin Craig heard something from Steve, and he heard it from Ross,' Gwen said. 'Don't know what's going on in that wee head of yours, but it has to stop. You're out of order, Niall. It's unacceptable. She's working so hard. You can't even imagine. It's mental.'

'If this project is too big for her, then perhaps she shouldn't have taken it on,' he replied with a dash of spite.

'Oh, do shut up! It wouldn't be if you weren't sabotaging her every step. Any other person could simply hire a contractor, some joiners and painters, maybe an architect, and get on with it.'

'Any other person would have either a lot more money or

know the right people,' Niall said. 'She's an outsider, in over her head.'

'Is she though?' Little bolts of lightning seemed to shoot out of Gwen's eyes in his direction. 'If you would stop revolving around yourself for five fucking minutes, you might see beyond your own nose. Did you know her grandda was from Kilcranach? He left in the sixties for Birmingham, married there and all that. He was a local lad. But even if not. what you're doing to Marla, that's pure cruel.' She threw her tea towel at him. 'I'm not gonnae tell her—yet—because I want to keep the peace in this village and don't want her to crazy-murder you, but you have to get yourself together, Niall McCarron.'

Now he fell silent. Gwen's words stung him like a forceful slap in the face. He suspected she might be right, but he couldn't bring himself to fully admit it. Gwen didn't know the entire story.

Was he being unintentionally cruel or simply rational and focused? He had justified his actions in his mind, and they had seemed perfectly reasonable. But hearing them spoken out loud by someone else sounded mean. Yes, he had been consumed by his own plans. But—

'And you already walked out on old Lady Hamilton like a wuss,' Gwen continued her tirade. 'So, whatever's happening, make it stop. You don't have to like Marla, but you mustn't bully her. She is a good woman. She is my friend. And as much as I can tell, life hasn't always been easy for her. She has no one. So be nice. You hear me?' Gwen's sweet and bright smile stood in stark contrast to her words.

Her comments echoed in his head. What did she mean by no one? Maybe he was being a bit petty. And maybe he had let Lady Hamilton down after… Niall mumbled something under his breath, feeling chastened by Gwen's words. An unsettling blend of abashment and irritation washed over him.

'Excuse me?' Gwen asked with her silvery voice.

'You might not be completely wrong in all aspects. Perhaps.'

'Good. Glad to hear it. Enjoy the Ceilidh. You don't have to dance, you know. But at least try not to spoil it for everyone else, Ebenezer.'

With heavy feet, Niall moved towards the back room, where the commotion was in full swing. Barclay followed, chomping on his second treat. The annexe was filled with people. Mostly locals dressed in festive clothes—Santa hats, sequins, and funny Christmas jumpers—and a handful of holiday guests, all dancing to the lively music under glittery garlands. Niall felt awkward and stopped in the doorway. Nobody on the parquet seemed to notice him. *Good.* They were too busy spinning around the room in pairs, falling over their own feet, laughing, the lively tune swelling around them, the notes bouncing off the walls. The two Mrs Bellbottoms had a good giggle when they bumped into Linda and Gary.

A Ceilidh is always a riot, Niall thought with a half-smile. Lots of people dancing in pairs and groups to jigs, reels, and polkas, following the caller's commands to live music. Jack was playing the double bass, Fiona her fiddle, and Bert his accordion. There used to be more musicians in Kilcranach, but they had moved or long passed away.

Then he saw her.

Marla was dancing with Mr Collins. Her hair flowed over her shoulders in waves of whisky-coloured silk. Her face was blushing with joy, bright with the glare of the warm lights and the shine of the holiday season. She had the most captivating smile, wide and carefree.

She was lost in the moment, being spun around the dancefloor.

And he was lost in the sight of her.

She wore skinny jeans and a simple black top with long sleeves and a plunging neckline that clung to her like a second skin, showing off every curve and movement. A sizzling shiver raced up his spine as he watched her move to the rhythm of the music. He wondered how it would feel to have her pressed against him, the silkiness of her hair between his fingers…

Niall shook his head and tried to push the thought from his mind. He couldn't let himself get carried away like this. He had no right to think this way about her. And he didn't want to. Not now, not ever.

Yet somehow, he couldn't tear his eyes away from what he saw.

Barclay interrupted his thoughts by nudging him on the knee.

'Look who's here!' said Gary with a hearty slap on Niall's shoulder before tousling Barclay's fur. 'Niall, man! What dragged you out of that cave of yours?'

'Heard you were in town and wanted to collect my debts,' Niall replied. All at once, eyes were on him. He wasn't used to being the centre of attention. It made him nervous.

Gary laughed. 'Glad to hear you're still half-funny, pal!'

Marla's heart pounded in her chest when she spotted Niall, standing in the doorway with Gwen's father. *What the hell is he doing here?*

He looked a bit lost and out of place in his black leather jacket, black turtleneck jumper, and jeans. A long past five o'clock-shadow covered his jawline, his thick hair tousled as ever. Nothing cheerful or festive about him. He seemed sad and lonely. And much, much too cool for a jolly Christmas Ceilidh in rural Scotland. The tune was ending, and Mr Collins gave Marla one last spin before bowing and thanking her for the dance. She curtsied and then made her way over to the tiny refreshment table to catch her breath. Her knees wobbled. *Probably too much carpet ripping and dance-floor twirling plus too little sleep.*

'Marla!' Gwen's voice brought her out of her reverie. 'Come try some of my famous mince pies.'

Marla grabbed a pastry. 'Delish! Thanks, Gwen.'

The musicians paused and loud chatter filled the room. Gwen fluttered around the room with her tray of mince pies, her mother with more mulled cider in tow. Marla closed her eyes as she bit into the buttery, crumbly, short-crust pastry, enjoying the spicy and fruity taste. When she opened her eyes again, Niall was standing next to her. Marla's heart stuttered for a few beats. She hesitated, wondering if she should do the polite thing and say something remotely nice. A truce, of sorts. But before she could make up her mind, it was Niall who broke the silence.

'Evening.'

'Evening,' she said, careful to sound neutral. 'What brings *you* here?'

He wrinkled his nose. 'My dog insisted. I couldn't refuse.'

'I suppose he is a more enthusiastic dancer than you.'

'Correct,' Niall said. 'He's also a lot more talented.'

'And much more popular, I bet.'

They both exhibited a reluctant smile. Marla quickly took another bite of her mince pie. Niall pushed his hand through his hair. 'You have crumbs on your top,' he said.

'I haff woff?'

'Crumbs. On your… um… top.'

Marla lowered her head and saw a trail of tiny pastry bits leading down the path between her breasts. Like a raunchy version of Hansel and Gretel. 'Oh. Oops,' she said.

Niall's eyes flitted over her face. 'Apart from that, you… you look nice.'

Was this really him talking, this gruff tree man who usually scowled as if competing for the grumpiest *Zoolander* impression? This was an unexpected compliment coming from him. Especially considering the traces of sleeplessness under her eyes. Expertly concealed, of course. Still.

'Who are you and what have you done to the village troll?' Marla replied. 'Because… well, you clean up nicely yourself.' Her tone was less sarcastic now.

Niall's gaze lingered on her lips as if expecting something else, and Marla felt her face turn pink. Because she knew he could see what she was thinking. About her hands gripping his amazing hair, his mouth pressed onto hers, burning lips that—

Where was this coming from? Up to now, she'd done her utmost to despise the guy, but something must have shifted when she heard about his hardships.

He grinned crookedly, a trace of the man she had met in the forest on her first day in Kilcranach.

'Took a shower today,' he said. 'Makes all the difference.'

And now she pictured him naked, eyes closed, water running over his muscular body…

Stop it, for Pete's sake!

'Niall, mate! You made it!' Jack headed straight towards them. 'I can't believe it! It's so good to see you here!' The two men hugged and there was genuine joy on the postie's face.

'Come on then, Niall,' Jack said, rubbing his hands together, 'You up for a wee jam? You can't just stand here and look pretty. All broody and moody. You're no Mr Darcy.'

Marla gave a snorting laugh, spewing crumbs in all directions.

'Naw, Jack. I haven't played in years. You know that. Don't put me on the spot.'

'What was that I heard?' said Janet Bellbottom, his former teacher. 'Niall is playing something for us? If that doesn't mean the world has come to an end, I don't know what does.'

'Hello, Mrs Bellbottom.' Niall shifted from one leg to another.

'Come on, it'll be fun. Bit like old times!' Jack said and grabbed Niall's elbow, pulling him towards the makeshift stage. 'Lucky for you, I brought my other guitar.'

Fiona and Bert were already preparing their instruments for the next round. 'Ah, Niall. Did your house burn down or… why are you gracing us with your presence?' Fiona said sternly. But the smile in her wrinkly eyes said otherwise.

They all really, really like him, Marla noted.

'Don't know if I'm up for it, folks,' Niall protested. But she could feel his resistance beginning to dissolve in the face of its futility.

'Come on, man. You used to shred like nobody's business,' Jack insisted.

There was no escape, so he gave in. 'All right then, let's try it. One tune. But don't laugh too loudly.'

Mrs Bellbottom clapped her hands in excitement, and Jack grinned. Amidst jeers, Niall took a seat on the wooden chair next to Jack on the small stage. 'It's tuned,' said Jack, and handed over his acoustic guitar. Niall lowered his head, closed his eyes, and took some time to feel the weight of the instrument. As if he wanted to get to know it first. He plucked at the strings, eliciting a few brilliant notes from her. 'All right, sweetheart,' he said. 'Don't let me down.'

Then he straightened his shoulders and played the first chords. Soon after, Jack joined him with his other guitar.

It took a bit until Marla recognised the melody. *Patience* by Guns 'n' Roses. When Niall started to whistle, Barclay perked up his ears. And after a while—where Axl Rose would have sung about taking it slow—Fiona's fiddle weaved its delicate sound into the melody, singing a song of longing and home that transformed a slow rock tune into a Scottish folk ballad.

It was utterly, unexpectedly beautiful, and it gripped Marla's soul.

Niall played as if he hadn't paused at all. His hands were agile, darting over the frets. He seemed one with the melody and the guitar. The music came from within him, streaming through him. The swift, delicate movements of his fingers hypnotised Marla. And as if that wasn't enough, the light cast a golden hue over his hair, like sparks flying from tinder. Only with a great effort of will could she take her eyes off him.

'Something good is happening here tonight, dearie,' said Janet Bellbottom to Marla. 'It feels like he's thawing. About bloody time after all those years!'

'Mhm.' Marla nodded absentmindedly and let her gaze wander over the audience. To the left of the stage stood a trio of female tourists, recognisable by their less-than-tacky, way-too-chic Christmas attire. They were leering at Niall with uninhibited fascination. Positively *ogling* him. A zing of awareness shot through Marla. Suddenly, she saw him with their eyes: a tall, broad-shouldered, fully-haired, stubbly-bearded, amber-eyed, sexy Scottish music god with nimble fingers and strong hands in a black turtleneck. Accompanied by his ridiculously cute dog. *Shit.*

Marla couldn't deny that there was something between them, even though she wasn't happy to admit it. At all. What precisely that something was, she couldn't tell. Her thoughts drifted to his playing fingers and what else he might be able to do with them…

Don't be absurd, she cautioned herself. A very sexy prick is still a prick.

He made her mad. He was bad news. So why was her heart drumming a staccato?

When the song ended, the room erupted in applause and cheering. Marla clapped along, nearly as enthusiastic as the others. She knew an excellent musician when she heard one. After all, she had dated enough of them. Interesting, exciting men with creativity, passion, and a whole range of problems. Narcissistic egomaniacs. Good in bed, bad for the heart.

Luckily, that was a while ago. And definitely never again.

Niall looked up from his guitar, caught her eye, and held her gaze for a moment before a smile formed on his lips. Her heart skipped a beat, and she felt a rush of heat pool in her belly. *That's it. No more mulled cider for me.*

Jack gave Niall a pat on the back, bringing him out of the trance. 'Bloody hell, mate. That was amazing. You still got it!'

Niall grinned, a trace of embarrassment flashing on his face. 'Thanks, man. It's been a while, but it was fun.'

Marla felt a twinge of disappointment when he got up and disappeared into the front room with Gary. Then there was a light tap on her shoulder. Turning around, she saw the trio of women who had been eyeballing Niall earlier.

'Excuse me. Do you know who that was?' one of them asked.

There was a pinch of jealousy. Marla knew it was irrational and stupid. But she couldn't shake the feeling that all the other women in the room were vying for Niall's attention. Except the two married Mrs Bellbottoms, naturally.

'That? Oh, just a stinky cow farmer. I would steer clear if I were you,' she lowered her voice. 'All he cares for are his heifers. I also heard he sold his soul to the Devil. Why else would he look so good *and* be able to play guitar like that?'

Chapter Ten

Barclay was having the time of his life. Surrounded by five cheering children, the border collie spun in erratic circles on the dance floor, like a will-o'-the-wisp, wagging his tail in excitement.

'You didn't exaggerate. Your dog *is* a groovy dancer,' Marla said to Niall, who had sat down next to her at the bar and placed his empty bottle of ginger beer on the counter. She was waiting for Gwen to get her coat. Time to go home. Her eyes would barely stay open.

'I envy him,' Niall said. 'He's mastering it on four legs. I can't even get my two to dance. And he loves to be the centre of attention.' He watched his dog with warm affection.

'I'd say you also look pretty in the limelight. What a performance. Do you sing, too?'

'Me? A little, back in the day.' His voice sounded strained. 'But not professionally or anything. Just in our school band.'

'Here you are, hen,' Gwen said with her signature smile, handing Marla her blue pea coat. 'I hope you enjoyed your first Ceilidh.'

'Thanks, Gwenny! And I did, very much so. We'll chat tomorrow.'

'Same time, same place. Lots of coffee,' Gwen said to Marla, and winked.

'So, Cinderella *is* leaving the ball before midnight,' Niall noted.

'Cinderella has neither fairy godmother nor prince and needs to take care of her own bloody castle tomorrow.' Marla shrugged in defiance. 'The struggle is real. Not that you'd care.'

'No need to get snippy,' he said. 'But if it's such a struggle for you, the least I can do is offer you my carriage.' Niall raised an eyebrow at her in challenge.

Marla couldn't resist the temptation to counter. 'Only if it's a pumpkin.'

'It's so old, it might as well be. But it should make it to Hazelbrae.' He got up and slid his arms into his leather jacket.

'I'm not sure if it's such a good plan,' she said, suddenly serious. Barclay came galloping towards them, ready to go. Marla fluffed his velvety ears. Niall driving her would save her from the tiring trek up the hill. Her feet throbbed from hours of dancing, and her muscles ached from weeks of labour. But the thought of being alone with him in his car, such a closed space… There was a tightness in her chest. She looked up at him, contemplating what to say.

Niall reassured her, 'Only if you feel comfortable. Whatever you choose is fine with me.'

There was something about the way he looked at her… Was he indifferent, or was he letting her take the lead, respecting her space and her decision?

The way he smells of pine, soap, leather, and something sweet.

Marla bit her lip, considering his offer. She wasn't entirely convinced of his nice and less grumpy side. His off-handedness was suspiciously nice. She wasn't sure she was ready to succumb to his charms, no matter how friendly he seemed right now. And then there was this flicker of something between them she was trying to ignore.

In the end, her weariness won.

She gave him a small nod. 'Alright then. But I'm warning you, Prince *Un*charming. I'm a terrible passenger. I might swear. A lot.'

'I'll try to keep the cause for swearing to a minimum, Cinder*hella*.' He flashed a smile, and it seemed genuine. Time would tell whether his friendliness would persist this time or whether the pesky Mr Hyde would return.

The December night was cold and quiet. As Niall drove along the narrow country roads, Marla fell asleep, Barclay's chin on her shoulder. Niall glanced over at her, head lolling to the side with each bend in the road. She looked peaceful, her chest rising and falling. He couldn't blame her for being exhausted. Niall wondered how she managed to still stand, let alone dance. Her resilience and self-sufficiency were commendable. He knew all too well what life here was like, what managing a rural estate truly meant. She didn't.

On top of that, however, there was a new feeling. An inkling of guilt, thanks to Gwen. Still, it wasn't that simple. Niall was torn between latent guilt and reluctant admiration. Between wanting to help and wanting to get away. He didn't know what to do next. Or if there was even anything to do. He lowered the volume of the radio. Marla and Barclay were snoring in perfect unison. A feeling of timelessness and tranquillity filled the car.

He slowed down as they reached the gate of Hazelbrae. Marla stirred awake, rubbing her eyes. 'Oh. Are we here already?' she asked.

'Aye, we are.'

'Sorry,' she muttered. 'I didn't mean to fall asleep on you like that. That's rude.'

'Don't worry about it,' he said. 'Are you sure you're okay? You seem a bit out of it.'

She yawned. 'Awfully tired, I guess.'

He nodded in understanding. But a nagging sense persisted in the back of his mind that he was at least partly responsible for her exhaustion. A feeling that he didn't like. The air between them was dense with unspoken things. Niall was the first to say something. 'You seemed to enjoy your first Ceilidh.'

'Man, that was wild. Honestly, I didn't know how much fun it would be,' she said. 'Makes me wonder what else I have missed by not growing up here.'

He leaned in as he turned off the engine and noticed her hands in her lap, red and roughened from days of relentless renovating. *She isn't that fine,* he thought. The stars mirrored in the many windows of Hazelbrae.

'Don't you feel alone in such a vast house?'

'There are plenty of ghosts, mice, and spiders to keep me company.' She exhaled. 'I was a lot lonelier in my tiny flat in London. A lot.'

As Marla spoke those words, emotion welled up inside her. She hadn't been aware that she had been bottling it up for weeks. Perhaps much longer. But a thousand microscopic cracks in the dam were enough. She tried to fight it down. The last thing she wanted was to burst into tears next to *him,* of all people. But she was helpless. The tears started to flow, hot and heavy, down her face. She tried to wipe them away with the back of her sore hand, but they kept coming. She let out a shuddering breath, and then another, until she was sobbing in earnest.

'Hey. Hey, it's okay,' he said.

Marla tried to speak, but her throat was tight and hoarse. She shook her head.

Niall took her hand. His touch was warm. She turned to face him, her eyes still wet with tears, and saw something in his gaze that she hadn't noticed before.

'I'm sorry,' she said, her voice choked with emotion.

'No need to apologise,' he said. 'Sometimes it's good to let it all out.'

Marla inhaled deeply and slowly through her mouth, attempting to compose herself. She could feel his eyes on her, and she knew she wasn't a pretty crier. Quite the opposite. When she cried, her face swelled up, her nose went bright red, and she morphed into a puffy snot monster.

'I hate… to say this… but… you might have been right all along,' she said with a cracking voice. 'It's all too much, and I should have left on my first day here. I'm a failure. No matter how hard I work, it's never enough. Ever.' Her shoulders trembled. 'But…. giving up feels like letting my grandda down. He was from here, you know From Kilcranach. This was his… he often… He died two years ago. My gran, too. I miss them both.'

The pain of loss made her fall silent. There was a grand-parents-shaped hole in her heart that would hurt forever and never be filled.

Niall still held her hand. Marla struggled for composure, too engulfed in her own pain to ponder this closeness. 'There must be an important reason Lady Hamilton left Hazelbrae to him and his descendants. Although I still have no clue. But if I fail in restoring and keeping Hazelbrae, I will let my family's legacy down. I'll let my grandda down,' Marla said, with her chin on her chest. 'I'd be a failure. I'd have to go back to London. To everything that happened there. And I don't want to,' she whispered, and her hand clasped his.

The city had suffocated her with its emptiness and stagnation after her grandparents' deaths. They had both been in their seventies. She should have had at least ten more years with them. Every inch of her flat, every sidewalk on her street, held a trace of her tears. Everywhere she went was saturated with sadness. Her breath caught like broken glass in her throat as she remembered the bus stop where she had sunk to her knees. Exhausted from sitting by her gran's bedside in her last hours. The shop on the corner, where she had heart-wrenching last words with her grandda over the phone before he passed away so suddenly, only seven weeks after his wife. Surely, of a broken heart. The windowsill where Marla had sat when someone, she couldn't even recall who, had phoned and informed her of her grandda's death.

Everywhere was poisoned with sorrow.

The weight of grief had been crushing her for two years. And she hadn't even noticed. She had been in such a dense forest of foggy numbness and withered prickles that she had forgotten the existence of the outside world.

But here, in Scotland, she had started to feel alive again. The pulse of its ancient landscape resonated with something in the depth of her soul, awakening her, and cutting through all the thorns. The warmth of its people thawing the ice around her shrivelled heart.

It was frightening. And wonderful.

Here, under the wide skies of Kilcranach, Marla could breathe again. The thought of going back to London filled her with dread. Even though Hazelbrae was draining her physically, mentally, and financially. She wasn't ready to give up. But she wasn't sure that she could go on for much longer, either.

'Marla,' he said.

There was something about the way he spoke her name that sent a jolt through her heart. It was long too late to deny the fact that she was attracted to him. Even though he was such an unspeakably irksome person who could make her blood boil with one look. Right now, every fibre of her being ached to fall into his arms, to be comforted by the calm rhythm of his heart. But she simply couldn't let herself get too close. Not when they had such different attitudes towards Hazelbrae.

Not when he was so changeable.

Marla pulled her hand away and kept her glance fixed on her knees, not wanting to meet his eyes. She was afraid of what he might see in hers.

'Not that you would understand, but I have to save this place.'

Niall opened his mouth to speak, but Marla cut him off before he was able to continue. 'Save it. I'm not giving up,' she said, steeling herself against any feelings of doubt or uncertainty that might be creeping in. 'This is my place now.'

'Seems like it,' he said. 'And although that makes zero sense to me, I'd expect nothing less.'

Niall tried to process what she had just told him. He understood what it felt like to be lonely. Be surrounded by ghosts of the past and the weight of loss. It was a feeling that clung to him, something he could never shake off.

Now he understood her determination to keep Hazelbrae, to make it into something meaningful and lasting. It was a challenge he respected. But it also worried him. He didn't want her to be tied down by the burden of someone else's legacy, to be trapped in a life that wasn't for herself, but for her dead grandfather.

Besides, *he* didn't want to be trapped in Kilcranach.

She looked up at him then, her eyes still glistening with tears, her nose red, her lips swollen. A part of him wanted to reach out and touch her face, to brush away the tears that still clung to her face, to pull her into his arms and comfort her and tell her that everything would be alright. But he knew that would only complicate things. He couldn't ignore the fact that they were on opposite sides of the fence when it came to Hazelbrae. Even more than she could have guessed. He cleared his throat, trying to chase away the thoughts that were clouding his mind.

'I'm sorry,' she said, her voice barely above a whisper. 'I didn't mean to unload all of this on you. It's… I don't know what to do. Also, it's embarrassing.' She sniffled. 'I'm so damn exhausted.'

'It's all right. Don't worry about it.'

When Barclay licked her salty cheek and Marla smiled with tears in her eyes, something twitched inside Niall. He swallowed hard, pushing down on anything that tried to rise to the surface. 'I'll come over tomorrow and have a look.'

Because at that moment, the solution was occurring to him. Helping Marla made perfect sense. If he could get Hazelbrae halfway repaired—just the worst of it—the chances of finding a buyer quickly were much greater. Which meant getting away a lot faster. She would be less exhausted and he would have less of a guilty conscience. If he went all in with those renovations, pushing them ahead, he could kill two birds with one blonde sandstone.

After that, Niall just would have to find a way to persuade her to sell. But he would think of something. Details could always be sorted out later.

Chapter Eleven

It was half eight and still dark. The sky was melting from pure black to an indigo that faded into a thin strip of periwinkle near the horizon, as if drawn by an artist's paintbrush. The morning star shone over the hills. There was a freshness in the air, the smell of a new day, of a clean slate. The world was silent but for some far-off birds chirping. Early risers. Like him. *Not much of an early riser when you didn't get to sleep in the first place,* Niall thought. He had been standing in the chill outside Hazelbrae's entrance for ten minutes at least. *Me lingering at doors. Eccentric new hobby.*

His mind kept replaying last night's scenes. The dance, the joy on her face, him getting lost in the music, filling a void in his soul that he hadn't even been aware of. Marla crying in the car, sharing her fear of failure, her hand in his… A string of emotions twirled around inside him. Awkwardness because they had shared this unexpected nearness, and he wasn't sure what to think of it. Confusion, as he grappled with the reality of what it meant. Did it mean anything? Did he *want* it to mean something? A seedling of joy reached out its tendril from the rocky cairn that filled his heart. This was uncomfortable, complicated, and downright dangerous territory.

And, of course, unthinkable nonsense. There was a line that shouldn't be crossed. Niall knew he had to be careful. And he was getting angry with himself. *Keep it together, man.*

He forced himself to take a deep breath, pulling himself out of his thoughts. It wouldn't do him any good to dwell on last night. He had a job to do. It was time to focus on that. Gritting his teeth, he prepared himself for the challenge.

'Did she not hear me?' Niall mumbled to Barclay, who tilted his head as if to say, 'I don't know, mate.' He had knocked seven times—Hazelbrae's bell wasn't working—and still nothing. As he was about to turn around and leave, the door opened with a creak. There she stood in white sushi jammies, dino slippers, and a unicorn robe. To round it all off, she had pillow marks on her face. Truly a sight to behold. Something tugged deep inside his belly. She looked incredibly cute.

'When you said last night "I'll come over tomorrow" I wasn't aware you meant in the middle of the night,' Marla said with a sleep-heavy voice. Then she giggled. 'A pencil tucked behind your ear *and* a flannel shirt? You look like Tim Taylor from Tool Time!'

'And you look like a freakishly tall four-year-old at a sleepover party,' he grumbled. Without waiting for her reply, he pushed a thermos into her hands and marched past her into the house.

'What's that? Beef tea?' she asked.

'Coffee.'

'Don't you know how to make a girl happy.'

As Niall stood in Hazelbrae's foyer, unmoving, a cascade of impressions and memory fragments pelted him. His heart dropped.

It was the same.

It was different.

The air was as musty as ever, and yet it smelled of paint and varnish. He hadn't set foot in Hazelbrae since the day he had come here to inform Lady Hamilton of Nathalie's death. He didn't remember the details. It was all a mist. A numb, grey, strangling mist.

When the two of them had discussed any work that needed to get done, they had met in the pub. And later, when Lady Hamilton was less well, in the old estate office at the back. Standing here for the first time in so many years made him realise Gwen had been right. He had let Lady Hamilton down.

Yes, he had kept the grounds in order. But that hadn't been enough, and deep down a part of him had refused to acknowledge that. She had said nothing. Lady Hamilton was classy that way. Much too kind to push him. She knew what had happened.

But now, seeing the stairlift, Niall understood that Lady Hamilton could have used his help a lot more than she had let on. A scalding stab of shame and remorse ran through him. He should have asked if she needed help.

No, he should have *insisted* on helping her.

'Are you okay? You look like you've seen one of the ghosts,' Marla asked.

Niall shook his head, snapping out of his thoughts. 'Just thinking. Let's get to work. I suggest we start with a list of everything that needs to be done and prioritise.'

She raised an eyebrow. 'Oh, you mean the list that I made weeks ago? Please, have a look. But I'm glad you're taking this seriously. You know what I am taking seriously at this time of day? Coffee.' Without waiting for his reply, Marla went into the kitchen, hidden away in the bowels of the house, and came back with two mugs. She led the way into the small yellow salon, which she was turning into a living room. Then she poured herself a generous serving and sank onto the daffodil-coloured ottoman. Niall sipped his while making a round of the space, surveying its condition.

'That's a pretty decent brew,' she said, breaking the tense quiet.

'Thanks,' he grumbled and turned to her. 'Do you intend to keep wearing that?' he asked with a disparaging glance at her unicorn robe and dino slippers. 'I'm not sure it's in line with health and safety. And it looks ridiculous.'

'Oh my. Bob the Builder prances in, and my personal anarchy is already history,' she said with a feigned sigh. 'It's early. You've woken me. This is me in my morning glory,' she yawned. 'Also, you don't get to judge what I'm wearing, Tim Taylor. But don't worry. I'll slip into something less comfortable and be right back.'

When Marla returned a good ten minutes later, she wore a striped Breton shirt, dark blue dungarees covered in paint stains, and worn-out trainers. She did a pirouette in front of him. 'See? All healthy and safe!' Barclay, who had been watching attentively, imitated Marla's twirl with great enthusiasm. His tail was wagging so hard that it was almost blurred out of sight. Niall rolled his eyes.

Goofballs, both of them.

As they inspected Hazelbrae inside and out, he saw what Marla had already done: the wooden panels were glistening and the paint was fresh, some windows were sealed, the furniture was reassembled and polished, old carpets were ripped out, rugs had been cleaned, curtains washed and mended or replaced. She had begun to fill the house with life. It was a good start, but there was still a ton to do. The wiring and plumbing needed an overhaul, a few new windows would have to be installed, some doors were in a sorry state, the doorbell wasn't working, the stairlift needed to be removed, all the chimneys had to be checked and cleaned. Niall had a notepad in his hand and was jotting down everything that needed to be repaired, replaced, or improved. He exhaled. *Well, needs must.*

A short while later, the two of them sat down at the heavy, oak kitchen table. Its surface was scarred with a century of marks and nicks. They discussed the tasks ahead. What materials were needed, how long each job might take, and which contractors would be available to help, including the estimated costs. Meanwhile, Barclay inspected every corner of the room with his nose pressed on the stone-tiled floor. Copper pots of all sizes hung on the walls, their gleaming surfaces dulled with age and neglect. They clanged together softly in the stillness, as if longing for the fire of a hearth to bring them back to life.

As far as possible, Marla wanted to keep all the historical features. Niall respected that. It showed a sense of tradition. She had done an impressive amount of research and even found some of the original blueprints.

'Let's start in the salon,' Niall said brusquely, turning to Marla with a look of determination on his face. 'We can begin by repairing the floorboards,' he glanced around and paused before adding, 'and I think it might be best if we concentrate on one room at a time, rather than trying to do everything at once, and leave the rest to the big boys with the pro tools.'

'I'm so glad to have a man in the house to tell me what I already know,' she said and caught her lip between her teeth.

It took him a second to realise that she was teasing him. Niall couldn't remember the last time that somebody had teased him as enthusiastically as she did. He wasn't sure how he felt about it.

The boards came up easily. Most of them needed minor repairs. Only a few were severely damaged. As they worked, Niall got into the rhythm of the job, the familiar motions of fixing something broken. It was cathartic. Barclay had taken up residence on a large, cushioned footstool, watching them toil away with one eye half open. As Niall was pulling up some boards, he noticed something glinting in the corner of his eye. Curious, he set down his tools. It was an old whisky bottle with a piece of yellowed paper inside. He turned it over in his hands. Carefully, he unscrewed the bottle and pulled the piece of paper out.

'Look what I found,' he said to Marla at the other end of the room. She put her tools down and came over. It was time for a break, anyway. Inside was a note that said:

> *James Grieve and Alexander Wilson laid this floor, but they didn't drink the whisky. July 27th, 1914. Whoever finds this bottle may think our dust is blowing along the road.*

This was a tangible piece of history. Of Hazelbrae's past. But that wasn't all it was.

'I think that might be my grandda's father,' Marla said, baffled as she glanced over his arm. She was so close that he could feel the heat emanating from her body, making him all too aware of her presence. What was it about this woman that made him so antsy?

He held the bottle like a valuable relic. 'Wait, your great-grandfather was here?'

'Seems like it.' Marla frowned and bit her lower lip in thought. 'I think my grandda's da's name was Alexander. I'd have to dig into the old family folder and see if I find any details. But that name rings a bell. That's odd.'

'Did you notice the date?' he asked with a sombre undertone. She shook her head. 'July 1914, one day before the Great War began.'

'Oh, dear. How do you know that?'

'History student at St. Andrews.'

'Ah, I see.' She rubbed her nose. 'I wonder if Alexander

enlisted right away, or if he was a conscious objector. He survived, because my grandda was born in 1942.'

'Then Alexander must have been an old father,' he said.

'Hm, intriguing. Once I find the time, I'll look into it. Likely within the next hundred years.'

While she held the piece of paper, Niall twisted the bottle in his hands. 'I know from family stories that my ancestors were enthusiastic about the Great War, like so many young men at the time. At least at the beginning. I think one of them was in the regiment of the Argyll and Sutherland Highlanders at the Battle of Loos.'

'War, what is it actually good for?' Marla asked in an obvious attempt to lighten the mood.

'Absolutely next to nothing, I'd say.'

She let out a long breath. 'I think after such excitement, we deserve a lunch break.' Then she turned to him, reached out, and brushed something off his face. As the outside of her index finger touched his cheek, his heart started beating erratically.

'Sawdust,' she said, and the bright smile she gave him made him feel fuzzy. *What, for pity's sake, is wrong with me?* Niall, for the life of him, couldn't wrap his head around why his obstructive neighbour affected him like this.

Ten minutes later, they were sitting next to one another on the ottoman, a couple of cheddar sandwiches on a plate between them. 'I wonder why my grandda never returned to Kilcranach, not even on holiday,' Marla said. 'He spoke about it often. It meant something to him. His family roots were here for centuries. Strange.'

'Perhaps it has something to do with Lady Hamilton and this inheritance?' Niall speculated.

'Yeah, that's possible. But I still can't fit the pieces together.

My grandparents were madly in love with each other. I don't think he had a secret affair or anything. But here I am, owning the very building where my great-grandfather most likely laid the floor. This is not just some general history. This is *my* history.' Marla took another bite of her sandwich and lowered her head.

Niall noticed the subtle change in her demeanour and gently prodded, 'Is everything okay?'

She hesitated before she said: 'You know that feeling when everything's going a little too well? It's like there's a balance to the world, and if we're too lucky, something's got to give.' Her gaze drifted off into the distance. 'Sometimes it's like life is a game of Jenga. Every time I start to build something, a piece gets pulled out from under me.' She blew out a long breath. 'I don't know why I'm telling you this. It's nonsense. Forget I said anything.' Her eyes flickered toward him, but she looked away again. 'I feel like Hazelbrae can be my anchor. A constant in my life that I can hold on to,' she continued. 'I suppose it's because I didn't have the typical home growing up.'

'How so? If you don't mind me asking.'

Marla grimaced. 'My mother died when I was about six and a half. And then my father left. He never came back. Don't know where he went. I don't care. My grandparents did their best, and they were fantastic. But they were getting older, and it was hard for them to keep up with a child and teenager like me.' She shook her head and put on a brave smile. 'Anyway, that's my sob story. I guess we all have our struggles, right?'

Niall noticed how her eyes twinkled with fierce determination, despite the pain that lay beneath. He saw that her stubbornness, defiance, and independence were no façade, but a result of the hardships she had faced early in life. There was more to her than met the eye. She was strong. He realised he was beginning to grow fond of her. Marla was the first woman he'd even noticed in this way since… And he couldn't resist liking her.

Which he wasn't supposed to.

Not if he went ahead with his plan.

Besides, he didn't want to feel that sort of interest in anyone.

To his amazement, he heard himself say, 'My father died when I was just about a teenager. Was a difficult time for our family. For me. And,' he said quietly, 'six years ago, my wife Nathalie died in a car accident. Not far from here.' He paused, lost in thought.

'Yeah, I heard about that. I'm so sorry, Niall,' was all she said, and it was enough because he knew she was sincere. It was curious. He could speak of Nathalie in front of Marla without the all too familiar rock of grief and guilt crushing his chest. Perhaps because she was so open with him about her own feelings and circumstances. This ease was new to him. It felt liberating.

'We had our wedding here at Hazelbrae. Outside, in the garden. It was summer. It was nice. Everybody was there.' He recited it all like a list of facts in a measured tone, but his heart was gripped with memories. Niall glanced downward, composing himself, and then continued in a low voice. 'I sometimes wonder what it would be like to live without grief.' He avoided looking at her. 'You know? To wake up every day without this weight. For once, not to remember what it's like to have lost someone you love.'

Marla reached over and placed a hand on his arm, giving it a tender squeeze. It was soothing, like a balm. And yet his pulse quickened.

'I understand,' she said softly. 'I've been there, too.'

Niall was relieved and grateful to see compassion and not pity in her expression. The truth was, he didn't mind the solitude of his life. He was used to it. After Nathalie's death, he had distanced himself from everyone. Better that way. Easier.

Only in some rare, dark moments, he longed for a connection with another soul. Preferably one that wasn't a dog.

Fortunately, this sentiment usually passed quickly. Like sunshine here in the Highlands. But he realised now, with her hand on his arm, that the one thing he was missing the most was touch.

The salon was quiet, save for Barclay's snoring. Marla and Niall sat side by side on the worn-out ottoman, their eyes fixed on the dusty floor. Late afternoon sunlight streamed in through the large windows, turning the dust particles into a golden glitter floating across the room. He toyed with a loose thread on his sleeve. She stroked the fur on Barclay's back. And in the salon's tranquillity, something made him want to linger. As if they were caught in the slow movement of an invisible tide.

Niall looked down at the pile of tools by his feet, then at the half-renovated floor. *Best to stop daydreaming and dawdling and get on with it.* He pointed towards the tools and turned to Marla. 'We should get back to work.' It came out harsher than he had intended.

It wasn't until after sunset that they finished the floor. By the time he and Barclay got back to the cottage, Niall was exhausted but content. They had made a lot of progress, and he felt a sense of satisfaction. This was a big, long-term project. But he was in for it. He was convinced more than ever that helping her ultimately meant helping himself. A repaired castle meant a quicker sale. It was for his own benefit, nothing more.

At least that's what he kept telling himself.

Chapter Twelve

Niall had proved impressively reliable and helpful over the past ten days. With the resolute presence of a man who knew what he was doing and didn't need to make a fuss about it, he unloaded his metal toolbox onto the stone tiles of the basement kitchen floor alongside Barclay. He took off his woollen jumper, squished it into a pillow, and lay on his back under the counter.

'Let's see what we got here,' he said, mostly to himself.

Marla had found a leaky pipe. The other workers had already gone home for the day. But Niall had promised that she wouldn't need to spend more money on a plumber when he could very well fix such a simple thing. Marla herself was handy. Painting, sanding, drilling holes… no problem. She could have fixed the pipe on her own, with the trusted guidance of random video tutorials. But Niall was so eager to help, she didn't have the heart to say no. He had been coming to Hazelbrae after work daily to see if there was anything to be done. There usually was.

Naturally, it had nothing to do with her wanting his company. Or vice versa.

Marla bit into an apple and watched him. It was nice not

to be the one toiling for a change. Astounding how he had transformed from an absolute pain in everybody's ass to a little fixer fairy. Albeit a moody one. Maybe Mrs Bellbottom had been right, and his default setting wasn't grumpy and gruff. His t-shirt rode up as he shifted, exposing a strip of toned abdominal muscles. Sculpted not in the gym, but by hard work.

Marla half-tried not to stare.

'The pipe is in worse shape than I thought,' he mumbled from below.

The same can't be said of you. She took a big bite out of the apple, the juice running down her chin. Niall slid out from under the sink and began rummaging through his toolbox, pulling out another wrench and a flashlight before getting back under the worktop. The next few minutes were filled with mumbling, clattering, and thumping. Marla stood there, savouring the movement of his flexing muscles beneath his skin. She justified it to herself by thinking that merely looking wouldn't hurt anyone.

Especially since looking was all she would ever do.

'This stupid thing won't budge,' he said.

'I don't appreciate the way you talk about me,' she said wryly. 'I'm standing here, minding my own business.'

He snarled in response. 'I think it's rusted shut.'

'Oi, that's no way to talk about a lady!'

'I wasn't aware you got the title with the house.'

'Touché,' she said. 'I am and shall forever remain an upstart crow.'

'Stop it with the Shakespeare blether and make yourself useful.' She heard the suggestion of a smile in his voice. 'Hand me a piece of cloth. An old tea towel or rag or something. Chop, chop!'

She did, and he continued to wrestle with the pipe, applying more and more force. 'Dammit!' he yelled.

Marla bent forward to get a better view of what was going

on that got him so worked up. In this instant, something cracked and gave way to Niall's continued jerks. Water gushed in all directions. 'What the actual—' He shot out from under the worktop. 'Where's the main supply?' he shouted.

'In the boot room. I think! Should I put the cloth on the leak?'

'This isn't *Grey's Anatomy*! There's no point in applying pressure to the wound!' he yelled while sprinting to the utility room.

It took a while, but when he returned, he had stopped the flood. 'It's off,' he grumbled and wiped his face with his fore-arm. 'But the damage is done. Going to take a while to dry out.'

Marla looked around, taking in the considerable puddle on the kitchen floor. 'Do you think it would be suitable for salmon farming?' she asked, squeezing water out of her bun.

'Salmonella farming, more like.'

She sniggered. 'I'd better get the mop.'

'And I'll fix what I broke.' He sounded apologetic. Barclay ran into the room and jumped into the puddle with a splash. Marla and Niall were facing each other. Water was every-where. Their clothes were drenched, their hair was plastered to their faces. She wiped her eyes free of a few wet strands and laughed as Barclay ran around them. 'Oh, shit! Look at us three wet poodles!' Marla took a swing with her foot and splashed water on his jeans. 'What a mess you made! Bad Niall. Such a bad boy.'

He crossed his arms over his chest and gave her an unim-pressed look. 'Oh, *really*? And who forgot to turn off the main *and* distracted me, hm?' he said and then retaliated by sloshing water on her. She squealed and within seconds, they were embroiled in a fierce water fight between them and Barclay. They tried to outsmart each other on their slippery battleground, both attempting to get the other wetter than themselves while dodging the splashes. Then Marla grabbed a salad bowl from the counter and said: 'Surrender, or else…'

Niall's wet t-shirt clung to his skin. Water droplets were cascading down his jawline, his eyes were full of mischief. This was a different side of him. Less restrained, less… What had Jack called him? Moody and broody. She liked this relaxed version of him. More than she should.

'Okay, okay. I surrender!' He tilted his head and lifted his hands above his head in defeat as Barclay barked.

'Very well. I accept your submission,' Marla said, dripping from head to toe. Then she stepped closer, licked her index finger, and poked his arm. 'Oh, no! Better get out of those wet clothes.'

With one swift move, he took off his drenched shirt and stood there, bare-chested, in all his Scottish sexiness.

And suddenly Marla couldn't get to the boot room fast enough. For a mop, a bucket, and some self-control.

After an hour of tinkering and cleaning, they got everything sorted, and Hazelbrae's kitchen looked civil again.

'I'm not only wet, cold, and tired, I'm also hungry,' Niall stated. He hadn't eaten since lunch. As much as he loved his dog, his peace, and the solitude, the thought of not eating alone for a change was a tempting one.

'I hear you, I do,' Marla said. 'But since the stove isn't working yet, I can only offer you a selection of cheeses, some bread, chocolate, and a few grapes.'

'Sounds French.' He raised his shoulders.

Her face brightened, and she clapped her hands. 'I have an idea!'

'Och, help ma kilt,' Niall replied. 'What now?'

'What do you think about an indoor picnic in the ballroom?' Childlike joy flashed across her face, and he didn't have the will to deny her. The sight of her heart-squeezing smile roused something inside him. He had to be cautious.

'You're doing my head in,' he said. 'First, I need dry clothes.'

She folded her arms. 'Fear not, I have the perfect thing.'

When she came back from her bedroom, she handed him an extra-large Beatles shirt, worn-out joggers—and her unicorn robe.

'I'm not wearing that. Under no circumstances. No way,' he declared.

Marla cocked an eyebrow. 'Are you sure? I think you would look dashing in it. And it's so fluffy!' She held the robe up in front of his nose. 'Technically, you're the only one here who should wear a unicorn robe. Because you're the one with the… you know… *horn*.'

'Please. *That's* where you're going with that? You're impossible.' He smiled and shook his head, but then he caved. 'Fine,' he said, taking the robe from her. 'But only because I'm shivering, and I want to be comfortable for this indoor picnic of yours. And strictly no pictures, you hear me!'

Marla grinned and led the way to the ballroom. They spread out several blankets on the wooden floor and surrounded it with pillows. Niall opened the wine, Marla arranged the bread, cheese, and grapes on a platter. In the shape of a grumpy face.

'This is you,' she declared. 'In case you wondered. You look sad because there's none of your disgusting rosé.'

'A fair likeness,' he countered. 'You really captured my essence.'

The grand ballroom was dimly lit. It surprised Niall how cosy and intimate it was.

'Thanks for staying. It's nice not to eat alone. But something is still missing.' Marla tapped her index finger on her chin.

'I know what's missing,' he said dryly. 'Chairs. And a table.'

'No, a movie!' she stated. 'I think I saw a projector in the old Butler's pantry the other day.'

He rolled his eyes. 'Does it ever end with you, woman?'

'Of course not. Let's get it!'

They made their way back down to the old Butler's pantry, now a storage room. Marla rummaged through the piles of dusty boxes until she found the projector. It was an old model, with a reel and a clunky lens. Next to it, they found a movie in a metal case. Niall watched as Marla set it all up on a side-table in the ballroom. It still worked.

'We'll use the curtains as a screen,' she decided and loaded the film onto the projector. 'Former side hustle in an art house film theatre,' she explained when she saw the questioning look on his face.

'Have you checked the movie title?' he asked with mock concern. 'What if it's a horrible medical training film about a lobotomy?'

'Course I have. It says *Greyfriars Bobby* from 1961. That's supposed to be a Disney film. But then again, you never know.' She gave a cheeky look. 'Sometimes, you just have to take a leap of faith.'

That's what I said to her when we met in the forest. A small flame flared up in his chest as if someone had lit a tea light.

When she switched it on, the projector whirred to life, and Hazelbrae's grand ballroom was bathed in a muted glow. Shadows flitted across the walls as the images of the old movie showed on the curtains. Niall settled against the pillows, his legs stretched out in front of him. Barclay snuggled up beside them on the blanket while they nibbled on bread and cheese. As Niall watched her laugh at a scene, comfort spread through him. This whole thing was unusual, but it was also nice. Marla wasn't unpleasant company. Not at all. Her presence radiated a glow that was new and familiar.

But that was surely a side-effect of the fluffy and silly robe he was wearing. All he knew for sure was that he didn't entirely hate sitting here.

He looked around the room again. Hazelbrae was changing. He had noticed that. Even the walls seemed lighter. Less serious and constricting. This change, as much as he could tell, was because of her.

What a pity that she would eventually have to sell it. Who knew what would become of Hazelbrae then? Another of the generic luxury resorts that peppered the Highlands. A playground for the super-rich. Something about this thought was dissonant and bothered him. Like a small stone in his boot. *Best not to dwell.*

Without warning, the characters on the curtain flickered one last time before they vanished, and the whirring died. With a ragged wheeze, the projector gave up the ghost.

'Aww, shame,' Marla said. 'Looks like movie night is cut short. Stupid old thing. We're lucky that we got about twenty minutes out of it.' She glanced around at the ballroom. 'I know it's a bloody grand house. But it's beginning to become a home, don't you think?'

'More than it did a few weeks ago,' he said evasively.

The way Marla was speaking about Hazelbrae made it clear once again that she had grown deeply attached to the place. Which made it more difficult for him to pursue his plan. For him, too, it was becoming harder to imagine anyone else owning this historic heap of stones. Least of all, a silly luxury hotel chain or anything like that. But there was no rush. Nothing to decide right now. Hazelbrae wouldn't be ready for months. And he liked to finish what he started before the next step. That was simply his way. 'Thanks for dinner. And this thing.' Niall handed her the unicorn robe.

'You're one of those people who looks good in anything. That's so mean,' Marla complained jokingly.

To his astonishment, he found his face growing hot.

'That goes for you, too,' Niall teased back, sliding his hands into the pockets of the borrowed jogging bottoms. His right hand touched something cold, smooth, and heavy. When he pulled it out, he held a small pocket knife with a red handle. 'What's that?'

'That's mine!' she said and snatched it from his hand. 'I mean, it was my grandda's.' She looked abashed, fidgeting in place. 'It's important to me. Like a talisman. Personal.'

'I'm sorry,' he said. 'Don't be miffed. It was in your pocket.'

'I know. It's fine. Sorry, I didn't mean to snap.' She tucked the knife into her own pocket and smiled apologetically. 'Thank you for indulging me and my inner child tonight. It was lovely.'

'No worries.' He replied with a lopsided grin. 'Wasn't too awful. But if you tell anyone about the robe…'

'I won't. Promise! See you tomorrow?' she asked.

'Aye, see you tomorrow.'

In his car, Niall rested his forehead against the steering wheel and let out a long, heavy sigh. He felt like he was being pulled in two opposite directions.

On the one hand, there was his initial plan of getting everything sold, including Hazelbrae, cashing in, buying a boat, and living out his days on the sea in peace and quiet. Free and independent.

On the other hand, there was Marla.

Chapter Thirteen

By mid-December, works at Hazelbrae were in full swing. The house bustled with activity amidst a flurry of progress. New windows were fitted, floors repaired, builders worked on site. It was a breakthrough.

Marla was taking a short break, sitting next to Barclay as she mowed down her turkey sandwich in three bites. Niall turned around the corner and into view, silhouetted against the winter light. He was wearing dark blue jeans and a light grey t-shirt, looking like a guy from one of those nineties Diet Coke adverts. Every muscle in his body moved harmoniously as he paced towards her, carrying a long, thick plank of wood with ease.

A wave of arousal shot through Marla's body as she observed him walking closer. The breadth of his shoulders, his muscles under his tight shirt, the concentrated scowl on his face. He paused, blew out a breath, and raked his right hand through his thick hair.

Damn, this man is sex on legs.

She needed to stop behaving like a cat in heat, get her common sense back, and quit thinking about him throwing her over his shoulder, carrying her away to his lair… That wasn't just stupidly archaic, it also wouldn't be good for anyone. It was opposite of amicable, let alone professional.

While she couldn't do anything about her attraction to him—or justify it—the least she could do was not give in to temptation. But each time their eyes met a hot flush roared down her spine. Marla caught herself biting her thumb. She didn't let herself dwell too much on what else drew her to him.

Because there couldn't be anything, could there?

Though exhilarated by the renovation underway, a slight headache was forming behind her eyes from the cloud of dust permeating the air. In the distance, a familiar leopard pattern began to emerge slowly approaching the pathway.

'Mrs Bellbottom, what a lovely surprise!' Marla said over the noise, hastening over to greet her fellow Kilcranachian.

'Hello, dearie,' she said, smiling warmly in return. 'I simply had to see how things are shaping up.'

'Did you come all this way by yourself?' Marla asked.

Mrs Bellbottom was breathing audibly. 'Aye, I did. Sylvia and Muffin are in Aberdeen, visiting her nephew. But I walked slowly. The doctor said I should exercise more. So, I'm trying to get my steps in each day.'

'Exemplary. If only every patient was so cooperative,' Marla said with a smile. 'Let me show you around and explain what we're doing.'

In the middle of the dusty construction site, surrounded by the sound of drills and hammers, they chatted about the project. Marla hinted at specific details and explained the work that had been done so far. Mrs Bellbottom listened intently, nodding and occasionally asking questions. Marla admired how poised, kind, and well-read the older woman was. Mrs Bellbottom pointed out some of Hazelbrae's features to Marla and shared one or two fond memories. As they walked through the ground floor, Marla noticed how the gruff men, covered in dust and sweat, would stop their work to give their former schoolteacher a warm nod or wave. She was a respected figure, even years after leaving her position as their teacher.

Suddenly, Mrs Bellbottom stopped, her eyes fixed on a particular worker. 'Is that Niall over there?' she asked.

Marla followed her gaze and saw Niall, his back turned as he spoke with one of the carpenters. 'Yes, that's him,' she confirmed. 'He's been helping me out after work. I mean, he's still Hazelbrae's estate manager. So technically, this is his work. At least, his salary was paid for another year by Lady Hamilton.'

Mrs Bellbottom's face lit up. 'Excellent decision, dearie. Very, very good. I told you he would help you.'

Marla watched as Mrs Bellbottom walked over to Niall, tapping him on the shoulder. He turned, a look of surprise on his face. When he smiled broadly, it almost knocked Marla off her feet. He looked downright boyish and sweet.

He must have broken a million hearts at school.

Marla couldn't hear what they were talking about, they stood too far away and the carpenter had just started the saw. But they both looked genuinely happy to see each other. Shortly after, Mrs Bellbottom returned to Marla with a twinkle in her eye. 'I like that boy, always have,' she said.

'I can tell,' Marla replied and smiled back at her. They made their way into the expansive ballroom, where the floor was being redone. Loose wooden boards had been laid down as a temporary flooring. Some parts had been rotting away for over a century and couldn't be salvaged.

One wrong step was all it took.

Under the weight of Mrs Bellbottom's foot, one loose board suddenly flipped up, throwing her off balance. She lost her footing and fell to her knees, throwing out her hands instinctively to catch herself. An old nail was protruding from one of the boards, and Mrs Bellbottom's left palm landed directly on the rusty point, with her full weight behind it. She let out an agonised cry as the nail drove deep into the skin between thumb and index finger.

Marla rushed over in alarm. Niall followed soon after.

'Are you hurt?' asked Niall with concern, kneeling down beside her, eyes filled with worry.

She was panting heavily, still visibly shaken from the shock. 'It hurts like hell.'

Marla immediately took charge, instructing one of the builders to bring the first aid kit. Niall gently held Mrs Bellbottom's uninjured hand and tried to calm her with distracting small talk. Marla quickly assessed the wound and saw that the nail had gone straight through, possibly hitting a nerve. She knew that Mrs Bellbottom would need stitches.

Turned out, the nail wasn't their most acute problem.

Mrs Bellbottom gasped for air. 'My… nitro… spray,' she uttered between desperate inhales.

'Are you an angina pectoris patient?' Marla asked nervously.

Mrs Bellbottom nodded. Marla looked for her red handbag and found it. Frantically, she searched for the nitroglycerine spray that would help. But there was none.

'What does she mean by nitro spray?' Niall asked.

'It's sprayed under the tongue so that the blood vessels dilate. This improves blood circulation and relieves the heart so it gets enough oxygen again,' Marla said and shook her head. 'It's not here. Fuck. We need an ambulance.'

'I'll call one,' Niall said, fumbled his mobile phone out of his trouser pocket, and went out the door for better reception.

'It's gonna be okay, Mrs Bellbottom. Don't you worry. Just try to inhale as slowly and calmly as possible,' Marla said, by now in full nurse mode.

The answer was a rasping, shallow inhale.

Niall rushed back. 'The ambulance will take over ninety minutes. We'll have to take her to Oban, that's less than an hour. Maybe forty minutes.'

Marla nodded. 'Right. First, I'll get the nail out. You talk to her, distract her. I'll do the rest.'

Niall's eyes were gentle and reassuring as he turned back to Mrs Bellbottom.

'Hey, Mrs Bellbottom, did I ever tell you about the time I fell off a horse and broke my arm?' he asked, his voice soothing.

Mrs Bellbottom's breathing was still ragged, but she managed a weak smile. 'No.'

With pliers and disinfectant, Marla got to work on removing the nail, trying to be as gentle and fast as possible.

'It was a wee bit embarrassing, to be honest,' Niall admitted. 'I was trying to impress a girl, you see, and I ended up falling flat on my face. Literally.'

Marla worked quickly, and soon the nail was out. Mrs Bellbottom's hand was bleeding. Marla knew they needed to stop it and clean the wound before they left.

'Niall, can you grab some bandages from the first aid kit?' Marla asked, and he quickly rummaged through the kit, handing her gauze and tape. She disinfected the wound, wrapped the gauze tightly around her hand, applying pressure to stop the bleeding. Mrs Bellbottom winced in pain, but Niall continued talking.

'By the way, it didn't work. I ended up with a broken arm *and* a broken heart,' he finished his story.

Mrs Bellbottom gasped for air.

'Okay, we need to get her to Oban. Now,' Marla said, standing up.

'Right. I'll drive. Alan, can you watch Barclay?'

Once they reached Niall's old Land Rover, Marla quickly opened the door, helped Mrs Bellbottom into the back seat, and then sat down next to her. Niall started the engine and pulled out of the estate's driveway. He drove the windy, bumpy roads with precision and care, avoiding any sudden jolts or bumps that could impact Mrs Bellbottom's condition. 'We'll get you there. Don't you worry.'

Marla took Mrs Bellbottom's pulse and watched as Niall kept a steady hand on the steering wheel, his focus never wavering from the road ahead. She turned to look at the older woman, who was clutching her chest with her uninjured hand, still struggling to breathe.

Niall spoke again, his voice low and soothing. 'It's okay. We'll take care of you,' he said softly. 'We won't let anything bad happen to you. We'll get you to the hospital and make sure everything is alright.'

She seemed to calm down slightly thanks to Niall's reassurance. But she still didn't get enough oxygen.

Soon enough, they pulled up outside the hospital in Oban. The drive had taken them less than forty minutes. Marla quickly jumped out of the car to flag down an orderly while Niall stayed with Mrs Bellbottom until help arrived. With care and efficiency, they managed to get her into a wheelchair and then into the crowded waiting room of the A&E. Mrs Bellbottom still couldn't breathe properly, let alone speak.

The room was packed with patients, nurses, and doctors who were coming and going with a sense of urgency. The air was thick with the all too familiar, tangy smell of antiseptic, sweat, and fear.

Welcome back to your old world, Marla.

She should have been used to it, but the smell made her nauseous. Although it had been her workplace for so many years, everything about being in a hospital made her feel sick. She had to close her eyes briefly, collect herself. *It's okay, you got this.*

Niall took a seat on a blue plastic chair next to Mrs Bellbottom's wheelchair, Marla sat down opposite them. With a feather-light touch, Niall stroked the back of his former teacher's hand, tracing delicate patterns with his thumb as he ran it along her petite palm. His free hand brushed against her cheek, caressing her face with gentleness as he spoke calming words of reassurance. Marla watched the tender moment between the two of them, her eyes welling with tears. It reminded her of many moments with her Gran Rose, where she had been the one holding a hand. Sadness tore into her chest. But there was something else, a sense of admiration. The empathy and care Niall was showing Mrs Bellbottom amazed Marla.

How lucky she is to have someone like him in her life. I wish someone would take care of me like that one day.

It wasn't easy for her to admit this to herself, but this man was more than sex on legs. A hell of a lot more.

Mrs Bellbottom was called forward. Marla followed behind as Niall pushed the wheelchair slowly towards the examination room.

Just then, a brusque voice shouted from the other side of the waiting room, 'Some of us actually need help here!'

It was a young, blonde man in a tweed jacket with a red face and a yellow jumper, busy with his phone. 'I've been waiting here for hours. Stupid old cow!'

Niall signalled for Marla to take over. The guy didn't see Niall approaching until he put a hand on his shoulder. He turned towards Niall, his face contorted with anger. 'What do you think you're doing?' he spat out.

Niall's voice was as cold as his stare. 'I think you owe Mrs Bellbottom an apology.'

The young man tried to brush off his words. 'Who?'

'Mrs Bellbottom. The wee woman you just insulted.' Niall's jaw tightened.

The young man rolled his eyes. 'Whatever, I was here first.'

Niall made no move to back away. Instead, his voice hardened like steel as he loomed over the man. 'That doesn't give you the right to be a dick. I'd apologise, if I were you.' He smiled, but made it look menacing.

The man blustered and squirmed in the face of Niall's stoic firmness, trying to backpedal. 'I didn't mean anything by it, man. I'm just frustrated—'

Niall cut him off. 'Aren't we all? That's no excuse for bad behaviour.'

'All right, all right. I'm sorry,' he mumbled.

'See, wasn't that hard,' Niall replied and gave him a cordial slap on the shoulder. 'Get well soon, lad.'

Even amidst the stress, Marla was struck by how confidently he handled the entire situation. By his kindness.

In the examination room, Marla gave the nurse a short overview of the events and symptoms. Then Niall and Marla were told to go back out and wait.

They found two plastic seats side-by-side. The warmth radiating from his thigh as it rested against hers sent her heart racing. Marla felt his muscles tense, then relax again. She looked at him out of her peripheral vision, noticing the way his gaze occasionally flitted over to meet hers. But neither of them said a word.

It was hard not to open up her heart to this man, who respected others, treating the vulnerable with dignity, who stood up for what was right, who showed care, love, and tenderness. She was grateful that Niall had been there with her every step of the way. Without him, all this could've gone much worse than it did. The side of him she had so clearly seen today was irresistible.

Sometimes, walls aren't brought down with a wrecking ball or battering ram, Marla thought, *but with the tiny gesture of stroking a distressed human's cheek.*

Without realising what was happening, she shot out her hand and entwined her fingers with his. His palms were callused but soft, and the feeling of comfort that came over Marla was indescribable. Every inch of her was at peace.

Except for the rioting silly heart muscle in her chest, that was.

She was so absorbed in the moment that she couldn't have guessed how much time had passed. But eventually, the familiar leopard pattern appeared as Mrs Bellbottom slowly walked back in from the examination.

'I'm so sorry for the fuss I caused, dearies,' she said with a worried expression. 'That silly old pump of mine refuses to work properly. But all is well, don't worry. It was just a wee fright. We can go home now.' An impish smile spread across her face. 'I have a hole in my hand that simply screams for a stylish piercing.'

Chapter Fourteen

Marla added the finishing touches to the table, making sure there was a Christmas cracker on each plate. She had invited the 'Kilcranach Clan,' as she called them, to bring their leftovers and eat them together at Hazelbrae on Boxing Day. A potluck to celebrate having help in the form of a contractor. But also to say thanks for welcoming her.

Despite the challenges she had faced so far, things were coming together.

The stairlift had been removed. Of course, the house still resembled a construction site. At least in part. In one end of the entry hall, heaps of new lumber and buckets of fresh paint were stacked up like tiny castles made from building blocks, under the watchful and, as Marla sometimes thought, disapproving eyes of the two large oil portraits. She hardly noticed the chaos of renovation by now. The dining room floor, sanded and sealed, creaked beneath her hurried steps. Marla had draped the George III mahogany table with a white linen cloth. It was flanked by sets of matching chairs with shield-shaped backs over threadbare drop-in seats. To add to the atmosphere, she had polished two grand silver candelabras—fished up from a forgotten corner of the old Butler's pantry—

and outfitted them with tall, red candles. On every available surface were tea lights in old jam jars adorned with tiny, tartan ribbons and painted snowflakes. Harvested from the grounds, pine sprigs and holly weaved their way around small red apples, creating a festive garland. A large Yule log burned in the fireplace. The chimneys had been given the all-clear right before Christmas.

The centrepiece, and Marla's pride and joy, was the crystal chandelier, painstakingly cleaned by her own hand. The faceted surfaces of the glass pendants were like the tiniest mirrors reflecting the candlelight and radiating rainbows into every corner. Looking around the room, Marla was fulfilled with a sense of belonging and achievement.

Yes, there were still challenges ahead, but optimism filled her heart. *It's okay to celebrate the small steps,* she told herself.

She went upstairs to get ready, putting on a simple, black-silk slip dress and a long mohair cardigan. After stepping into matching black ballet slippers, she dabbed some gloss onto her lips and put a dash of mascara on. Something she had stopped doing when her grandparents died. *What's the point if you're assaulted by grief at any moment?* With care, Marla donned her gran's simple necklace, which she had taken home from the hospital the day she passed. The last things she'd owned, remnants of a life, stuffed into a plastic bag. Her heart tightened. Rose's necklace was simple, but beautiful. A fine gold band and an oval moonstone surrounded by minuscule zirconia stones. Next to Gordon's pocket knife, it was the most precious thing Marla owned. Even more valuable than Hazelbrae.

Merry Christmas, you two. I love you.

The doorbell rang, and Marla rushed down the stairs of her castle.

Her castle.

She smiled, the tears that had almost come still heavy in her eyes.

Jack and his three kids, Jack Junior, Beth, and wee Phil, were the first to arrive. 'Excuse the menace. They're still on their sugar high from Christmas at their maw's house,' he explained.

'So glad you made it!' she said, beaming.

'The house looks alive,' Jack said. 'Well done, lass!'

Marla's chest swelled with pride as she led them through the entrance hall into the decorated dining room.

Shortly after, the other guests arrived. The two Mrs Bell-bottoms with Muffin and a tray full of Ecclefechan. Gwen, Gary, and Linda, carrying heaps of roasties and sprouts. Fiona and Bert McIntosh with vegan haggis bonbons and some leftover curry. And William Collins, whose call had been the spark for everything, with what looked like a bucket of gravy. Marla greeted them all, excitement building inside her with each arrival. She couldn't wait to share Hazelbrae with them. A part of her wondered what the two people in the enormous portraits would think of this unconventional collection of riff-raff gobbling up leftovers at their fancy dining table.

When Marla heard the hum of a certain car and the crunch of gravel, her pulse quickened.

I forgot how stressful it is to have guests.

Niall and Barclay were the last to arrive, just as Marla had worried whether he might have changed his mind at the last minute. He wasn't exactly the sociable type. 'Good to see you,' she said. 'Come on in!'

'Food is a strong pull factor.' Niall grinned. 'Didn't recognise you in not paint-stained dungarees.'

Marla blushed at the compliment. She shouldn't read anything into it. They had been working together every day for three weeks now. They had got used to each other, that was all. He had brought a bottle of wine, some stew, and a small potted Christmas tree.

He handed it to her. 'My humble contribution.'

'Awww, how cute! I hope you didn't kill its mother,' Marla said as she took it out of his hands.

'I think I probably might have,' he said, and his mouth curved in amusement.

'Then let's call it Bambi!'

He let out a laugh. 'You're insane.'

'I know.' She gave him a bright smile. 'Merry Christmas!'

The sound of laughter and chatter filled Hazelbrae's dining room as old friends caught up, wrapped in the cosiness and goodwill of the season. While her guests mingled and talked, Marla noticed how her gaze was drawn to Niall. She was doing her best to be an attentive hostess, but she found herself watching him from the corner of her eye. Something about him had changed, but she couldn't put her finger on it. He seemed lighter. But also distracted, not fully present somehow.

Once or twice it seemed as if his eyes were wandering in her direction, as if giving her a sideways glance, when he turned his face away a little too quickly. A part of her wondered if he was experiencing the same irritating magnetic pull to her that she felt for him. She refused to ruminate too much about what drew her to him or him to her or anyone anywhere.

That's nothing but hormone-driven, holiday-induced silliness.

After they had put the leftovers on the table, they all sat down for dinner. Marla closed her eyes, trying to soak up this special moment. She knew that life was never perfect. It wasn't supposed to be. The temporary absence of disaster and suffering was all any human could realistically hope for. A breather, a sliver of peace, an up in the endless cycle of ups and downs. *Don't jinx it.* Marla ignored the sinking feeling in her stomach, like an elevator coming to a halt.

'I have not been up here in ages, Miss Wilson,' said Mr Collins, folding his napkin. 'But I must say that the house already looks better than I thought possible.'

'Thank you, Mr Collins. We still have a long road ahead of us.' Marla smiled and looked in Niall's direction. He was busy pulling Christmas crackers with Jack Junior and Beth.

'It must be lonely here, all by yourself,' said Sylvia Bellbottom with concern in her eyes.

'I suppose it is, sometimes. But I'm either insanely busy or deadly tired,' Marla said. 'There's not much time to think.' One of the things she liked about this project.

'I don't want to pry,' asked Janet Bellbottom, 'but do you not spend Christmas with your family, dearie?'

Marla shook her head. 'I'm afraid not. There's no one left. As far as I'm aware.' She intended the joke to cushion the inevitable consternation. The room fell silent, and Marla felt everyone's eyes on her. She was so used to being alone in the world that she always forgot how alienated it could make others feel. She didn't mind. It was a lot more annoying when people looked at her with pity. In the need to fill the silence, she spoke up. 'But it's okay. I'm fine. I enjoy my own company.' She paused and gave everybody what she thought was a winning smile.

'Don't you want a family of your own?' Sylvia, the other Mrs Bellbottom, asked.

Ah, Christmas! The time of unbridled joy, children's smiles, and well-intentioned intrusive questions, Marla thought while ripping her bread into tiny pieces. 'I don't, no. It's not that I'm opposed to it or anything. But why do people naturally assume that a woman's happiness must lie in a relationship or family? For some it does, and that's great,' she declared, 'but for others, it doesn't, and that should also be okay. To each their own.'

'Hear, hear!' said Gwen and raised her glass. Barclay, as if in agreement, barked.

'Good for you, love! We didn't want children, either,' said Mrs Bellbottom. 'There was only space for the two of us. And we have Muffin. Also,' she gave Marla a serious look, 'you're one of us now. Part of the clan. We're all Jock Tamson's bairns.'

Marla smiled with relief as they moved on to lighter topics.

While they were devouring the delicious Ecclefechan, Janet Bellbottom shared some village folklore. 'I remember hearing stories about your Grandda Gordon Wilson. And Lady Hamilton, too. Vaguely.'

Marla perked up at the mention of her grandda. 'Really? What stories?'

'I was a child at the time,' Mrs Bellbottom replied, 'but I remember some sort of scandal involving the young Lady Hamilton. At least, there was a lot of gossip. The adults were all hushed when they talked about it, so I never understood what happened. What I do recall is that there was a conflict between the young woman and her parents, especially her father. And people talked about Gordon and his contact with her. That was frowned upon in the early sixties. Like so many other things,' she said with a knowing look to her wife, Sylvia, who kissed her on the cheek.

The group pieced together what they knew of Lady Hamilton's life. 'Her parents died early. She never married, and there's no heir, as you know,' said Bert.

'We lived in the same village for decades, and yet we hardly were acquainted,' added Janet Bellbottom, shaking her head in disbelief. 'She was nice, walking around in her wellies. And, as far as I know, she dedicated her life to charity work.'

Jack chimed in. 'What about your grandda?' he asked. 'What do you know about his past?'

Marla took a breath. 'My grandda left Kilcranach when he

was about twenty,' she began. 'He moved to Birmingham to work in the steel industry. Then he met my Grandma Rose at a dance. They married quickly, and soon my mother was born.' Her eyes glazed over as she drifted into memories. 'They were very much in love,' her voice faded, and sadness settled on her shoulders like a coat of lead. 'My grandda never wanted to go back to Kilcranach. They only went to Scotland once, on holiday to East Lothian, after he retired. But he never told us why he didn't want to return to the Highlands. I guess I never asked.'

The group fell silent, the mystery of Hazelbrae lingering long and heavy in the air between them. Even the kids were quiet. The only sound was the crackling fire and the occasional clink of cutlery.

'I think they were shagging,' Fiona said abruptly.

'Language!' Mrs Bellbottom exclaimed, while Gwen and her parents started laughing, and even Niall tried to hide a chuckle behind his fist.

'That seems to be the most plausible explanation,' Marla said. 'But if *I* bequeathed everything I own to every guy I've ever—' she looked at the three bairns, '*befriended*, then I wouldn't be able to keep up with the rewriting of all the wills. No, there must be more to it.'

Now everyone at the table was cackling.

'I guess we'll never know Lady Hamilton's secret,' Jack said, 'and that's fine. Some mysteries are not to be solved.'

Marla cleared her throat, stood up, and tucked a strand of hair behind her ear. 'Speaking of unsolvable mysteries… Thank you all so much for coming here tonight. You're the best village people ever. But I have not only invited you here to celebrate Christmas with you and to thank you,' she said, her eyes darting around the room. 'I also have an announcement to make.'

'Good grief! You're not leaving here already, are you?' asked Fiona. 'We've just got used to you, love!'

Marla gave a reassuring smile. 'Not to worry, but I wanted to tell you officially what I'm going to do with Hazelbrae.'

The room filled with palpable tension. 'Be gentle, I'm on new heart meds,' said Janet Bellbottom.

Marla straightened her shoulders before continuing. 'As you might know, I was a nurse for a long time before I got here. And this house is obviously way too huge for one person to live in. Even Miss Havisham would feel out of place. Hazelbrae would eat me alive, financially. It must support itself. So, I will turn it into a retreat for NHS personnel. For them to recharge, to look after their own well-being for a change. I finished a solid business plan. It's happening.' She paused. 'There, I said it.' Marla held her breath.

'Brava!' shouted Janet Bellbottom. 'What a marvellous proposition!'

The entire table erupted in chatter. 'How are you going to do it? I mean, what's the plan?' Jack asked.

'It's going to be mixed-use, funded by a combination of sources. The core thing is providing space for nurses, midwives, carers, and doctors to unwind,' Marla explained. 'But there will also be workshops and courses on wellness, mindfulness, and stress management. And I will offer private rooms for tourists on a B&B basis when it's quieter. To generate some extra income.'

Gwen lifted her glass and smiled. 'I think that sounds fab.'

'The NHS is the most important institution in the country,' said Linda, Gwen's mum. 'That's a bloody brilliant idea, hen.'

The only person who didn't say a word was Niall.

But Marla didn't have time to think about it. Not right now, when she was filled with the satisfying radiance of a worthy cause that had found her people's approval.

❄

When Marla later rose to carry the dishes into the kitchen, Niall was the first to offer his help. 'Let me do the washing up before I go.'

He knew Hazelbrae and the path into the souterrain well enough by now. As he took the tray with the dirty plates from her, his fingers brushed hers. The shock of the instant tingle almost made her drop everything. Their eyes met and for the shortest and longest second, there was a glimmer of amazement.

They both couldn't look away quickly enough.

Still, Marla was grateful for his help. Not just with the dishes. When they stood in the kitchen, surrounded by copper pots and the aroma of leftover dinner, she felt a closeness between them. Her heart raced as she stole a glance at him, taking in his handsome features in the kitchen's dim light. The tools from when he had fixed the stove a few days ago were still scattered on the counter. 'Hey,' she said, turning to him. 'It's not much, but I wanted to give you something.' Marla opened the drawer and handed him a wrapped package. She had never been stellar at expressing her feelings through gifts, but she hoped this one would show her appreciation.

Niall looked surprised as he opened the package and revealed a handmade leather tool holster. 'Oh. Wow, Marla,' he said in honest amazement. 'That's very thoughtful. Thank you.'

It was the first time she'd seen him blush. 'I don't think I've thanked you properly for your help during the past weeks,' Marla said.

'Och, don't worry about it. We seem to work okay together.' He averted his eyes.

'True. We've been surrounded by sharp tools and not ended up on the evening news. That must count for something,' she said. And after a pause, 'You know, for a while, I thought you were a massive ass. But you're not so bad.'

He grinned. 'I thought you were a silly cow. And you're not so bad, either.'

As their smiles faded, their eyes met again and a serious silence fell between them, conveying everything for which they had no words. The distance between them began to narrow. Blood rushed to her face as she gazed into Niall's eyes. Marla found herself leaning in closer, drawn by an irresistible force. She shouldn't… This was madness. But if it really was, why did it feel so natural, so right, to be near him? His delicious scent pulled her in like an invisible thread. The warmth of his breath brushed over her lips. Infinitely gently, the tip of his nose grazed hers. She closed her eyes, and she could feel the heat radiating from his body, engulfing her. He was close, so very close. The world seemed to fade away as they stood in perfect stillness, savouring each other's breath for the first time, on the threshold of something new and irrevocable and—

… infernal barking and a deafening clang interrupted the scene. Barclay and Muffin scurried into the kitchen, fighting over a stolen piece of cold meat. And, by the looks of it, Muffin was winning. In the fervour of their argument, the two pups knocked over a metal bucket. Niall backed away and awkwardly ran his hand through his hair. 'Barclay! You bloody daftie!'

The spell had been broken. He went over to investigate the commotion while Marla turned to the dishes, grappling with relief and embarrassment. Although neither of them said anything, both were aware that something had shifted. But they had a job to do, and they couldn't risk any deeper complications.

Actually, it was her heart that couldn't risk any deeper complications.

Because how often can something break before it turns to dust?

❄

Their goodnights that evening were awkwardly polite. Marla closed Hazelbrae's massive oak door behind him and leaned her back against it. *What on earth happened?*

Marla knew that kissing that man was the last thing she should do. They must have got carried away by the entire Christmasiness of it all. Yes, that was it. The wine and the company and all the talk of shagging. Tomorrow, all would be fine and friendly-professional again. She would make sure of it. There was too much at risk, not just with Hazelbrae. Feelings were far too dangerous. She couldn't get involved with anyone. And Niall had already got way too close. One more loss, one more heartbreak, and that would be it. She needed more time to heal and be safe. Perhaps forever. With a long sigh, she buried her face in her palms.

Marla had to protect her heart. No matter, what her vagina said.

But when she lay in bed, the air around her still buzzing with the excitement of the evening, she couldn't shake the memory of the way he had looked at her. And although it was a frosty December night in the Scottish Highlands, her skin was burning like fire.

Chapter Fifteen

It was one of those endless Scottish January nights. The forest outside the window had been shrouded in black for hours. A chilly draught drifted through the cracks in his cottage. Niall sat in his leather chair next to the log burner with a cup of tea, lost in thought. The model sailboat, with its half-painted deck and un-tied strings, lay abandoned on the wooden table, gathering dust. Darkness was crushing in from all sides as if to punish him for not going to bed.

But he couldn't sleep.

Every time he closed his eyes, all he could see was the curl of Marla's lips. So close to his own. The memory replayed in his head, over and over. Taunting him. He shifted in his seat, feeling restlessness and sorrow. Like an itch that he couldn't scratch. The tea was too hot. He sipped at it, anyway. It burnt his tongue.

They had been working together for over a month. He had used his connections, and Marla was getting on fine on her own with the contractors. Niall popped in whenever he found the time, which was more frequently than he had anticipated, and helped wherever possible. Taking deliveries and signing them out, talking to the joiners… wherever he was needed.

There was always something to do at Hazelbrae. He still hoped the castle would go on the market at some point. But there really was no rush at all. Niall had been waiting for years. He was able to wait a little longer.

Provided that he kept himself in check.

They had been getting more comfortable in each other's presence. More at ease. Yet he was careful not to get too close. A delicate balance that seemed to hold.

Until Christmas, that was.

She had looked so radiant, so happy. Beautiful. Her silver eyes, the curve of her mouth… But it had been the simple gesture of giving him a gift, heartfelt and thoughtful, that had caught him off guard and wiped away the barriers he had erected.

He should have had himself more under control. He was a grown man, not a hormonal teenager. She was the first woman since Nathalie that he had almost… What the hell had possessed him? What if they had *actually* kissed?

This was thin ice, and he knew it.

Niall hadn't seen or spoken to Marla since that night. She had gone down to London for a week or so to spend Hogmanay with her friend and tie up some loose ends. He wasn't sure when she would be back, and he was reluctant to ask.

Through his large window, Niall watched roaring black clouds close in overhead. There had been a red weather warning for this part of the Highlands. He got up and walked toward the window. The outdoor light seeped into the fringe of the dark forest. He was just about able to make out the branches of the tall pine trees as they whipped back and forth. Snow swirled in the air. With the storm picking up pace, he was worried about Hazelbrae. They had put scaffolding up on one side of the building to work on the walls. *Better make sure the house is all right,* he thought.

Niall put on his coat and boots, picked up a sleepy Barclay, and headed out into the storm. Chilled gusts numbed his face, snowflakes peppered his skin. He got into his car and slowly drove up the road to Hazelbrae. The racing clouds let little moonlight through.

He arrived in time to see Marla staggering down the drive with a torch in her hand.

'What are you doing here?' she screamed against the wind.

'Checking on the house!' he yelled. 'I didn't know you were back!'

'What?'

'I said, I didn't know you were here!'

'I came back this afternoon!'

Driven by the howling wind, they both strove toward the scaffolding. Some nets and ties were already loose. Niall helped Marla secure it. It was good to be distracted, so neither of them had the time to deal with or even think about what had nearly happened at Christmas.

Niall stepped to the side to secure the outer corner, when he heard Marla scream, 'Watch out!'

The next thing he knew, she tackled him to the ground. With a muffled bang, a heavy sandstone pine cone fell to the ground. Exactly where he had stood a second ago.

That was a damn close call.

'You have to stop jumping at me, woman,' Niall said.

'And you have a funny way of saying "thank you for saving my life",' she replied, still lying next to him on the snowy gravel.

He tried to get up. 'Killed by an ancient ornament. Would have been an interesting obituary in the *Oban Courier*!'

'You're bleeding.' Marla's face was worried. 'Let me see,' she said and took off his beanie. 'Right. We'll need to get you back to the house and take proper care of this.'

❄

With a laboured breath, Niall sunk into the worn Chesterfield couch. Barclay curled up into a ball at his feet. Flames licked the logs in the fireplace in Marla's bedroom, where she currently lived amid all the renovations. The storm had cut the power off, but this clearly wasn't Marla's first time without electricity. Candles flickered on the Victorian writing desk, on the windowsill, on the floor, on the sideboard, on the night table. She stood in front of him, preparing to take care of his scratch. Rubbing alcohol and band-aids were at hand on a small side table. When she leaned in closer to clean his wound, the fragrance of her skin overwhelmed his senses. Dashes of vanilla mixed with a lick of salt. Her presence was perilously near and intoxicating.

'Ouch. You're well equipped, I see.'

'I wouldn't think about renovating without a proper first-aid kid at hand. Also, I'm a nurse, as you know.' Marla's words were light, but there was an undercurrent in her tone he couldn't grasp. Her fingertips brushed against his cheek as she applied the band-aid to his temple. *Is she so gentle with all her patients?*

'You won't need stitches. Lucky boy. How do you feel?'

'Aside from the searing headache and the stabbing pain in my side? Grand! Never better!'

'Do you feel sick or nauseous?'

'Sick of being asked daft questions and treated like an invalid? Aye, I am.'

'Less of the cheek, please,' she said. 'How many fingers do you see?'

'How many fingers do you *want* me to see?'

'Only this one,' she smiled sweetly as she held out her middle finger. 'Do as I say, Niall McCarron!' Marla examined him further. 'Your head is made of tough stuff, but you might have a concussion. I can't let you drive home alone like that. Out of the question. Besides, there's heaps of snow out there. You have to stay here tonight. To be safe.'

Niall opened his mouth to protest.

'Shush! Nurse's orders!'

'Then I suppose I have no other choice.' He leaned against the back of the sofa. 'Who would argue with a medical professional?'

'You'd be surprised. You can sleep in my bed. I'll go on the couch,' she said in her sternest tone, blighting any notion of objection. 'Now it's time for your unofficial medicine. And mine.' Marla grabbed a bottle of Burgundy and two glasses from the sideboard. 'Only a sip for you!'

It was as if this January snowstorm had lifted them into a realm where the rules of daily life didn't exist, and time didn't matter. Wind and wine had induced a sense of liberty as if their minds were untethered from reality. Niall became outright chatty. And Marla was an eager listener. They shared bits of their lives, anecdotes neither of them would remember. He was sitting on the couch, she on a pillow on the rug next to the fireplace, legs curled under her. Barclay snored, most likely dreaming of sheep and squirrels. Marla's medicine worked. He no longer felt anything of his headache. Occasionally, Niall brushed his thumb over the stubble on his jawline, a movement that seemed to fascinate her.

'I'm glad we don't have any ancient champagne in the castle cellar,' she said, curling her finger around a lock of hair that had slipped out of her bun.

'Agreed. Bubbles are not for me. But why are *you* glad about it?'

'There's this quote. "Burgundy makes you think of them, Bordeaux makes you talk of them, and Champagne makes you commit follies".'

Committing follies.

The candlelight painted a soft glow on her cheekbones. And the way one corner of her mouth curved up more than the other when she smiled made her look like she was up to something. *Was she aware that her eyes darkened whenever they caught his gaze?*

'I can get us another bottle, but I'm not sure if that's a wise thing to do,' she said and stood up. 'Our tomorrow-selves might thank us more for some today-water.' Instead of going to the carafe on the sideboard, she went to the window and watched the storm. She was standing with her back to him. The way she carried herself emanated strength and grace. Just like the wind on the outside, something was raging inside Niall. And he was beginning to realise what it was.

The woman he was getting to know was self-reliant and strong. A fighter full of kindness. Yes, he had started to admire that side of Marla.

That wasn't all, as he was coming to understand. Not by far.

He also *desired* her.

So much so that it physically hurt.

As she leaned there with the empty bottle dangling in her hand, the light from the countless candles illuminated her figure under the white linen shirt. He could make out the silhouette of her body, the outline of her curves. He let his gaze linger on her. She was nothing so simple as pretty. Nothing like accessible. She was extraordinary. Niall's stomach tightened, and a fierce flame arrowed through his body. It might have been years since he'd been intimate with a woman, but… he remembered.

Yes, he wanted her.

Desperately.

He had for a while. Since the day they met. Admitting it to himself was a surprising relief.

Consequences be damned.

The zipper of his jeans was painfully tight. He shuddered. His desire felt alive, a creature that had slept for millennia—

only to be awakened by this… *hunger*. That wasn't like him, not at all.

And yet he couldn't remember the last time he felt so much like himself. What Niall didn't know was what Marla was feeling. And that unsettled him even more than her unbelievably sexy shape.

Through the window, Marla saw a crack in the sky as if some great hand had ripped it open. A formidable power made her heart thunder.

But it wasn't the Highland snowstorm.

She had forced herself to put some distance between them. His scent was so magnetic it made her dizzy. The sound of his laughter reverberated through her body. His eyes were radiating an intensity that could scorch the air. And the sight of his strong hands on his knees—hands that swung an axe to fell majestic trees, but also caressed a guitar to coax music from it—made her feel like jelly inside. Her cheeks flushed and this time, she didn't even try to tell herself that it was the wine.

Because it wasn't.

It was him.

It had been him from the moment he had caught her in his arms.

Marla squeezed her eyes shut, trying to ward off the dizziness. She could physically feel his presence humming behind her back and his glance resting on her like a touch.

Even Barclay must have sensed the tension, because quietly, he had left the room. *Clever creature, much more receptive than us.*

Niall's sonorous voice cut through the haze. 'Are you okay?' She blinked, and everything came into focus. A shiver ran down her spine despite the fire. Marla turned around.

And what she saw in his eyes sent a current up her spine and through her whole body.

It changed everything.

Tenderness. Heat. Hunger.

He knows. He feels it, too. We mustn't…

Slowly, she moved through the room towards him. 'Let me see if the wound—'

But she couldn't finish.

It was as if buried parts of them had been waiting for this, and now that they were here, there was nothing else that could be done. Their bodies knew a secret and were fulfilling a promise made long ago. Marla could only watch in wonder as Niall's hand rose and followed the line of her chin. His fingertip rested on her lower lip. He whispered her name like an incantation. 'Marla.'

With the raw sound of longing in his voice, the last of her walls crumbled.

Her fingers curled around his wrist as his hands encircled her waist. He pulled her closer, burying his face in her belly, and she felt him inhaling deeply. She ran her hands through his hair, tugging gently. It was thick and velvety and wonderful. Then she eased herself down, settling onto his knees. 'Hi,' she said.

Carefully, he pulled out her scrunchie and laced his fingers through the fall of her waves. 'It does feel like silk,' he mumbled. 'Been wondering.' He pulled her close and kissed her so delicately that his lips barely touched hers. And yet she felt everything, thousandfold—his hot breath flowing into hers, the firm softness of his lips. There was restraint in his kiss, the subtle promise of something wild. His stubble scratched her chin, his calloused palm was coarse on her nape. And all she wanted was more of him.

'Kiss me deeper.'

Niall pulled away. He looked at her with veiled eyes. 'If I do, this will lead to more.' His voice sounded hoarse and serious. 'Because I want you, Marla. I want you so badly that I can barely breathe.'

'I want you, too, Niall McCarron.'

He inhaled sharply. 'Are you sure?'

'God, yes. I am. Very, *very* sure,' she whispered into his ear.

She didn't have to say anything else. Niall traced a line across her collarbone, grazing her skin with his lips. As if he was trying to restrain himself.

'Are you ready for this?' she asked him, her lips curved with humour.

'Mmm, we shall see.'

'I promise,' she said lowly, 'that I'll control myself and be gentle with you.'

'Don't. Because I can't be. Not one more second.'

And with that, Niall finally let go. He took her face in both hands and kissed her again, wild and hard this time, with an all-consuming passion. He tasted sweet, hot, and rich. Like honey and wine. Marla's tongue delved deeper into his mouth, conquering it, making it hers. She shivered as his fingers trailed down her back, awakening every inch of her.

When she thought she couldn't take it anymore, she rose from his lap. Even this short distance between them was enough to make her body ache.

She *ached* for him.

Marla unfastened her shirt, one button at a time. She didn't avert her eyes. Not once. The linen fell to the floor, and she pulled the lace straps of her white bra over her shoulders, one after the other. Then she stripped off her leggings and underwear. Still holding his gaze, she let her hand wander down and began to touch herself.

She saw myriads of unspoken things blazing in his eyes—and she understood them all. 'I'm ready for you', she said softly. Then she turned around, reached for her handbag on the floor, and pulled out a condom. 'This is a giveaway from a pub. It'll have to do.'

'Shut up and come here,' he said with ragged breath.

She did as he asked.

Her entire inside pulsed. Marla let out a gasp as his fingers dug into her hips, pulling her in. She moved against him, kissing him fiercely as she opened his trousers. 'God, Marla,' he groaned. 'I need you. Now.' There was so much urgency in his words. Liquid fire coursed through her veins, and she didn't care if it complicated things. Because she needed him just as much.

She heaved a long sigh as he finally pulled her down, completed her.

This was it.

His breath came fast against her ear as she moved in a rhythm as old as time. The fire popped, casting dancing shadows on the walls. The hail was still beating against the windows, the wind still howling outside, but inside the castle, it was only them. As they clung to each other, rocking against one another in unison, she felt his heart pounding as wildly as her own.

Marla put her palm on his chest and looked into his amber eyes. His gaze was full of wonder, charged with a desire as vast as the universe.

This feeling… she never thought she'd have that again.

There was joy. Pure pleasure. Nothing more, nothing less.

It was enough.

It was everything.

'You're driving me fucking wild, Marla,' he murmured against her neck. She felt his lips close around her nipple so tight it almost hurt. Each flick a lightning bolt that lit up the pathways in her body with an electric current, connecting it all. She sensed him *everywhere* at once. A husky breath escaped her throat as she grabbed his head and pressed him closer, yearning to dissolve into his mouth.

'You feel so good… so good…' she moaned and meant it. His warm skin on hers, his hands on her hips, guiding her movement. Both of them joined. They shared in this, shared each other. Finding solace in one another. Warmth flooded through her. She was melting, lost in it all.

His rhythm slowed, and he lifted her up—he was that strong—and carried her to her bed. Without leaving her. He was a part of her now.

'Do you want me to go on?' He laid her down and his voice was deep.

'Niall, if you stop now, I will die. And then I will kill you. Don't stop… Please… Don't…'

He smiled with contentment. 'Never.' And then he did go on. Exactly how she needed him to, as if he could read her body, as if he was made for her. And he claimed her completely. Marla lost all sense of time. Everything was now. Everything was feeling. Everything was him, and he was everything.

Oh yes…

It felt so good to be alive. Right here. Right now. Forever.

Please don't stop…

Two beings becoming something else. Something pure and real. His heat radiating inside her. His hands cupping her face, his thumbs on her chin, as her centre began to pulsate and release in unstoppable surges. She was more than the sum of her parts. Her shell dissipated, her soul expanded, it beamed out of her heart and filled the room, the entire world.

Somewhere in the distance, she heard him call her name. And for this moment in time, all was well.

Chapter Sixteen

Marla awoke with a start, as if someone had flicked a switch inside her. At first, she didn't remember where she was. Then there was a warm wetness on her face. She opened her eyes to find the source of the sensation and saw Barclay next to her, licking her face with enthusiasm. She grinned sleepily and stroked his glossy fur. Niall's dog seemed delighted about waking her. Barclay ran circles around the room, waiting for her to follow.

Niall himself was still fast asleep. His chest was rising and falling in a steady rhythm, and his eyes were closed, heavy with sleep. The dim morning light shone on his content face. The shadows of sadness and wariness had vanished. Marla let her eyes wander over his body The sheets only covered his lower half. She rested her chin on her hand and allowed herself to marvel at his broad shoulders, the firm muscles under his pale golden skin, and his wide chest with curls that gleamed like copper in the morning light. His lashes cast shadows on his cheekbones, his lips were slightly parted, and his tousled hair was wild and wavy. He was a beautiful, beautiful man. Marla felt a mix of heart-wrenching tenderness and awe at the sight of him. Usually, she wasn't able to sleep next to another human being. Too much movement, too much breathing, not her thing. But to her astonishment, she had slept like a rock. *Probably all the wine and physical exercise.*

Niall shifted in his sleep and let out a soft grumble. He looked so peaceful. A lot less like the ardent lover who had—for lack of a better word—worshipped her last night with breath-taking fervour. His raw desire had swept her along like a tidal wave. And she had been all too happy to sink into it.

They really had made maximum use of that one condom.

As she watched him sleep, she thought about what last night meant. Or didn't mean. Marla had had her share of dates and lovers. Some better suited than others, some closer and more lasting, some passing passionate encounters. But this was different. She sensed it in her bones. With each heart-beat, it had been like two pieces of a puzzle clicking together seamlessly. Marla didn't like to compare lovers or experiences—sex wasn't a competition—but this had been a night she wasn't likely to forget. She was fulfilled and sore, satisfied and hungry, all at once. The air around her seemed to be made of a million fluffy, languorous bumblebees.

Don't be so hasty, she cautioned herself. Yes, she might be the accidental owner of a castle. That didn't mean that she was a princess looking for her prince to give her a happily ever after. She saw that as her own responsibility.

But still.

For the first time since she cared to remember, Marla could remotely picture a guy being a part of her life. This guy, to be precise. As he had already been for weeks now, anyway. He had gone out of his way to help her. He was kind, funny, ridiculously good-looking. Marla smiled. *And oh, the way his skin smells. Like sun-dried laundry and cinnamon buns on a pine forest peat fire.*

She peeled herself out of bed and tiptoed to the large window behind the desk. The sun was rising, the winter morning light streaming through the glass. She hadn't got around to removing her Christmas decorations yet. Cascading strands of fairy lights embraced the window frame. A gilded wreath with crimson velvet bows and clusters of shimmering gold ornaments still hung at the centre of the window. As she stood there looking out at Scotland's serene winter landscape in its post-Christmas beauty, the ground powdered with frosty icing, the peaks in the background blanketed in pristine white, she was calmer and more at peace than she had ever been before. Realising that this was what contentment must feel like, she closed her eyes. Barclay nudged her with his nose. 'Aww, you must be a hungry chap,' she whispered. 'Let's go downstairs and see what we've got for you.'

She slipped into a t-shirt and her unicorn robe, and together the two of them quietly made their way down into Hazelbrae's kitchen. The house was huge and empty, with echoed rooms and endless hallways that should have been populated by occupants, guests, visitors, and workers. But Marla was used to it by now. It was so quiet she heard Barclay's paws clicking on the floor. Since he had become a frequent houseguest, she made sure she always had something for him to eat in the kitchen.

As she poured Barclay a portion of dog food, Marla decided to prepare breakfast for Niall. After all, he had worked hard for it. She let out a little giggle.

When she brought the tray with coffee and a bowl of porridge up to her room, Niall was already out of bed and dressed. Marla paused, surprised to see him up and about. 'Morning,' she said with a smile, setting the tray down on the bed. 'I thought you might be hungry after last night's exhausting late shift.'

'Hey,' he said with a pressed voice. She could only glance at him sideways while he was buttoning up his shirt, but she was able to tell that his shadows had returned. She took a step towards him and reached out to touch his arm. 'What's wrong?' she asked.

Niall stepped back, out of her reach. 'Nothing.'

She bit her lip, unsure of what to say, while he put on his boots without another word. The silence between them was suffocating. Marla frowned. 'Niall, what's going on? Don't shut me out.'

'I'm not,' he said, still not meeting her eyes.

'Yes, you are.'

'Marla.' There was a tinge of pain in his voice. And something else, something indefinable. 'Marla, we need to talk,' he said in a serious tone.

Her heart sank. 'Okay,' she said. He sat down on the edge of the bed, his face grim. She sat beside him, her heart hammering in her chest. 'What is it?' she asked, trying to keep her voice calm.

He took a breath. 'Last night was incredible. I've never experienced anything like that. Ever. But—'

'But what?' Marla cut in, her heart descending deeper. She had a feeling she knew what was coming.

Niall took another breath before continuing. 'You are incredible. You really are. But I can't do this. I can't be with you. Not like this.'

'What do you mean?' she asked, her voice sounding hollow in her own ears.

He looked away, unable to meet her eyes. 'You're the first woman I've touched—the first woman I've *wanted* to touch—since Nathalie. But—' It took a moment for him to continue. 'I'm not right for you,' he said. 'I'm not what you need. I'm not what you *think*.'

The pounding of her heart was so loud that Marla couldn't hear anything else. 'Please. Spare me the "you're too good for me" speech,' she said. 'I heard that in lower sixth and I didn't fall for it then!'

Niall flinched at her tone, but he didn't back down. 'It's not that. It's… I can't… It's not a good idea, for a million reasons.' He lowered his head. 'Last night was unbelievable. But I… it was a mistake. It could complicate everything. Don't you see?'

Now anger flared up in her chest. 'I hate to inform you that this train has long left the station,' she said and saw him wince. 'Things already *are* complicated. And don't patronise me, Niall!' She was on her feet now. 'Maybe I don't want commitment. Maybe I want to enjoy what we have right now. Or maybe I want something different. But that's not something that you get to define or decide for me!'

'I have to go,' he said, standing up from the bed. 'Marla, I have to leave. I can't stay here. Truly, I'm sorry.' His breathing was heavy, and he sounded agonised.

By now, the rage was so seething inside her that her ears rang with fury. 'Don't you dare walk out on me now! How old are you, fifteen?'

But he turned and left, with Barclay in tow. And without another word.

Marla watched in disbelief as he walked away from her. Again. Her body felt like stone. She stared ahead, unable to move or speak.

This wasn't the first time someone she had opened her heart and soul to had walked out on her. Everything had started with her scumbag of a father. It was as if she was trapped in a recurring nightmare. Fury boiled in her veins as she realised the truth about the situation. And herself. She should have known better than to let him fool her into thinking there was a genuine connection between them. There was none. At least not from his side.

Not that she had a problem with one-night stands. They could be fun. And not that they lived in the nineties when kissing meant going steady.

No, what made her so mad was that this had felt different.

It had a different premise. The way he had held her in his arms last night, the way he had kissed and touched her, the way he had set her body ablaze and made her soul sing. It had been more than a good shag. And they both knew it. Or so she thought. Bitter tears welled in her eyes. No matter how hard she tried to understand him, he remained an enigma. The only thing she knew for sure was that her initial impression of him as a fickle ass had been spot on all along. He didn't even try to talk about whatever was going on with him.

And she deserved better. She dug her nails into her palms.

How could I be so stupid?

Then, in a burst of rage and hurt, she swept the tray off the bed and with a clang, the coffee mug, the porridge bowl, and the last intact pieces of Marla's heart lay shattered on the bedroom floor.

Niall drove home through the melting snow in a state of turmoil, tires crunching over the slushy mess. His hands clutched the steering wheel with tension. There was a chill inside his bones as he thought about how he had betrayed Nathalie. By sleeping with Marla. By enjoying it so much. He had felt more than mere lust. Lightness. Wholeness. Fulfilment. For a few hours, he had forgotten.

He had forgotten about his wife. His *wife*, for fuck's sake!

An unforgivable sin.

How could I be so disloyal?

Guilt twisted in his heart like a knife as he remembered the vow he had made at Nathalie's grave. He had promised that he would be true to her memory and honour the love they shared. That he would make up for letting her drive that night. That promise was all he had left, and now it was broken because of one night's pleasure. He cursed himself for being so careless as to let down his guard like that around

Marla. He wished he could take back what he had done. She was right. She deserved better. Niall's mouth was dry, the metallic taste of regret and shame lingering on his tongue. It felt as if he was swallowing broken pieces of glass with each breath.

But still.

When he remembered Marla's sweet murmurs, how she had given herself to him without reservations, all of her, the way her body moved with his, her eyes gazing up at him with such intensity. A fierce longing ignited inside him again. Thinking of it filled him with a chaotic tempest of emotions. Desire, guilt, and an aching urge. Niall gritted his teeth in frustration. He tried to push the thoughts away, but they kept creeping back in.

One-night stands weren't his thing. Never had been. This wasn't like him.

He knew that given half a chance, he would lose himself in her embrace again, in her gentleness and intensity, her softness and strength. This was precisely what a part of him had feared. The growing realisation that there was something between them that couldn't be denied. But he couldn't afford to get attached. This woman could cost him his solitude. His freedom. God knew what else. He had to stay away from Marla. For both their sakes. Niall let out a suppressed growl. He couldn't allow that to happen again. Ever.

Not just because of Nathalie. That was only part of it.

No, he couldn't because of his other secret.

He hadn't told Marla that he wanted her to sell Hazelbrae. That he needed her to sell it so he could sell his land with it and get away from Kilcranach. Hadn't told her his true intentions. No. He had her led to believe that he was helping her out of the goodness of his heart. When all he had really been doing was acting in his own interest. He had told himself that getting away was all he needed to feel unstuck. That helping her with the house meant getting closer to freedom and peace.

Now these half-truths and concealed lies were like weights dragging him down into murky depths. He was in way too deep, and they both would have to pay dearly if he wasn't careful. What he needed to do now was focus on repairing the damage done by his recklessness and selfishness.

Taking a deep breath and letting it out slowly, he knew there was only one way. He had to keep his distance no matter what.

The only thing he didn't understand was why the thought of it stung so much.

Chapter Seventeen

'Niall McCarron!' He heard Janet Bellbottom call from some distance away. When she used her teacher's voice, tried and trained in front of generations of students, he would never *not* feel like he had forgotten his homework. Niall was sitting on a wooden bench on top of one of the hills surrounding Kilcranach, overlooking the picturesque village. Until ten seconds ago, he had been lost in thought. Lost in general.

Niall had tried to get back to normal after what had happened with Marla ten days ago. But normal, whatever its definition these days, seemed out of reach for him. He couldn't focus on work. Although he had got round to getting some bookkeeping done and some drainage work organised. Still, his mind was all over the place. *Not just your mind,* said a nagging voice inside his head. He refused to listen. He had always been adept at ignoring the darker, aching parts of himself. Eventually, they would fall silent and blend into a manageable background noise. Worked for him. This was how he had made it through his adolescence, after all. Especially growing up in a village like Kilcranach, where everyone knew everyone else's business. Where everybody always needed to meddle and bring old stuff up. As well-intentioned as it might be.

Mrs Bellbottom was getting closer now. He spotted her leopard coat. Niall knew he couldn't avoid talking to her. Muffin came running up to them and greeted Barclay with a few assertive barks. It was clear who was boss, and it wasn't the three-times-bigger border collie.

'Mornin' Mrs Bellbottom.'

'Mornin' Niall! What a braw day, eh?'

She was right. It was almost February, and the glistening winter sun painted Kilcranach in a mantle of gold. Last night's icy hail was already forgotten. Small, sodden pathways meandered through the fields. Smoke twisted up from the chimneys of the tiny houses dotting Kilcranach's peaceful roads. The backdrop was the uncompromising majesty of the Highlands. It was picture-perfect. Idyllic. Mrs Bellbottom settled down next to him on the bench. Between them on the backrest was a shiny plaque, proclaiming that this seating was dedicated to Ethan Harris. He had been Niall's predecessor as estate manager and had already worked with Niall's father, before taking the younger McCarron under his wing. Despite an unhealthy fondness for whisky, Old Harris had died eight years ago at an impressively old age. Hence the name. But he wasn't sorely missed.

'I often like to come here on a nice day,' Mrs Bellbottom said with a smile and slightly out of breath. 'Sadly, we don't have too many of them.'

'Och, you know how it is round here,' Niall gave a resigned shrug.

'I do, I do,' she said, her gaze drifting towards the horizon before returning to him. 'So, how's work on the castle going? Did you find more historic treasures?'

Niall flinched. 'It's going fine, I suppose.'

'You suppose?'

'I haven't been on site since before Christmas,' he admitted, playing with Barclay's leash. There was no point in lying. This was Kilcranach. People were always talking.

'You haven't? Aha,' Mrs Bellbottom raised an eyebrow. 'Are they all finished, then?'

'Not yet, I suppose.'

'You suppose?' Mrs Bellbottom was not one to stop prodding once she had picked up a trail. Niall fidgeted on the bench. Why did this seem like an exam?

'Weren't you *supposed* to help Marla?'

'I was, aye,' he said. 'But I changed my mind. She's getting on all right. Doesn't need my help anymore.' Niall held his breath as Mrs Bellbottom digested this information in silence. There was not much more to say. Not to her, anyway. Niall stared at the landscape of jagged grey mountains stretching beyond the horizon. A few snow-laden pines clung to the side of the hills, not quite ready to let go of winter.

'Old Harris was a bit of an arse,' Mrs Bellbottom said after a while, with a glance at the plaque between them.

'That he was.' Niall nodded, surprised by the change of topic.

'Always grumpy and a bit mean. A know-it-all and a proud man. Annoying. But he was one of *our* arses,' she added. 'And so, my dear boy, are you.'

'Beg your pardon?'

'You heard me well enough.' There was that teacher's voice again. 'You see, I'm getting old. I don't have oodles of time left. So, let's cut the crap and get to the point. What's *really* going on?' She put her small hand on his arm. It wasn't heavier than a child's. There was something about this gesture of compassion, echoing Marla's the other day, that cracked his shell open. At least open enough. Or perhaps he had been ready to spill after all these years.

Either way, spill it did.

'It was my fault,' he said, a choked sob trapped in his chest. 'All my fault.'

'What was your fault, dearie?'

'Nathalie. The accident,' he said through gritted teeth.

'What… God, my boy. Is *that* what has been keeping you so terribly down?' she asked with sincere concern. 'Oh Jesus. Niall, no. No. There was nothing you could have done. You must know that!'

'Wasn't there?' His voice was bitter and fraught with sorrow. 'If I had driven her that night… You know she asked me to? Or if I had taken her car to the shop. It was rusty and needed repairs, and I'd been putting it off again and again.' His jaw clenched as he remembered their heated argument. 'We had a fight right before she left. Before it happened. Nothing serious, only nonsense. But—'

'Oh, my dear, dear boy. None of it is your fault.' Mrs Bellbottom kept her voice gentle now. 'It was such a tragedy. But there's no point in torturing yourself with a million possibilities. It would have been something else. When our time runs out, it runs out. That's how it always has been and always will be. There's nothing any of us can do about it.'

He grunted in frustration and shook his head. 'Such a fatalist thing to say.'

'Possibly. But I'm right. You know I am,' she asserted. 'We can't turn back time. You keep punishing yourself for something that was neither your fault nor within your power. For something that you can never, ever change. No matter how relentless or everlasting your self-punishment may be. It has absolutely no effect. None. Except one.'

He slowly raised his gaze. 'Which is?'

'You're dead, too. At least you try to be.' She stared straight into his eyes. 'Do you even realise you stopped living the instant she died?'

His heart caught in his throat as her words registered, a chill was snaking up his spine. Mrs Bellbottom's face mellowed as she spoke. 'Let me tell you this, and you better listen closely. I knew Nathalie. She was a kind and generous soul. She wouldn't have wanted this,' she made a sweeping hand gesture from his feet to his head and back, 'bleak shadow of an existence for you.'

'I'm trying to honour her memory—' Niall broke off and swallowed hard.

Mrs Bellbottom smiled. 'Oh, but you're not honouring her memory by shutting yourself off! It's the opposite, actually. One reason being that you don't do all the marvellous things that she would do. If she could. She never had the chance to live her life. You still do. But you refuse to enjoy life. Plain and simple.'

He hung his head and said nothing. Because there was nothing to be said. Stillness lay over the valley, the calm only punctured by birds in flight and occasional creaks from the old trees. Until Mrs Bellbottom broke the silence and spoke with conviction.

'You're alive, Niall. She's not. And you're wasting your precious time. Although you should know better. Nobody can tell how many or few years we have left.' She paused, gathering her thoughts. Then she said, 'Hiding and isolating yourself won't bring her back. It's been so many years. You have to put her to rest, my boy. You must. It's time. It's okay.'

Her words echoed in his mind, resonating in his core. It was like putting on glasses and seeing sharply again. A painful clarity that cut into his soul. He couldn't help or understand it, but something in him agreed. And given the sudden sense of relief, he realised that a part of him must have been waiting for six years to hear those words from another human being. As if he needed permission to live again. Niall felt like he'd been bound in thick, rough ropes, and now they were loosening, thudding to the ground. His skin ached, his blood itched, and he didn't know if he could stand upright on his own.

But for the first time, he was willing to try.

'Now, what about that Marla?' Mrs Bellbottom asked. She

really didn't waste any time. Niall was wary and not ready to touch on that subject. Ashamed of how cowardly he had behaved. But he couldn't let Mrs Bellbottom see or know that. So he asked as neutrally as possible, 'What about her?'

'Don't even try. I saw the way you two looked at each other at the Ceilidh and on Christmas. It's obvious that there's something going on.' She gave him a conspiratorial look. 'I know these things. Always have. Got it from my gran.'

These people. Their meddling.

'Not much,' he said, trying to evade the topic.

'Ah, I see. Well, not much is *not* nothing. She's a great young lady. So capable. And gorgeous! If I was about twenty-five years younger and not married to the most wonderful woman alive…'

Elbows on knees, Niall propped his chin on his clenched fists and surveyed the muddy ground in front of the bench.

When it hit him, the realisation was a biting, bitter shock. But there it was. Clear as day. 'Mrs Bellbottom?'

'Yes, dearie? Get it aff yer chest.'

'I think I screwed up.'

'Oh, you *think*?' She rolled her eyes. 'Niall, nobody even mentions your name around her anymore.'

'You knew all along?' He turned towards her. 'Of course, you did.' He let out a long breath. 'There was… We had… The other night…'

'I'll stop you right there, young man. I think I see what you're getting at. And I won't meddle. I never do. But know this. It's possible—and, if you think about it, only logical—to have more than one love in your life.'

Niall kneaded his hands and cracked his knuckles. He thought it had taken him an eternity to climb out of the abyss after Nathalie's death. Now he wondered whether he ever had.

But there was something else.

Rationally, he understood it was close to impossible that

he would lose someone else in the same brutal, abrupt way. But he wasn't convinced that his heart was strong enough to take that chance. Even a slim one. 'What if I'm scared witless and what if—' He stopped.

Mrs Bellbottom was able to read all the unsaid things on his face. 'Pain and loss, that's the price for joy and love. You can't have one without the other,' she said. 'If that's what you mean.'

He nodded, and Mrs Bellbottom took his hand.

'Opening your heart to someone, loving another human, doesn't take away any of the love you had for Nathalie. There's not a finite amount of love and when it's spent, it's spent. And love is not linear. You don't have to stop loving someone to love someone else. There's enough room and love in that giant heart of yours for Nathalie and someone else. Love is a strange, vast beast.' She gave him an affectionate smile and squeezed his hand before speaking again. 'You deserve love, Niall. You do. Yes, you're a bit of an arse. But like Old Harris, you're *our* arse after all.' Her small hand patted his. 'You have a good heart, even if it's been broken into pieces. Time to get out the broom and sweep them up! And you know what Dostoevsky said, "What is hell? The suffering of being unable to love."' Mrs Bellbottom managed to sound wise and silly at the same time. Then she added, 'Whit's fur ye'll no go by ye.'

It began to sink in that she was right. He had been wrong and blind and dead inside for years. For understandable reasons. Was possible that survivor's guilt played a part in all this, too. He had shut down, withdrawn, and hidden. First like a wounded animal, then like a coward. And yes. He had been a bit of an arse. To the people of Kilcranach, to himself, to Marla.

The more he realised it, the more it hurt. His heart coming back to life meant that all the pain was coming back, too. Which was what he deserved.

Because, as he now began to see, he had treated a good person, who had opened herself to him, with unjustified and reckless unkindness. Out of fear. He wished with all the bits and pieces of his fractured, twitching heart that he could undo it. Or even make up for it, somehow.

But it also dawned on him it that was probably too late.

Chapter Eighteen

The delicate heads of snowdrops stretched through the vanishing slush left by one of winter's recent interludes. Here in the Highlands, it was rarely very cold for very long. It was rarely anything for very long. The mountains, the sea, and the air were embroiled in a perpetual, age-old battle that could never be won. Not for any length of time, at least.

Niall's heavy boots made smacking, sucking noises with every step through the wet grass. An 'awfy splorroch,' as his father used to say.

But Niall's boots were not the only thing that was heavy.

His heart felt as though it were made of rock, dragging him down with each beat. Even Barclay was grumpy. They had started taking their daily walks along the sheep pastures about two weeks ago, and he had to be on a leash. Niall was sorry for his stray-happy buddy.

But he wanted to avoid the wee forest.

He wanted to avoid *her*.

This was much easier physically than mentally, he had found. His thoughts kept returning to Marla. But no longer because of any plans or intrigues or even flare-ups of attraction. No, all this had given way to something much more profound and real.

He truly cared for her.

He cursed himself now. That had not been the plan. And he should have seen it coming. He would have, if only he had paid closer attention. But he had been too wrapped up in his escape dream.

During the past months since her arrival here in Kilcranach, they had become closer and closer. They had worked together, got to know each other. Enjoyed each other's company. And for one incredible night, they had lowered their walls. Temporarily.

Niall sighed. Marla was independent, determined to the point of stubbornness. Clever, but not arrogant about it. Sexy. And such a dork. A smile flitted across his face. But no matter how good she was at masking it, he sensed that she was hurting inside, that her life had been as challenging as his own. In a different way, of course. She seemed to be searching for something, although he wasn't sure for what. A stable home, perhaps? A place of belonging? And yet she seemed so independent. In spite of this, at some point a part of her must have decided to let him in. A little.

What have you done? he thought, a knot writhing in his stomach. Not sure if he meant her for letting him in. Or himself for screwing it up.

Things had been unravelling inside him. Memories had been returning since his encounter with Mrs Bellbottom. As he trudged along the narrow, sodden path that hugged the hillside, he took in the striking landscape, the sharp ridges touching the sky and the uneven winter pastures. Droplets of the sea laced the air.

This had been his home since… forever. He was born of this land. He was shaped by this land. He remembered how it had felt when he and Nathalie had returned to Kilcranach after their graduation and a year-long trip across South America. When he had started to work with Old Harris, learning the ropes of managing the Hamilton estate and his own bit of land. Coming home, finding his purpose, really growing up. How the landscape had whispered to him, sung within him. When the wide skies above him, the hills around him, and the earth beneath him had made him feel like a tree—with deep roots and unrestrained branches.

Until Nathalie's death had felled him with one swoop.

Since then, he had lain motionless on the forest ground like a decaying log. Overgrown with moss. Rotting. And although, in reality, these logs were nurturing, protecting havens for all sorts of wildlife, he had been no such thing for anyone. Not even himself. His longing and pining for the sea, Niall thought, came from his urge to sever his connection to the land. He had been dead inside for so long that the prospect of feeling alive, rooted, and connected filled him with fear and dread. And Marla had made him feel alive in a way that he had never experienced before. She was an unstoppable force of life. Just like spring.

And he had been a coward. An absolute arsehole. Niall had seen in her eyes how much he had hurt her when he walked away.

He had been buried in the stillness and darkness of his inner ashes. And now... His world felt as slippery and muddy as the ground on which he was walking. In truth, he simply didn't know what to do. To face her, he needed to collect his thoughts. His courage.

When Niall turned the corner, lost in his own mind and with a surly Barclay plodding alongside him, his heart nearly leaped through his ribs.

Only a few metres away, Marla was headed toward him.

And judging by the expression on her face, which rapidly changed from shock to anger, she was just as startled and a thousand times less pleased to meet him. Niall's chest tightened at the sight of her. He felt like an intruder, like he didn't have any right to be here. On his own land.

'I can't believe this,' she said. 'Why are you not on your usual path in the forest?' Icicles seemed to grow in her silver eyes. Barclay, blissfully unaware of human problems and happy to see her, ran in circles and she gently rubbed his ears. Niall hesitated before finding his voice. 'I was trying to avoid any awkwardness,' he said, his shoulders slumping.

'So was I.' Her tone was caustic. 'Brilliant plan. Worked out splendidly.'

'Marla, I—'

'Don't even speak to me,' she said. 'Let me pass and move on.'

'As you wish.'

Niall and Marla intended to push past each other on the tight path without touching. They kept trying to create a safe distance between them. Each time one took a step backward or forward, so did the other in a stumbling tango of avoidance. The thawing ice had made the trail slick and treacherous. It was Marla who lost her footing first and lurched forward, arms flailing. Without thinking, she grabbed onto Niall for support. They tried to keep their balance before gravity won out, sending both of them splashing into the mud puddle.

'What the fuck is wrong with you!' she shouted.

'*This* is not my fault,' he said, trying to keep his cool and ignore the wet water that was seeping into his jeans. '*I* didn't slip.'

'I'm not talking about the fall, you idiot!' Her voice got even louder.

'Oh.'

'Damn right, oh! Why did you walk away? No, don't answer that. I know. It's because you're a coward!' She glared at him. The air quivered around them as she seethed in anger. 'This,' she pointed at him and herself, 'was something good.

Something new and real. We could've... And I did nothing wrong. *You* messed this up. This is on *you*, Niall McCarron!' She slammed her hand into the puddle, and mud splashed everywhere. 'I deserve to be treated with honesty and respect!'

'I agree. And I'm sorry,' he said quietly. 'For what it's worth.' He saw the pain and the anger seizing her face. It hurt him so much that he wished he could melt away like the snow and disappear into the ground.

'I tell you what it's worth—nothing!'

'Aye, I get it.' He ducked his head. 'But let me explain—'

'No! You had your chance to explain, and you decided to bloody walk away!' In her rage, she tried to stand up. Her trainers found no grip on the slippery soil, and she skidded again. This time, she fell onto his lap.

'Ouch! Marla, if you would just listen for—'

'No!' She yelled and tried to wrestle herself away from him.

'Dammit woman! Haud yer wheesht and listen!' Now he was getting mad, too. 'You deserve the truth. And I'm ready to tell you the truth now. If only you'd fucking let me!'

Her face was bright red and sprinkled with mud, her eyes full of icy fire as she stared at him in silent ire. Niall took his chance. 'I lied to you. And I'm ashamed of it. But it's not what you think!' He inhaled. 'This is difficult for me, but—'

'Yeah, because it's such a breeze for me!'

He ignored her stinging sarcasm. 'See, when Nathalie died, I died, too. Part of me, at least. And I felt responsible for her death. I—' His words were choked with guilt as he cast his eyes to the ground. 'Everything here reminds me of her. Our life together. That it was gone. That *she* was gone. And that it was my fault. I thought it was. Maybe I wanted to think it was.' He looked up and his pain-filled gaze met hers. 'This place suffocated me. So, I wanted to get away. No, I was desperate to get away.' He noticed her features easing slightly.

Which would make the next part even tougher, so he braced himself. He had to come clean. And who knew if he'd ever find the courage again to tell her the whole truth.

'A while ago, a big developer approached me. They wanted to buy my land, and I was more than happy to sell. I wanted to get myself a boat, take Barclay, leave, and never look back. Getting rid of all the baggage. Never having to work again, just drifting on the sea. But—' He paused and swallowed. 'They wanted Hazelbrae, too. That was their condition. It sits right in the middle, and there was no deal without the cherry on the icing. Lady Hamilton refused to sell. And after she died, I thought… I hoped that…' Anxious, he tried to gauge her reaction before continuing.

'What *exactly* are you trying to tell me?' she asked with a scowl of dread on her face.

His body tensed. 'There's no good or easy way to say it, so I'll just say it. You came here out of nowhere and you stood in my way. I'm not proud of it. But initially, I wanted you to fail. And I made sure you would. By telling everybody not to work for you. All so you would be ready and willing to sell. Then I could have sold my land to the developer, too. I could have escaped from here for good. But you…' He faltered and bit his top lip. This was hard. 'You were… I didn't expect to develop *feelings* for you.' He pronounced the word as if it were something altogether exotic and outrageous. Which it was to him. 'It changed everything. Believe it or not. But it took me a while to see that.' His breathing quickened as his emotions took over. He wanted to turn away to hide the pain on his face, but then stopped and looked straight at her. 'That's what I couldn't tell you the other morning, after our night together. That's why I couldn't look you in the eye. That's why I left.' His voice cracked at the end. 'That's the reason I'm not good enough for you.'

Her face was as white as the last bits of melting snow. 'Niall. What have you done?'

'I didn't know what to say to make it right. I was in too deep. So, I said nothing and ran away. You're right. I'm a coward. And I'm sorry. So sorry.'

His stomach dropped as she shouted, 'How? How could you betray me like that? I thought you were *helping* me!'

He felt the full force of her hurt and fury, and he deserved all of it.

'Dammit! I trusted you, Niall. I opened up. Do you understand how hard that is for me? I was so stupid to see you as anything else than a vicious, pompous, self-serving ass!' She managed to stand up and gain a firm footing. With blazing cold eyes, she looked down, and it seemed as if she was about to kick him. She didn't. But she might as well have. Her eyes weren't silver anymore. They looked dark and dangerous. Like gunpowder.

'I wish I'd never met you! You're a liar, a coward, and insane. How dare you tell me you have *feelings* for me and that you betrayed me *in the same breath*? What am I supposed to *do* with that now? I can't even. I don't want to see you ever again!' She turned around to leave, but then looked back over her shoulder. 'And yes, I know this is a tiny town. But try to stay the hell out of my way!' Marla stormed off, her feet squishing on the wet trail. She stomped on a patch of snowdrops, crushing their fragile petals. Niall remained sitting there, soaked in icy, dirty mud water.

And with every fibre of his wretched being, he knew she was right. He had ruined it before it could even begin, and that was that. After everything during the past years—maybe he was the one who didn't deserve better.

Chapter Nineteen

Icy rain pelted her from all sides on the walk back to Hazelbrae. Marla had long got used to the mad Highland weather changes—one day, it had hailed under clear and sunny skies—but she still wondered how it was possible for it to rain from the bottom up. The fierce wind whipped the raindrops into her face like a thousand pinpricks. It was precisely what she needed, washing away her grudging, acrid tears.

The things Niall had just told her were inconceivable.

What bothered Marla most was the powerlessness and confusion. She had let him in, against her better judgment. How could she have been this wrong about him? He had been so supportive, so helpful, so sweet. It all had felt right.

But if she was honest, she still scarcely knew him. Not really.

She most certainly hadn't known anything about his secret agenda. Sabotaging her to get her to sell Hazelbrae so that he could buy a stupid boat, all the while pretending to help her. How was that even supposed to work, why would he help her when he wanted her to fail? What kind of twisted person would do such a thing? And now he told her he had feelings for her. *That's one messed-up dude.*

Her taste, if one could call it that, in men was reliably abysmal. That much was obvious. Everything inside her was raw and inflamed.

After entering Hazelbrae's hall, Marla wriggled herself out of her wellies without using her hands. She had neither the strength nor the will to stoop. Then she dropped her dripping rain jacket on the marble tiles. *Who cares? My castle, my mess.*

And what a mess it was. Because there was the leak.

This one fateful night of the heavy post-Christmas storm hadn't only rattled her heart, body, and her judgement. No. She had learned two days ago that the winter winds and continuous rain were causing considerable damage. Water had been leaking in for weeks. It threatened the stonework and needed fixing. Immediately. Marla had called in a surveyor for this morning.

This was the hour of truth. With trembling, frosty fingers, Marla typed the number from the business card into her phone. Her heart sank into her stomach with each ring, dreading the outcome of this call.

Finally, a voice answered on the other end.

'Hello? This is Marla Wilson. I'm calling about my property damage. Hazelbrae. Someone was here today.'

The surveyor rustled some papers and, sighing heavily, informed Marla of the estimate. 'It looks like it will cost around 100,000 to fix up your place,' he said.

Fighting back tears, Marla's throat tightened. She had assumed it would be expensive but hearing it out loud was too much. 'That's... that's a lot more than I was expecting,' she stammered.

The surveyor responded sombrely, 'I know, it's substantial. But these old buildings... they can be tricky.'

One hundred thousand bloody pounds. That was much, much more than her savings. He went on to explain what kind of work they would have to do, the costs associated with each task, and how long everything would take. The list was endless and her stomach twisted at the thought of it. Marla tried to take in all the information. When he finished speaking, she thanked him and hung up, feeling even more overwhelmed than before. No, not overwhelmed. Defeated.

Because to make matters worse, as she had found out just this morning, the insurance wouldn't cover the damage. She had taken out a new insurance policy for the castle in her own name after the inheritance was settled. But pre-existing and unreported damage to the exterior of the building was excluded. Before the inheritance, another surveyor had examined Hazelbrae and apparently missed a pre-existing leak in the roof. How some people did their jobs… As usual, they hid the catch in the small print. Also as usual, Marla hadn't read it too closely. But freaking out about it was obsolete. Especially since she had to admit that, according to her own experience so far, in such an ancient and immense house all kinds of surprises and secrets lurked, waiting to reveal themselves at the worst times.

It didn't look good.

Even selling both her kidneys wouldn't get her close to the money she needed. Plus, there would be the minor inconvenience of her being dead.

Her castle-shaped Jenga tower had crashed with a bang.

After Marla had made herself a cup of tea and slipped into her fleece sweatpants, she threw herself onto her bed with a grunt and dug out her mobile phone. High time to make a long overdue call to her best friend. They hadn't spoken since January, when Marla visited London for New Year's. *How did I let that happen?*

When Trish appeared on her screen, Marla could hardly keep it together.

'Jeez, Marl. You look terrible. What's going on?' The

default sunshine on Trish's face had made way for an expression of serious concern.

'Everything is going to shit. That's what's going on,' Marla said.

'How's that possible? When you were down here, you were so optimistic. Unusually so, to be honest.'

Marla groaned. 'You better sit down. This is going to be a long conversation.'

It took over fifteen emotional minutes for Marla to explain the complex situation to her best friend. She closed her monologue with '... and that's it. I fell for a liar, and the castle is ruining me. Unless I find a miraculous source of money—a billionaire, hidden treasure in the cellar, or something like that —I'm finished here.' She buried her face in her hand. Not that Marla was consumed with self-pity. That was not her style. But this situation couldn't be glossed over or sugar-coated. Not even by Trish's built-in sunshine and optimism.

To Marla's surprise, there was none of that.

A resolute Trish stared back at her on her rectangular phone screen. 'Stop it,' she said. 'Dry your eyes, Marl, and get over yourself for once. You always do that. Something happens, and you erupt like a jack-in-the-box. And then you run. That has been your MO ever since I've known you.'

Marla was stumped. 'Sorry, but he lied to me because he wanted me to fail and go bankrupt. That's not a tiny thing, Trish. That's downright devious.'

'Yeah, perhaps. But he seems to see what he did wrong. He seems to have his reasons. And, from what you told me, he seems to regret it. Also, he admitted everything to you when he technically didn't have to.' Trish raised an eyebrow and Marla wasn't able to brush off her logic completely. 'And if you did have to sell the castle, even for pennies, you would cash in. What is it worth? A million? Two? Even if you had to throw it away for half a million, that's half a million more than you had before. Minus what you already spent, of course. I know nothing about properties and taxes. I'm just saying.'

'Trish, I'm not in it for the money.'

'I know, babes. But what's the worst case here? You sell it, you come back. No harm, no foul.'

It was clear to Marla that her friend had a point. But why did the thought of selling Hazelbrae and moving back to London not only feel like failing on an epic scale but also like a piece of her heart was being ripped out?

'I don't know, Trish. For the first time in a long while, I feel like I have a good purpose again. Something bigger than myself. It's hard to explain. I'm connected here.' Marla rubbed the bridge of her nose between her fingers.

'Fair enough, hon. We'll figure it out. We always do. But back to your hot Scot drama for a minute. Do you remember Dan?'

'He's not *my* hot Scot.' Marla winced inwardly. 'Dan? Of course, I do. Unfortunately.' He had been her longest relationship. They had dated for about seven months. It went fairly well. Until she found out that he had a teenage daughter whom he had kept secret and, on top of that, didn't want her to meet anytime soon. 'What does *he* have to do with anything?'

'Same thing in green. You dumped him without further ado. You didn't even consider working through it. I think that's your way of protecting yourself. Before anybody can come too close and do any actual damage,' Trish sounded uncomfortably stern now. 'And I get that. But what you have to keep in mind is people have shit going on, they have to figure things out, they make mistakes. I know I do. What matters is whether and how they learn from it. What they do to make it right. Which can only happen if you let them. Provided they're serious about it, obviously.'

'I really, really don't appreciate your truth bombing right now.'

'Fine. But I'm not your friend only to tell you what you want to hear. Sometimes I have to tell you the things you need to hear. Even if you don't like it. Marl, you haven't let anyone in—like, ever—but especially since Gordon and Rose passed.' Her gaze softened. 'I think you're hurting, babes. A lot. And you're in sheer terror of not surviving one more loss.'

It was as if an enormous fist had just socked Marla in the stomach. But Trish wasn't done yet. 'Here's the thing: all that pain that you don't want to feel? That's the price you have to pay for love.'

'Oh, please. Motivational quotes, is it now? Where did you read that—on Instagram or Pinterest?' Marla snapped.

'Be as snippy as you like. That's okay. I know you're still grieving. For your mum, for Rose and Gordon, maybe even your dick of a dad. But think of all the love you and your grandparents shared. The life you had together. Your bond. You wouldn't want to miss any of that, right? I mean, if you could go back in time and choose?'

An iron ring was tightening around Marla's chest. Fragments of precious memories passed her inner eye. The tree house her grandda built her, dancing in the kitchen with her gran, birthday parties in their garden. How her gran had always given Marla the bowl with the biscuit dough to 'clean' with a spoon, even when Marla had long since grown up. Her grandda teaching her to whittle with his pocket knife. Sunshine threaded through the inky ribbon of grief. 'You're not totally wrong,' was all Marla was able to say.

'Good. I have one more question.'

Marla sighed. 'Good grief. Go on then.'

'Do you like him?' Trish looked right at her through the screen.

'Who? Oh, right. Yeah, the sex was phenomenal. I have to give him that.'

'That's not what I asked.'

Marla squinted her eyes. 'When he's not plotting against me, he's handy with tools.'

'I see. That all?' Trish kept probing.

'Not sure. He also smells nice?'

'You're still not answering my question, Marl. Do you *like* him?'

'What is this, a police interrogation? What is it you want me to say, Trish? That I have an infallible radar for guys who are unavailable, unstable, and dysfunctional? With soap-opera-style secrets? Drama written all over them? Oh, I do. And so yes, of course I like him!' The second she blurted it out, she knew it to be painfully true.

This and a lot more.

'It's not just liking, Trish.' Marla confessed and closed her eyes. 'I can't stop thinking about him. His kisses, his addictive scent, the sound of his laugh, the way I fit snuggly into his arms, his cute freckles. How he cares for others. The way it makes me feel when he holds my hand or how he looks at me. His jokes. His grumpy stubbornness. All of it. He's everywhere, inside and out.' She paused and continued with a low voice. 'I was falling for him, Trish. As hard as never before. I thought this would be different. I really hoped… Shit. Seems I was wrong. I didn't want to hurt again and now…' Sobs were welling up inside Marla and she had to fight hard to suppress them. 'Fuck.'

Even Trish seemed to realise that she had hit a sore spot with her friend. 'Oh, love. I'm so sorry, Marl. I didn't mean to upset you. I just think you keep running away. Honestly, I think you should talk to him. But don't worry, babes. You'll sort it out. The castle as well as the guy and yourself. You'll see. And I'm always here if you need me. You know that, right? Even if you hate me now. I'm here.'

'Thank you, means a lot,' Marla said, sniffling. 'I don't hate you. Even though I sometimes wish for a less wise-ass friend.'

'No, you don't.' Trish smiled from ear to ear.

'Yeah, okay. Probably not. Whatever,' Marla said. 'Damn, you're annoying.'

'I'm aware. That's why you love me so much!' Trish wiggled her impressive eyebrows, and Marla couldn't help but smile back at her.

'Awww, there she is!'

When Marla was sitting at her desk later going over her budget for the umpteenth time, a futile endeavour if ever there was one, she thought about how talking to Trish had equally comforted and confused her. Niall had tried to apologise to her when they bumped into each other. He seemed sincere. A part of her even bought his reasoning, although she didn't completely understand it. And it didn't make it right. Of course not.

Marla's nose twitched. There was something else. She traced the course of the Victorian desk's elegant intarsia. 'By their deeds, you shall know them,' her gran had always said. Or, as Marla used to re-phrase it, 'What have the Romans ever done for us?'

Dubious motivations aside, Niall had helped her. As a matter of fact, every day. Sure, no aqueducts. But pipe repair. He had fixed this and sorted out that, organised here and there, made calls, called in favours, signed off on deliveries when Marla was busy. Followed through on every promise. He had listened, shared his stories, put up with her whims, and put on a unicorn robe. Why? She couldn't make sense of it. But those had been his deeds, factually speaking. That's what made it so difficult for her to understand. Why bother?

Then there were his other deeds, of course. The deeds he had done with his fingers and his lips and all the rest of his stunning, strong, enjoyable body. The mere memory of their night was enough to make her heart beat faster and a hot, tingling sensation fill the area between her legs. Again. Something briefly tempted Marla to indulge her desire with some serious self-care, but she decided to ignore it. Again.

She let out a long breath.

She was missing him. A lot.

Trish had pretty much hit the mark.

Because there was another thing gnawing at her wobbly moral high ground.

Escaping and running away from pain and grief—like Niall had planned on doing—was the exact same thing that Marla herself had done. She knew how it felt to be reminded of loss on every corner. How the urge to get away from the pain could fog and suffocate everything. No, she hadn't planned it like he had. Yet she had jumped at the chance all the same. Her anger softened a little. Despite all understandable motives, his behaviour was still no trifle. Someone who played such a double game was not to be trusted readily. Even though he smelled nice, was handy with tools, and a total phenomenon in bed.

Even though he had managed to capture her heart against her will.

Apart from all that, Marla had also made a proper fool of herself with her massive tantrum. A sense of embarrassment rose up inside her as she thought about her defensiveness. She recalled Trish's words about Niall. Should she talk to him?

No, that ship had likely sailed. And her temper had lifted the final anchor. She couldn't imagine that he would ever want to speak with her again.

First, he had ruined it by walking away. Then she had. By stifling any chance of reconciliation.

Maybe it's for the best after all. Who knows?

Her mobile phone rang and interrupted her pondering. It

was the bank. Marla's stomach turned. As if this day wasn't awful enough.

The bank adviser made stale conversation at first, but then she got to the inevitable point. 'We're sorry, but your financial situation doesn't allow for a loan. Especially considering that you have currently no income.' The formulaic explanations went on for a few endless minutes, but Marla wasn't paying attention to the adviser's voice, so professional, so indifferent and cold. She had already figured that. Eventually, she mumbled some standard response and hung up. Her eyes filled with tears.

I'm so, so sorry, Grandda.

This last rejection fitted neatly into the picture. There was also no government funding—nor any funding—because Hazelbrae did not meet the relevant criteria. Marla needed an investor or a miracle. And soon. Yesterday would be great. Or Hazelbrae would have to be sold for a song at auction.

'Fuck!' Out of sheer frustration, she slammed her hand on the desk. So hard that her palm stung and her entire arm vibrated.

Click.

Marla tilted her head. *What's that sound?*

It seemed to have come from within the desk. Which didn't make sense. Then she noticed the misalignment. The slim, ornately carved wooden trim in the middle protruded slightly. Which, as Marla could have sworn, it hadn't done before. There was a subtle yet visible gap between the front and the surrounding frame of the desk.

Holy shit. A secret compartment?

A jolt of excitement raced through her. Part of her wasn't surprised. As she had learned in these past months, this was a grand house full of history and stories, of strange objects and remnants of bygone times. And countless secrets. She tried to widen the crevice, but the wood wouldn't move.

Who knows what's in there, perhaps a hidden treasure of

£100,000 in numbered notes? Marla gave a laconic hiss of a laugh. *Dream on.*

She fished Gordon's knife out of her pocket, squeezed the blade into the narrow slot and began to wiggle, using it as a lever, careful not to break anything. It worked. Another barely audible click and the gap widened enough to hook a finger in it. The wood had warped over time and was a bit stodgy, but this wasn't broken. It had been designed that way. Marla used the index and middle fingers of both hands to pull.

Not too long after, she stared into the shallow drawer, clad with beautiful red velvet. And it wasn't empty. It didn't contain any jewellery or money. Of course, it didn't. No, the main compartment held something much more intriguing. A simple, leather-bound notebook, its cover embossed with the cursive golden letters 'H. C. H.'

It only took her a few seconds to figure that one out.

Helena Cecilia Hamilton.

Marla felt a peculiar mixture of awe, curiosity, and remorse, unsure whether she should touch it or not. Let alone open it. But Lady Hamilton had left her whole cursed money pit of a castle to Marla. Including all of its remaining contents. And problems. And leaks. She would have known that she was also leaving this. Or maybe she had long forgotten it was here? Because the book seemed like it hadn't been touched for decades. There was a small hole punched in its right side, where a tiny lock must have protected it from prying eyes. This little leather book had all the bearings of a diary or a journal.

For a while, Marla grappled with herself. *Should I really?*

But curiosity got the better of her. Partly because right now, she needed any distraction she could get. And also, because this might shed some light on who Lady Hamilton had been. Perhaps even on why she had bequeathed her estate to Gordon and his descendants. *What kind of person would find such a thing and* not *look at it?* Not her, that was for sure.

Gingerly, Marla lifted the book out of its drawer, blew off the dust, and placed it slowly onto the inlaid desk—the same location where it must have captured the thoughts and feelings of Helena Cecilia Hamilton many, many years ago.

With trembling fingers, Marla opened to the first page.

Chapter Twenty

The handwriting was expansive and sweeping, but not floral. Although faded in spots, Marla could read most of it. The letters had an upward and downward movement, as though they were written in a hurry or distress.

July 1, 1962

I wish I was dead! I feel so weak and horrid. I can barely hold the pen. So, I will only write what's necessary. L. is to be wed to an American heiress next month. After all the letters in which he wrote he missed me. He said he does not love her. But what does it matter? It is decided. As I write this, he has already departed for New York. He writes that I should not write to him anymore. 'It is for the best, Pebble.' Those were his words. I disagree! At seventeen and a half, I know my own mind. How can he do that to me? Why does he not stand up to his family? The pain leaves me hollow. My life is over. Over!!!

As Marla's index finger touched the yellowed pages, a wave of sympathy for the heartbroken teenager washed over her. Who was L.? Young Helena's pain was obvious from her words, and Marla remembered her first heartbreak around the same age.

It was a guy from school, Mike. They had done all the things typical teenagers do. Go to the movies, hang out in malls, play video games, and make out at every opportunity. He was a sweet first boyfriend. For three months. Until Marla heard from his mate Rob that Mike was moving from Birmingham to Sheffield because his mum had got a new job there. He hadn't told her anything about it.

Marla vividly recalled the sense of betrayal and the hurt that she had experienced when she broke up with him. She had stayed in bed for days, curled up into a sobbing ball. Her grandparents had tried their best to cheer her up. But the first broken heart hurts like nothing else.

Surreal how old heartbreak can sometimes creep up again as if time itself didn't matter, Marla thought. But which one of all the heartbreaks was creeping up again right now eluded her. She shook her head and continued reading.

July 17, 1962

Mama is urging me to eat every day, but I cannot. No appetite. I feel like a ghost in these halls. Still no word from L. Today I wandered through the hazelnut grove all by myself. The place where I once knew happiness now mocks our love. Nothing will ever be the same again. And I cannot help but wonder what L. is doing in New York. Is he thinking of me, or has he forgotten all about me? I wonder, I wonder… Maybe one day I will look back on these words and laugh at myself. But now all I can do is cry, cry, cry.

• • •

August 9, 1962

Dear diary, this is farewell. I cannot go on anymore. The pain is too much to bear, and the future holds nothing for me. Yesterday, mama spoke of a possible marriage with Mr Abernathy. 'A fine match,' she said. Because he is wealthy. He is twice my age! But even if it is not with him, I realise that I am to live a trapped life in a gilded cage, loveless and unhappy. That is not something I can do. Yet I have no say in it. Unspeakably unfair! I will not stand for it. It is decided: I will take my fate into my own hands. And I have a plan. I will hurry now, there is much to be done.

August 13, 1962

What a foolish child I was! I wanted to run away to America. It was all well thought through. But alas! I was discovered and caught. Papa was very cross. He said that I bring shame to our family. 'Ungrateful wretch' he called me. What does he know of shame or wretchedness? My plans are dust. My heart is broken. The walls of this room seem to close in on me with every passing minute. I am utterly alone. Feeling dead. Dead!!

Arranged marriage? That seemed downright medieval to Marla. It was odd, but she had never thought about the life of the privileged in that way. They had everything that made life easier—enough wealth, status, and connections to always get by. Perhaps that was true. But it wasn't true for everyone, was it? How much say did women have in these matters, even in the 1960s? Marla continued to flip through the pages. Until she saw something fascinating—her grandda's name.

August 19, 1962

Dear diary, as I write these words I am still recovering from recent events. I am pouring my heart out to you, the only listener who will not judge me. As you know, I was very, very low. My love is unrequited, my escape was stopped, my future is bleak. So, in the depth of my despair, there was only one solution. In the wee hours of the morning, I snuck into the kitchen and grabbed Missus Fergusons' sharpest knife. Later, I made my way to the Hazelnut grove. I lay down in the spot where L. had promised me his love with all his kisses. There was solace in the thought that it would all be over soon. My hands shook as I held the blade against my wrist. The pain was sharp, but it was nothing compared to the pain in my heart! Blood came rushing out, and I felt dizzy. I do not quite remember what happened then. Only that a boy came from somewhere. 'Dinna fash, lass,' he said. 'I'll git ye tae the doctor!' Then he picked me up and carried me all the way to the village. 'No, leave me!' I cried, but he held me tightly and kept on. His name is Gordon Wilson, and he saved my miserable life.

Marla exhaled heavily. So that's how they knew each other. Not what she would have guessed or expected. Poor young Helena. Now Marla was hooked. With jittery fingers and a prickling stomach, she skimmed the lines.

August 20, 1962

My strength was not there completely, so I had to stop my writing yesterday. I will tell the rest of the story now. While he was carrying me and I cried and bled into his shirt, I made the boy promise not to tell what I had done. He swore. And he kept his word. At the doctor, he said he found me cutting some hazel twigs, and I slipped and had an accident. The doctor is a slow fellow and did not suspect a thing. The boy named Gordon stayed with me and then escorted me home when I was not quite stable on my legs. He was very concerned about what I had done. 'Makin' wey o anesel. It's a sin,' he said seriously. Foolish boy! What does he know of my suffering? I do not know him. He told me he has started helping our gardener. 'Why haven't I seen you before?' I asked, and he said, 'Cause yer folks disna uisually fraternise wi' the likes o' us.' He is a peculiar young man.

Spellbound, Marla devoured the pages written in Helena's curved handwriting. She was deeply and honestly sorry for the young woman, so privileged but also unfree and lonely. And it was both weird and exciting to read about her grandfather as part of another human's story. As if she suddenly had the chance to travel back in time and meet Gordon as a young man. Marla was desperate to know if there was more, what happened next. Did Helena and Gordon end up being lovers? And why did her grandda leave and never return?

September 5, 1962

I have recovered, and the wound on my wrist is healing. The wound in my heart not so much. But I am glad that Mama has not brought up Mr Abernathy again. Awful man. Today, I saw the gardener boy, Gordon, again. He was kind and asked how I was doing. I did not feel like I had to lie to him, so I was honest. He looked concerned. This made me feel a bit better. Later, he came back and gave me something. 'Ye leuk sad, here's somethin' to lift yer spirits,' he said and gave me a record. Can you believe it! He wants it back, but I can listen to it, he said. The band is called The Beatles (what a ridiculous name!), and the song is *My Bonnie.*

September 15, 1962

Sorry for not writing in such a long time, but I have been distracted. Some days I am so tired that I cannot get out of bed. On others, I listen to the music Gordon brings me. He really seems to like the Beatles. And now I do, too! We discussed the meaning of the song. Gordon insists it is about Bonnie Prince Charlie. Ha, if Papa knew I was liaising with a Jacobite! But I like to think of L. as my Bonnie over the ocean, who is by now married to another girl. My heart still weeps for him.

September 29, 1962

Today, I have concluded that I am not sad about being alive anymore. Not all the time. Gordon has become a confidant. We meet every other day in the garden, talk about life and music and all things. He is so different from everyone I know. For one, he does not indulge in any flattery. Some people would think it crude. Those people are ignorant. I think he is an honest boy and the first friend I ever made who is true and kind. He even knows about L.—not his name, though. There are some secrets one should never share. But he knows of my broken heart. He says that it is normal, and that true mutual love is rare to find. I think pain is easier when you can share it, when you can speak about it, instead of trying to deal with it all on your own. It is nice not to feel so alone anymore. I will always be grateful for his friendship.

❄

Marla had to put the journal down to wipe her eyes, a smile on her face. This was so much like her grandda! He had told her the Jacobite story of *My Bonnie*, too, when she had been a little girl. It was as if Gordon was coming to life again on Helena's pages. A different and younger version, naturally. But it was all there. His kindness and generosity, his determination to help others, his ability to comfort, his stubbornness once he had formed an opinion.

October 8, 1962

The Beatles have a new song out!

October 11, 1962

Oh, dear diary! Papa thinks I have taken Gordon as my lover, and he will not listen to reason! It was awful, awful! Someone must have told him we often meet in the garden. Because when Gordon brought me the new record, Papa came storming toward us with his hunting rifle! He threatened to shoot us both! Papa was beside himself, with a bright red face and a foaming mouth. He shouted at Gordon to get out of Kilcranach and never come back or he would shoot him. I screamed and tried to talk to him, but he would not listen. He would not listen! Gordon was as white as a sheet. 'My laird, I havna din anythin' improper. I wouldna!' But in vain! Papa yelled that he could shoot scum like Gordon anytime and no judge would convict him. And if he would not go away and leave me in peace forever, he would make life hell for the Wilson family. He cursed him! Gordon was shaking like a leaf, but he got up and told me I could keep the record. Then he left. Oh, I swear I will never stop hating my father. NEVER! He has always been a cruel man. Now he has chased away my only friend. I will NEVER forgive him!!!

It was getting dark and too hard to read now. And Marla was shaken. There were only blank pages after that. Now she understood why her grandda hadn't returned to Kilcranach for decades. What had happened to his family? From his stories, she remembered he didn't have many direct relatives up here.

Marla didn't know how long the old, nasty Lord Hamilton lived or what happened later in Helena Cecilia Hamilton's life, but she wanted to find out. Maybe she had written other diaries?

Gordon had saved Helena's life. Not only by taking her to the doctor, but by being her friend. Their connection was what helped the young woman feel less alone and devastated. Ultimately, that must be the reason Marla had inherited Hazelbrae.

Perhaps her grandda's legacy wasn't the grand house itself. But the kindness and openness he had shown. Sadness encompassed her. It felt less like grief and more like regret. Now that she knew at least a part of the story, she wished even more that she could keep Hazelbrae.

With a last, weak glimmer of hope, Marla took her phone and made a call.

Chapter Twenty-One

'This whole affair is most unfortunate.' William Collins looked at Marla over the rim of his round spectacles. His face showed sincere concern and empathy. Marla considered him a friend. Not a bosom friend, but a friend, nonetheless. Who was, despite his neat and proper appearance, a surprisingly ferocious dancer.

Sadly, that was of no help at all right now.

'This is a small business community. There's not much money being moved around.' He sniffled. Because of all the dust. 'As we discussed, I have put out my feelers. But it seems that interest is rather low.'

Marla hung her head and stared at the documents that were scattered across the floor and on any other available surface in Mr Collins' tiny office. Lazy sunbeams rolled through the small window and dipped some of those impossibly high file stacks into glares before the clouds closed in again.

This is where it all began.

Is it ending here now, too?

Asking him for help had been her last straw. Marla had run out of ideas. 'I understand,' she said. But she wasn't sure she did. Why would the universe give her this opportunity and then take it away again?

I guess that's life. The good stuff rarely lasts.

'What happens next?' she asked tonelessly. Her mind wandered off while Mr Collins held a monologue on the various options of sales and auctions. She could spot a chunk of a hill through the tiny window.

Kilcranach.

How quaint and strange this little place had seemed when she first walked its streets last November. And how familiar, normal, and homely it all was now. 'Eddie's Chippy' with the blue window frames, crowned with a sign depicting a fish that looked disturbingly psyched to be fried. And Eddie's neighbours, the ice cream parlour 'Pinocchio' with gelato to rival any in London, owned by siblings Doug and Sophie, Scots with Italian roots. Behind the lemon-yellow window frames the wee charity shop that provided a never-ending supply of affordable books, clothes, crockery, and toys for the entire town and any tourist curious enough to enter. Not to forget Bert's bookshop across the road with Fiona's café inside. Both were passionate advocates for Kilcranach's rich history and culture, keeping its strong tradition of Gaelic song and poetry alive.

The thought of leaving made her queasy, like a million moths gathering in her stomach. Her hands were numb and her throat tight. Marla had never felt so connected to a place before. She loved the people of Kilcranach who had welcomed her as one of their own. For one, the magical creature that was Gwen, a kind soul and such a mouth. But also, the two Mrs Bellbottoms who, next to her grandparents, were the happiest married couple Marla had ever met. Jack, of course, devoted single dad of three, deliverer of parcels, and strummer of guitar riffs.

And Niall.

Nope, she couldn't. It hurt too much, like a buzz saw spinning in her chest. She couldn't go there. Marla bit her bottom lip until she tasted blood.

Think of something else.

Oh, the land! Marla loved this land. It was as though the landscape was alive, breathing, pulsating with energy, speaking to her in an ancient language that only she could understand. Scotland hummed in her blood and in her bones. It was the truth.

Then there was Hazelbrae. Marla felt another searing pang in her heart. Its ivy-clad walls, portraits and chandeliers, its creaking wood, nooks, crannies, dead wasps, and many, many wonders. It was like living in an adventure playground, which was also a construction site and a haunted house. A bit like a gothic Pippi Longstocking. She thought of Helena Cecilia Hamilton's incredible friendship with Gordon, her gratitude and loyalty, her tragic story… Marla felt like a part of it all. And she didn't just feel it. She was. For a brief part of its long existence, Marla had been part of Hazelbrae's history. A part of Kilcranach's community.

What a joy.

What an honour.

And what a failure.

Regret enveloped her, suffocating her like a heavy, woollen blanket. She had been Hazelbrae's guardian, and she had messed up. She had put her heart and soul into the castle, pouring every penny and ounce of her energy into it. For nothing.

Stupid, cursed storm night!

For more than one reason.

But Marla pushed down the sting of a different kind of hurt. She had enough to worry about as it was. Like losing her home, for example. It would have been fair of Lady Hamilton to consider that Gordon Wilson's descendants would likely not play in the same trust-fund-sponsored league as her own peers and that the upkeep of such a house would be ruinous even for financially stable people. But Lady Hamilton didn't have anybody else, and she wanted Hazelbrae to remain a private property, not a museum.

Marla let out a long and laboured sigh.

And him. Always him. If only she could trust him enough.

'Miss Wilson?'

Mr Collins brought her back to the present. 'Oh, I'm sorry. I was thinking about what you said,' she fibbed.

'There's one more thing we can try,' he said. 'There's a regional investment firm. I'm acquainted with the CEO. A lovely woman, might I add, excellent business sense, very connected. I will not pester you with the details right now, but there might still be a way.' He frowned as he was musing, then he said, 'I would hate for you to lose Hazelbrae, and I will do the utmost to prevent such a tragedy from happening. However, you have to understand that I cannot make any promises. There might be a chance, but it is minuscule.'

Marla waved her hand, resigned to her fate. 'Fine, then let's try this.' She thanked him and left. What else could she have done?

After this appointment, an all-encompassing fatigue rolled over Marla. A numbing nothingness. Instead of walking all the way back to Hazelbrae, she decided to stop by the pub for a chat with Gwen and a coffee. Preferably with a generous shot of whisky.

Never mind the coffee. Whisky should suffice.

Marla walked straight up to the bar, threw her purse on the counter, and proclaimed: 'Whisky. Neat.'

'Marla, hi! Wait, what? Are you serious?' Gwen looked startled.

'I always wanted to say that.' Marla crooked the corners of

her mouth into a fl[illegible]ing, tired smile. 'But also yes, I am. Deadly serious.'

'It's not even noo[illegible]ove.'

'So? It's five o'cl[illegible] somewhere,' Marla replied in dissonant gaiety.

Gwen flipped he[illegible] long green braid over her shoulder. 'Now you sound des[illegible]rate.'

'Bingo! I am. Wa[illegible]a know why? Because I fucked up. Royally. More than I[illegible]nce Harry!' Marla laughed, short and hard. 'Nothing agai[illegible] Prince Harry, though. I think everybody who gives th[illegible] toxic family the finger should be applauded.'

The Blue Bonnet [illegible]as still empty. Gwen had just opened for the day. It was a [illegible]Wednesday in early February, and the season had not pic[illegible]d up. Only one couple was staying overnight. They wer[illegible]oth wrapped from head to toe in functional clothing, equi[illegible]ed with Nordic walking sticks, and about to leave for a long hike.

No one here to judge the day drinking, Marla thought. *Ideal.*

There was a smooth rumbling sound as Gwen slid the glass across the wooden countertop towards Marla. '*That's* the spirit!' she exclaimed and giggled again. 'No, that's literally the spirit. Ha!'

Gwen raised her eyebrows in alarmed suspicion. 'I've known you long enough now to understand that when you're making *that* sort of joke, shit is hitting the fan. Spill!'

'Do you remember the leak I told you not to worry about?'

'The one on your roof?'

'Yep, that's the one!' Marla said over-cheerfully and downed her dram in one go. She slid the glass back across the bar to Gwen and pointed two fingers at it, gesturing her to top it up with a nod. 'Well, I lied. You *should* have worried about it. And so should I.'

Gwen frowned while she poured another wee drink. 'Elaborate.'

'Long story short, it's eating the stonework, and I need a hundred thousand pounds to fix it. Or it will all turn into a heap of mushy castle-crumble.' Marla briskly tipped the second Scotch and slammed the glass onto the counter. 'Fun fact,' she then said, wiping her mouth with the back of her hand, 'not only do I not have a hundred thousand pounds, I also don't know anyone else who has that kind of money. Aaand... everybody else is a lot smarter than me and stays the hell away from castles.' Marla pointed her finger at her empty glass again. 'There are no funds, no investors, nothing. Sooo...' she imitated a drum roll on the edge of the table with her two index fingers, '...I will have to sell Hazelbrae!'

'What?' Gwen had started pouring the third dram and stopped. 'What the—'

'Precisely!'

Still shocked, Gwen grabbed another glass and filled both generously with whisky.

'But Gwen,' Marla said mockingly, 'it's not even *noon*.'

'Shut up and drink. And then explain yourself.'

Half an hour later, Marla had moved on from whisky to Scotland's most famous soft drink Irn-Bru and indeed laid out the entire situation. 'And that's why I have to move back to London, you see. It's over. Over and done with!' She made an awkward, sweeping gesture with her hand and nearly knocked over the tall glass of orange liquid in front of her. There still weren't any other guests around.

'If you want to stay, I'm sure you can find work round here. We could all pitch in and help,' Gwen suggested. But they both knew it to be more wishful thinking than anything else.

'Thanks. But there are no jobs in the Highlands, that's what everybody is always going on about. And I couldn't live with myself here after... after everything. Tsss... The stupid, naïve, big-city girl ltzing in, playing castle and getting kicked in the butt. Ri ly so! Right. In. The. Butt.'

Exactly as Niall l prophesied. *Niall.* Marla buried her face in her hands. Th she opened her fingers and looked at her friend. 'Oooh… d there's another thing. A bad thing. Badly bad. I probabl nouldn't say a-ny-thing.'

'Now you definit should say something.'

'Okay, okay.' Tha s to the whisky's persuasive powers, Marla was easily sv ed. 'Here it comes.' She cleared her throat and took the ands of her face. 'I… I… slept with Niall.' She squinted e eye and held her index finger up. 'Just once.'

Gwen's face rem ned thoroughly unimpressed as she stated, 'Finally.'

'Huh?' Marla saic

'Hen, the tensio was thick between yous. Everybody sensed it. I could on just about manage to stop the village from setting up a be n when it would happen. And I'm not sure that they didn't it behind my back anyway.'

'Wowza. I did *not* pect that. Sneaky bunch!'

Gwen grinned, sh casing her chipped tooth. 'Not to pry, but as it's out now ar vay… How was it?'

'Cheeky you!' M a snorted. 'But yeah, it was nice. No, I'm lying. It was a-m zing! Except that he ran away the next morning. I spooked l n. As if he'd seen a ghost. And then he left. Rude! But every ng before that… I liked it. He was so good at…' She circl her pelvis on the chair, almost losing her balance. 'Oops! n not sure whether he liked *me* or whether he pretend so he could…' she said solemnly and sipped on her drink. id you know? He wanted me to crash and burn so I would ve to sell the castle and then he could sell all his land als nd then buy a stupid boat and then skedaddle for good. h an arse. Amirite?'

'Naw, that's not n ,' Gwen agreed. 'But didn't he change his mind and help yo '

Marla slowly moved her head up and down. 'Yeah, he did, he did. A lot. Every day. Still no idea why. Maybe so a prettier castle would sell faster? Niall and his shitty schemes. Such a wonderful guy. Such bad plans.' She lowered her gaze and whispered with a slur. 'Evil, evil, sexy man.'

Gwen let out her bell-bright laugh. 'Marla, you're steamin'.'

'So what? I have every right to be as pished as a fish! This is a free country!'

'Is it, though?' Gwen said under her breath. 'Anyway, what about a glass of water for good measure, hm?'

'Nope. That's where the fish fuck in. Gross.' Marla shook her head vigorously, narrowed her eyes, and then said with pouty lips, 'You see, I met him the other day in a puddle, and he talked about *feelings*.'

'Ew, *feelings*!' said Gwen ironically.

'Yeah, right? Ew!' Marla rested her head on her folded arms on the sticky wooden counter and fell silent.

'What about *your* feelings, then, love?' Gwen asked.

'Can't,' Marla mumbled, with her head still buried. 'Hurts. I'm in love and it hurts.'

When Gwen put a full pint of good Scottish tap water in front of her, Marla was already fast asleep.

The pub was quiet when Niall came through the door of the Blue Bonnet to collect another parcel. Not a model sailboat this time. A bunch of books. He had picked up reading again, brushing up on a few classics like Dumas' *The Count of Monte Cristo*, Lawrence's *Lady Chatterley*, Stevenson's *Dr Jekyll and Mr Hyde*, and some self-help stuff about loss, grieving, and healing. Mrs Bellbottom had recommended a few titles. At first, he had felt an inkling of clumsy embarrassment and the need for secrecy. A bit like watching porn for the first time at thirteen. But, as witl orn decades ago, that sentiment had eventually passed. Tl e was nothing wrong with wanting to heal and grow. *Bette te than never*. Still, he didn't want the ever-meddling peopl f Kilcranach to know his private business. Not more than y already did. Hence the online order and not Bert's booksl .

Barclay, keen on tting his usual treat, led the way. But then he went to the l before he reached the bar.

That's odd, Niall t ught. He turned his head to see what had caught his dog's ention.

It was Marla.

His hands droppe o his sides, and his heart fluttered like a hummingbird in l chest. Marla was half-sitting on the bench in the booth, h head leaning against the wall, and her feet up on a chair. Sh eemed to be sleeping.

Even odder.

Gwen's pointy ha eeked up from behind the bar.

'Hi, Gwen.'

At the sound of l voice, she rose and gave a faint grin. 'Oh, hullo. You're he or your parcel, I suppose.'

Niall pointed tow ls the booth. 'What's going on there?'

'Oh, *that,*' she saic nd blinked multiple times.

'Gwen?'

She looked at hin ith perplexity. That was something he hadn't seen in her be e. 'Och, Niall! It's a right mess.'

'What is?'

'Everything. And u, my grumpy friend, seem to be right at the heart of it.'

'I have neither ti nor energy for riddles today,' he said with a strained voice o if you could speed things along and tell me?'

'As you wish. E you're not gonnae like it. Or who knows? Maybe you v .' She threw Barclay his treat. 'Because honestly, the biggest dle here is you.'

Gwen did her be to summarise the situation for Niall.

She told him about the leak, the £100,000, and that Marla would have to sell Hazelbrae after all. She closed with '… so I think you got what you wanted all along.'

He felt bloodless and must have looked the part, because Gwen's expression shifted from slightly irritated to strongly concerned.

'That is not what I want,' he said, crestfallen. 'Not anymore.'

'But it's the reason poor wee Marla over there had to numb her pain and anger with whisky and is now knocked out cold in the middle of the day. Alcohol is never the solution, but it lets you forget about the problem.'

Niall tugged on his earlobe. 'Did she say anything, um… else?'

'Aye, she said many things.' Gwen's gaze now pricked his skin. 'But I doubt she'll remember any of them. She talked about *feelings*.' Before he could open his mouth, Gwen continued. 'I'll speak plainly—'

'… as if you would ever speak in any other way.'

'… it's clear as day that you two have a massive thing for each other. It's also clear that there's something in your way. So, I'd suggest that yous get over yourselves and sort it out, for fuck's sake.'

Niall turned his head and looked sideways, downwards. 'Not that it's any of your business. But no point. I blew it.'

'Ah, I wouldn't be so sure if I were you.' Her pointed hat appeared a tad witchier than usual.

These people and their goddamn meddling.

'Anyhoo, if there's not a miracle, she'll go back to London. And that would be a real shame. That's all I'm saying. That's it. I'm done.'

Back to London. Gwen's words sank into his chest like red-hot hooks, tearing him apart. So far, he had told himself that it would all go on, that *he* could simply go on. But the thought of Marla disappearing for good was unbearable. He let out a breath. She had mad difference here. With Hazelbrae, with the people of Kilcra h. And in his life. She had awakened something in him. Th was no denying it.

'Och, dinna hing lugs,' Gwen said and handed him his parcel. 'It'll all be w I'm always right about these things and I have a *feeling*.'

On his way out, ll stopped at Marla's table. For a few moments, he watche ner as she slept. Snoring quietly, with her lips parted, a fu ow between her eyes. Careful not to wake her, he picked her navy-blue peacoat from the chair and gently placed it er her shoulders. 'Sleep tight and get some rest, love. That ngover will be a bastard.'

And even though ings were tense and broken, a sense of peace and calm settl over him. 'Come on Barclay, let's go!'

They left in a hur

There was somet g he had to do.

Chapter Twenty-Two

Marla collected half-empty glasses and wiped down the wood tables. She had been helping Gwen in the Blue Bonnet for a few days. It was the end of February and tourism was picking up in the Highlands. Kilcranach was no exception. All the tables were packed. It was the monthly pub quiz night, hosted by Fiona and Bert, who were testing the patrons' knowledge on an ever-rotating list of topics. It drew people in from the entire area.

In a corner, the two Mrs Bellbottoms gazed into each other's eyes on their weekly date night. Gwen was pouring pints behind the counter while Marla took orders and cleaned up. The thought of drinking even one sip of whisky made her stomach turn. Her last hangover had been monumental and kept her in bed for two days. It had been entirely her own fault, and it wasn't an experience she was keen on repeating. Definitely not anytime soon.

It doesn't get easier when you're in your thirties. Nothing does.

The two of them were a good team, a well-oiled machine. Since Mr Collins had told Marla that the regional investment firm wasn't interested in Hazelbrae after all—and thus her last straw had combusted—she had been trying to keep herself busy so as no think about her inevitable, imminent departure. Let alone. *im*. Conscious denial, as she called it.

It didn't work too ell, though.

A harsh tug prick at her heart. *I'm going to miss this wee place so much*, she tho ht and fought back the tears.

Just this place?

She had spent t past weeks organising, settling bills, paying the rest of at she owed the tradespeople, and getting a surveyor in ish had come up to Scotland for a few weeks and returned London only yesterday. She wanted to see Hazelbrae for he lf before it got a new owner. But Trish was more than mor support for Marla. As a professional photographer, Marla d tasked her with taking pictures of the grand house that uld show it in its best light.

For the website. T ell it.

After that, Trish Marla had taken a road trip through the Highlands along e North Coast 500. 'You need to get your mind off things rish had stated, hauled Marla into her car, and driven off. T had talked, they had kept quiet, they had revelled in Scot d's incredibly beautiful landscapes. A farewell tour of sorts arla's chest tightened.

Now it was time ack up. She wouldn't let herself think about it or she woul cry and never stop. It was surprising that she still had any rs left inside.

Marla had listen to snippets of conversation all night. She hadn't intended eavesdrop, but was so attuned to the rhythms of the pu Just then, Marla heard his name mentioned. Her hea kipped a beat. She couldn't catch all the words, but she o heard someone say, 'That Niall sold a chunk of his land the her day.'

He had?

They were two er Scots with weathered faces. Marla had seen them here few times but never spoken to them before, aside from th ccasional 'Awrite, lass?' Crofters from the area, most likely.

Marla's interest was piqued. Of course, it was. She tuned in a bit more closely. There hadn't been a day in the past weeks when she managed not to think of him. Of his helpfulness, his sense of humour and sweet seriousness, his lovely hair and sexy stubble, his… She shook her head as if midges were sitting on her nose.

Every day, she had thought of his clumsy attempt to explain everything and her own excessive, immature reaction. What if she had listened to him and tried to find common ground? That wouldn't have magically made up for everything. She wasn't that naïve. At least they could have talked about it and then seen where they stood.

But her old fear of loss had controlled her. She saw that now. That was why she had reacted as she had always done—attack and flight. By trying to protect her heart, she had messed up colossally. Marla had to take a few breaths. Every single time, the cognition burned like acid inside her core. And with each passing day, she dared to face him less and less. The mere thought of being rejected a second time was too much to bear. Not that it mattered much.

I'm going back to London, so what's the point?

Although nothing would ever happen between them ever again, she still took an interest in how he was doing. And since she wasn't able to ask him—or anyone else in Kilcranach—directly, eavesdropping was the next best thing. However pathetic.

The table next to the two men had just been vacated. Marla suddenly found it to be *extremely* dirty.

'Hope he hasn't sold it to one of those environmental capitalists from doon south,' the one in a white Aran jumper said with unveiled disdain in his voice.

'Aye, they promise wildflowers and butterflies and carbon credits and all that. Sounds pretty,' the other man said. 'But what we end up with is fancy houses to make a return for the investors and rows (plastic tubes instead of trees sticking out of the ground. Sh ıe.'

Marla kept wip ; the same spot with unwavering concentration.

'Or holiday lets. al shame,' said the man wearing the Aran jumper and toc ı sip from his pint. 'We're not daft. It's not about biodivers man. It's about profit. That's what Scotland has always l :n about for *them*.'

The other man sl ɔk his head. 'I know, mate. The land should be returned t(rofting, to the people whose ancestors fought for it with bui ng dykes and such.'

'I hope that McC :on did the right thing, I do,' his pal grumbled. 'But I gue: ve'll see.'

'We'll see. It's not ıt anyone ever asks us.'

They finished th(pints. 'Mony words, muckle drouth. Anither?'

'Aye.'

'Oi, Marla! Are u done polishing that table?' Gwen called out to her acrc the room. Marla's face heated up and she hurried back to tl ɔar. 'Coming!'

When the pub quiz ıs over and the Blue Bonnet quieted down, Marla and C en joined the two Mrs Bellbottoms, Fiona, and Bert, at :ir table. It was a bit crammed, but Marla's imminent de :ture seemed to draw them together.

'Did you know N l sold some of his land?' Marla asked the group. Her que: ɔn elicited a wide spectrum of facial expressions, from aw ard to sheepish.

Janet Bellbottom ıs the first to fold. 'I did hear something, yes.'

'So did I,' added I t, and stared at his pint.

Marla propped h(chin into her hand. 'Why did nobody say anything?'

'It's fairly fresh,' Gwen explained evasively. 'I just heard about it yesterday.'

'Please, go on,' Marla insisted. 'What do we know?'

Gwen lowered her voice. 'Apparently, he sold about hundred acres to an enterprise that wants to revitalise the wild forest in the area. They are expanding. It all went astonishingly fast.' She clasped her hands together. 'So I've heard.'

'Hundred? That must be no small chunk of his acreage,' Bert said and scratched his head.

'Och, don't worry about him,' said Janet Bellbottom. 'That boy still has enough land. Not as much as the Duke of Buccleuch or the Danish guy, but enough.'

'What'll happen now?' Fiona wondered. 'What kind of enterprise is it?'

Gwen, well-informed as usual, jumped in. 'I already checked their website. They are all about habitat restoration and in some sort of cooperation with the reserve on the other side of our wee forest. They want to run a tree nursery plus an educational thing that includes a Gaelic resource centre.' She gave an indifferent thumbs-up. 'They also want to sequester carbon and split the credits with the community—aka us. Apparently, they're doing a similar project on the Isle of Lewis.'

Fiona flashed a knowing smile. 'We shall see about that Gaelic centre.'

'What I'm wondering,' ruminated Bert, 'is why he's selling in the first place. That's not like him. He had been holding on to his land for dear life.'

'I suppose,' said Sylvia Bellbottom, 'that this must have been a lucky opportunity. Land in the Highlands is not easily sold so quickly if it's not a large croft or a plot with existing planning permission. Maybe he sold it cheap.'

Marla was asking herself the same question as Bert. If Niall had sold a piece of his land to an ecological enterprise, that most likely meant that the deal with the developer was history. The memor was vague in her head, but if she remembered it right, ey had wanted it all—all of his land, all of Hazelbrae. Anc iall had wanted to sell it as a complete package. *Very strange,* ie thought.

Marla was on her wa home to Hazelbrae. It was past eleven when her phone vibr ed. Such late calls used to send shocks through her nervous stem because they usually meant that there was an emerge with either her gran or her grandda. But over two years l passed since she lost them, and her panic at unusual ca times had given way to harmless, regular confusion.

It was William Co is, her solicitor.

'Mr Collins,' Marl aid as she picked up. 'Is everything all right?'

'Miss Wilson, I an orry to disturb you at such an ungodly hour, but I thought ou would like to hear this instantaneously.'

Marla frowned. 'H ir what?'

'We have a silent estor. You will not have to sell Hazelbrae, if you do not w to do so.' There was an unmistakable note of celebration his voice. 'However, I cannot stress enough that the enti matter depends on the utmost discretion. The investor ins s on remaining anonymous or the deal is null and void.'

'I see,' she replied utiously.

'Miss Wilson, do u understand what I am trying to tell you?'

'Yes, I believe I ' she said, and relief started to flow through her. 'I promi not to be too nosy. I have one question —is it a Nigerian prir ?'

'Pardon me? Is t another of your humorous remarks

that elude me because I am not up to snuff with your popular culture?'

Her smile got wider and wider. 'It is indeed. Never mind, Mr Collins. You're a darling. And for the record, there's nothing wrong with Nigerian princes. Provided they're real.'

'Now that we have cleared that up,' he said, 'when can you come to sign the papers?'

By now, she was beaming. 'How about tomorrow morning? No time to waste.'

'Splendid!' he said, sounding as if he would have liked to clap his hands. Which someone like him would never do. 'How do you always say—let's do this!'

Marla laughed into the darkness of this wonderful, amazing, life-changing, star-glittering Highland spring night. There was hope, after all.

Only what she was really hoping for, she wasn't sure.

She was up with the birds and made her way to Arniston Solicitors in Kilcranach's centre. The early morning sun glowed orange as it rose above the horizon, its rays spilling golden onto the landscape. The spring air was alive with the trilling of birds. A mild breeze rustled through the branches. As she made her way down the hill, Marla noticed the sweet aroma of fresh coffee and Scottish morning rolls wafting from the bakery. It had all the markings of a glorious day. For the time being.

Marla arrived at the office before Mr Collins or his secretary Catriona, feeling hopeful and relieved, but also tense. She wanted all the required ink on all the papers. Then, and only then, would she allow herself to celebrate. The possibility of losing Hazelbrae had been looming over her for weeks, crushing her, threatening to take away everything she had worked for since November. Her purpose. But now, with the silent investor, she h a chance to hold on to the estate and continue her work. create something that would make a small difference for a nch of people.

People like her. I austed and tired in service to others and in need of som vell-earned respite. *One can only pour from a full jug.* And rla had made it her mission to fill all those little jugs to the im. At Hazelbrae.

Shortly afterward Catriona turned around the corner, her red hair glowing in th sun. 'Mornin', Marla. You're early,' she said while she dug t key out of her huge handbag. 'I hear there is good news.'

'I think there is. T re is indeed.' Marla smiled so broadly that her face hurt.

When Mr Collins rived a few moments later, he was all smiles and handshak 'Miss Wilson, a delightful morning to you. I trust you slept ll?'

Marla smiled. nsurprisingly, I did. Thank you. Yourself?'

'I cannot complai he said, leading her up to his office. 'Shall we get on with then?'

This was the thir ime that Marla sat in the chair across from his desk in the uttered attic room. A trace of ink and dust lingered in the r. 'Here.' He pointed to a dotted line and then turned the per. '…and here…,' he flipped another page, '…and here, .' Marla signed the papers without hesitation. Her hand hook slightly as it moved across the lines, the scratch of h pen the only sound in the small room. In the universe, ever As she handed the documents back to Mr Collins, she coul feel the slight weight of them in her hands.

'Excellent,' he sai ooking over the papers. 'Hm. There is one thing missing.' Mr Collins hunched over his desk, moving his hands fr n one paper to the next. 'Excuse me please. I thought I s it here last night. How curious.' He squinted through his asses, mumbling to himself. 'It seems I left it in the printer. Excuse me, I will be back in a jiffy.' He rose and scurried jauntily out the door.

Marla sat in her chair and picked at a loose thread of her coat sleeve. She was saved, Hazelbrae was saved. And now that the initial relief was dissipating, another thought arose… *by whom*?

She knew with absolute clarity that anonymity was the one key condition for this deal. Yet she found herself wondering.

Then her heart nearly stopped.

Because the entire file was there on the desk. Even the documents she didn't have to sign. All of it. Right in front of her.

She was alone. Her chest was pounding.

Before she knew what she was doing, she had grabbed the cardboard folder and begun flipping through it. With one ear, she listened like a lynx to the creaking floorboards that would announce the return of Mr Collins. She was looking for a name, anything, but it was all small print and lots of long and complicated words. No names, as far as she could tell, only 'parties.'

When she finally spotted it at the bottom of one unassuming piece of paper under the small print, she couldn't believe her eyes.

At the same time, it was like she had known all along.

She knew this signature.

She had seen it on delivery notes for construction material at Hazelbrae.

It was bold and straight and all too familiar.

N. McCarron.

Before Marla could give in to the freakout that was surging up inside her, she heard the wooden floor creaking and threw the file back on the desk like it was lava. When Mr Collins entered his office, she pushed a strand of hair behind her ear and sat, legs crossed as if nothing had happened. He would most likely at bute her flaming red face to her relief and happiness. But i ruth, a storm of contradictory feelings raged inside her, whi she was hardly able to contain.

It all made perfec nse.

It didn't make ser at all.

Niall must have s l his land to invest in Hazelbrae. And he didn't want her to ow.

Well, she knew n . She had tasted the fruit of the Tree of Knowledge and it wa ittersweet.

The only questi was... what was she going to do with it?

Chapter Twenty-Three

The single-track road stretched away into greyness. Already the morning sun had given way to suffocatingly low and heavy clouds again. The hills and mountains were drenched in mist. Marla's teeth were grinding as she fumbled with the gearshift. The only things she heard, besides the blood ringing in her ears, were her car's rumbling engine and the hiss of water spraying from the tyres. Her hands held the wheel tightly as if to wring every bit of control from the situation.

Marla was on her way to Niall, and she was upset for various reasons. *What does he hope to gain from this? What's his plan this time?*

It seemed that he had given up his grand scheme of selling all of his lands as a bundle to some developer. Which also meant that he wasn't trying to get Hazelbrae sold any longer. Was he staying here in Kilcranach, even though he had made it more than clear that he didn't want to?

On one hand, Marla was grateful that he had come to her aid. There was no way to sugar-coat it. He had saved her ass. Temporarily. To be honest, she would have been extremely glad for anybody's help in this situation. Who wouldn't have?

On the other ha , it was him. *Him.* His money. His investment in Haze ae might have saved the castle for another day, but it t her to him. Financially, at least. She didn't want that. N after what had happened. Although, technically, she wasr even supposed to know that he was the silent investor. I had done it over her head, without even trying to talk tc er. Was he that repelled by her embarrassing tantrums?

Water droplets s ttered the windshield, obscuring her vision until she swi ied on the windscreen wiper. Marla couldn't for the life c ier figure out why he had done it. But she needed to know at was going on. What was behind all this. Another secret a nda?

This concerned h iome *and* her heart.

But part of her v glad that she now had an excuse to face him. Even thoug he felt deceived by his secrecy again.

Damn, Niall!

Marla turned ont he drive to his cottage, as Gwen had described it. After a metres, she saw the crouched, white-stone house and its ssy slate roof nestled against the edge of the forest, as if tr g to hide. Like its owner. Its insufferable, beautiful, bewil ring, secretly-investing, money-squandering, giant-hearted se of an owner.

She got out of he ar and slammed the door behind her, leaving a short, d echo. Drizzle settled on her face. Marching towards th ront door, she noticed two chattering magpies sitting on w t looked like a broken sail peeking out of a trash bag aside t jute doormat. *Nothing shiny here for you guys,* Marla thought.

She lifted her fist knock and paused, unsure of what to say first. She probal could have walked in. People here never locked their dc . Marla inhaled to gather her courage. But before her knuck touched the wood, the door opened.

There he stood.

She hadn't seen h in a while, despite Kilcranach's small-town awkwardness. His russet stubble was longer than usual, his broad shoulders slumped. He wore nothing but grey joggers and a bit of chest hair.

He wore it well. Only too well.

Even through the lens of anger and confusion, he looked ridiculously hot. Marla's knees felt as if they were buckling. *Seriously, get a grip, girl.*

'You,' he said.

'That's right. Me. You remember me? The girl whose castle you just bought. Partly,' she said, narrowing her eyes at him. 'We need to talk.'

He stepped aside, avoiding her eyes. 'Come in, if you must.'

'Yes, Niall. I must.'

She stepped inside. Barclay was there to greet her, and she wouldn't let anything stop her from fluffing her furry friend's ears, however briefly. She crouched and took the opportunity to survey Niall's abode. Living area with an open kitchen. Polished hardwood floors. A large wooden dining table, a cracked and faded leather chair in front of a small wood burner, whitewashed walls, some bookshelves. Also, a few doors. One was partially open, allowing a glimpse of what appeared to be his bedroom. The cottage's most stunning feature, though, was an entire wall made of glass. It was a simple, tasteful blend of rustic and modern. Inviting. And so clearly meant for one person.

'Christ, it smells like a bear's den in here.' As she got up, she noticed a pile of unfolded laundry on the leather chair.

He shrugged. 'Perhaps I *am* a bear.'

'I'm not Sir David Attenborough, but I believe bears don't sell their land to become silent investors in their arch enemy's castle business without so much as uttering a word.'

'Dramatic much? You're not my arch enemy, Marla.'

'Oh, no?'

He scoffed. 'How ld are you—seven? And how do you even—?'

Marla felt her blo boil. 'I've never met anyone as arrogant and secretive ar .. vexing as you.' Through the clouds of her disgruntlemer a less disgruntled part of her became uncomfortably awar f his bare, toned chest and muscular arms. 'And why, pr tell, are you prancing around half-naked in the middle he day?'

'I live here. It's m day off,' he said dryly. 'But give me a second. I'm going to ut a shirt on so you can calm down.' Niall went into the be oom.

Calm down? M a didn't want to calm down. But perhaps she needed A little at least. For several reasons. While she waited for m to return to the kitchen, she spotted a neglected potted p it on the windowsill. She reached out and removed the dea eaves, stuffing them into her pocket.

'So, I believe you ve questions?' Niall asked as he came back and walked up his kitchen counter, now wearing a tartan flannel shirt.

'I know you sol part of your land and invested in Hazelbrae.'

'Aye, I did. But n you'll also know that you weren't supposed to know.' e stirred a cup before taking a sip. 'Shite, that's cold. Do u want fresh coffee?'

'What? I'm not for coffee!' she blustered. 'But yes, please. That would lovely. Sip of milk, no sugar.' She seized Gordon's knif n the pocket of her jeans. 'Is the deal null and void now?'

'No, Marla. It's t.' Niall still hadn't looked at her. 'Unless you wish it to . So how *did* you find out?'

'You could've... y didn't you want me to know?' she asked quietly.

He shook his hea 'It's not polite to answer a question with another questio Has nobody ever told you that?'

Marla folded her ms. 'I figured it out. Wasn't that hard.

When Gwen confirmed that you suddenly sold a piece of your land—it was the talk of the town—and Collins told me he had spontaneously found a silent investor, I had my suspicions.' She pursed her lips. 'Then I saw the signature on the document. I wasn't supposed to, but Collins' office is a mess. The opportunity appeared. It was all there. What can I say? I recognised one of the signatures.'

Now he looked at her. 'Oh, right,' he said in a flat tone.

'Seems that your Machiavellian side might need a bit more training.'

Niall said nothing. He turned back around and filled the coffee machine with beans. Marla, however, wasn't prepared to let go. 'Didn't you tell me you wanted to sell everything, all of your land at once, to a developer because you were saving for a yacht or something? Because you couldn't wait to get away from here?'

He turned half around to her, his head hanging low. 'Aye. Wanted to. For years. But if you'd listened closely, you would know that I changed my mind.' Niall walked over to the sink, turned on the water, and splashed it on his face.

'Did you, though? All I remember is you sitting in the mud, talking about *feelings*.'

'Don't mock me to lash out, Marla. That's low. No need for that.'

Scathing shame flared up in her chest. He was right. 'I didn't mean to be mean.' Or maybe she did. Maybe she wanted to hurt him as he had hurt her. An eye for an eye, that sort of thing. Low? Yes, very. But understandable.

No, that was her old defensiveness.

While the coffee brewed and neither of them spoke, Marla noticed the green and white mug of a football club in the cabinet. She took it out, examining the cracks. It was an old piece, chipped and stained. 'Scottish Cup Winners—season 1987-1988.' She didn't take him for the sentimental type.

'Belonged to my a.' His tone made it clear that he'd rather not go into fur r detail.

Marla put it bac before she said, 'Correct me if I'm wrong, but you gav up your dream of selling your land, buying a boat, and g ng the hell out of here all just so that I don't have to give up azelbrae?'

'That's right.' Ni poured the coffee into mismatched mugs, spilling a bit to the table. Two tiny coffee puddles converged into a littl rown loch.

Marla and Niall s down, and she was even more baffled than before. 'But that nsane!'

'Possibly.' Barclay proached Niall and rested its head on his lap.

'Sorry, but it does t add up.' Marla gripped the knife in her pocket. 'Why do u even care?'

'I have my reason

'No. No, not goo nough.' Marla said. 'Why did you do it? Tell me. Please, I n d to know.'

Niall averted his ze. 'I guess I couldn't stand seeing you lose your home. Not er you put so much work and money into it.' He traced hi ingers along the grain of the wooden surface around the fee loch. 'And compared to me, you truly seem to like it h .'

They both took a . The warmth spread through Marla's body. It was soothing

'Guess what it co s down to is…' He paused and stared into his mug. 'I didn' ant you to leave.'

'I don't understan she said.

He sighed. 'It did feel right. The thought… This whole place wouldn't feel ri t without you.'

'I still don't see y you… What does that have to do with anything?' Gest lating, Marla knocked over her coffee cup. The brown liqui lowed towards a pile of papers on the table. 'Oops. Shit, I sorry!' she said and lifted the pile hastily. A bunch of loose note paper fell out, floating to the floor.

They were doodles. Drawings.

Drawings of… her?

Marla's heart rapped against her ribs as she picked up the papers in slow motion, studying each one closely.

A sketch of her standing on an oak tree branch, desperately hugging the tree trunk.

She in her unicorn robe, resting on the ottoman, peacefully sipping coffee with a half-curved smile.

A close-up portrait of her face with a serious, heavy expression, looking out into the distance, oozing all-encompassing, life-devouring sadness.

She was stunned speechless. He had captured her essence in each sketch. Viewing herself through Niall's eyes made her feel strangely seen. Recognised. It felt like being caught. He had looked at her. Closely. Intimately. All of a sudden, there was no more room for ire and posturing. Something else entirely had opened up, and it took her breath away. 'Niall… what is this? Why did you draw these?' she whispered.

'Are you seriously that slow, or are you taunting me on purpose?' He looked at her, his face a grimace of anguish. 'Because I'm in love with you. Dammit!' He had blurted the words out, but out they were. There was no stopping him now. 'I loved you from the moment you jumped at me in the forest. Took me a while, aye. But there it is!' He was yelling now, unable to contain his emotions. Barclay, sensing the tension, whined. 'And I'm terrified, okay? You terrify me! Do you know that?'

She did not.

The shock of what he had said rippled through her body, followed by a wave of anxiety. But it wasn't him that scared her. It was herself. 'You have a weird way of showing all that,' she mumbled.

He lowered his head again. 'I thought I ruined it—'

'You walked awa

'And yet I still di t want you to leave. Nor do *I* want to leave. I want to stay. the off chance of bumping into you in the pub. In the fores n a mud puddle. Or at the supermarket.' He scoffed. Hur ckered across his face. 'It's stupid and ridiculous. But in spi of everything, I still want to be here. In case you ever need s eone to catch you.'

Marla let go of th ocket knife.

He continued, hi oice hoarse. 'I think about you from the second I wake u I fall asleep. It's annoying. I'm pining for you like a teena .' He held his mug with both hands now, his knuckles w . 'You make me laugh. You make me mad. And yes, you ke me randy. I didn't know there was any of that left in me ou made me feel joy again. Joy, Marla! You brought me back om a deep, vast darkness I didn't even realise I was in. You rought me back to life. Just by being here. By being you. at's why I didn't want you to leave. That's the truth.' His est was heaving.

Single sunbeams ut through the thick clouds and streamed into the age through the oversized window pane. Inside Marl an all-consuming, vibrating hum emanated from he heart, like waves of warmth, like sunshine.

'Say something. P se, Marla.'

She wanted to, d perately, but the words were slipping through her mind, ne r reaching her lips.

'If you don't feel thing for me, if you can't forgive me,' he pleaded, 'then I p nise to leave you alone. If you wish, I will never speak to u again. But I need to know. Did I imagine it?'

Finally, after wh seemed like a hundred years, she looked up at him at l and whispered, 'You did not.'

'Did not what?'

'Imagine it,' she with a lump in her throat. 'But how

can I trust you, Niall? Your track record in that department isn't exactly stellar.'

'Fair enough. I made a mistake.'

'Yes. Yes, you did. That was the worst thing, turning around and leaving me like that.'

'I know. God, I know. And I deeply regret it. A thousand million times. I promise I'll do better.' He looked at her. 'But I guess ultimately you won't find out until you try.'

She saw him. Truly saw him. Sitting there, hands shaking. Looking at her with his head bowed, a strand of his hair falling over his left eye. Breathing heavily, his face etched with regret and pain and uncertainty.

'I wasn't fair to you', she said. 'I should've listened. I behaved like a defiant, silly child. My mistake. I'm not proud of it.' With that, Marla pushed aside her fears, her doubts and gathered her remaining courage. In her pocket, she felt the calming weight of her grandda's knife.

And then she jumped again.

'It really is annoying, you know.' Marla moved next to him on the bench and took his hand.

'What is?' he asked.

'This thinking about someone all the time thing. The pining.'

He looked stunned. 'What… Do you mean—?'

'You daftie.' She smiled despite the numb weakness in her limbs. 'I admit to having *feelings* for you, too.'

'I thought the only feeling you'd have for me now is disdain,' he mumbled, his thumb stroking her palm. 'Wouldn't blame you for it.'

'Niall, can't you see?' She heard the anguish in her own voice. 'I'm even more terrified than you. So fucking terrified.'

He cocked an eyebrow. 'Impossible.'

'Try me!'

They looked at each other with open hearts, open wounds.

It was as though thei uls made a pact—and then both began to laugh with relief, nished by joy. For a timeless moment, they sat side by side i ilence. Holding hands and breathing in sync. Barclay, sensing e shift in energy, curled up at their feet.

'I guess we both broken people,' Marla stated after a while.

'I guess you coul y that.'

'It's not going to easy, considering our pasts and all that.'

'No. It's not,' he s . 'But that's okay. We'll figure it out.'

Looking across t room, Marla saw a framed photo of Niall and another w an on the wall, slightly crooked. She got up and straight d it. 'Speaking of the past., Is that Nathalie?'

'It is, aye.'

'She is beautiful, e looks classy and also warm,' Marla said. 'I want you to ow something, Niall. It's important,' she said earnestly. 'Y can always talk about her if you wish. Share your memorie want to honour them with you. She's part of your life's sto Part of you.' She saw how his expression changed. His fe res mellowed, shedding the last of its armour. 'You don't h e to, of course. Not if it hurts. I don't want to pry, ever. Bu ou always can. Never think you can't. Okay?'

'Okay. Thank you His eyes were glistening. 'Thank you. Truly.' He took a de breath and added quietly: 'Nathalie loved crossword pu es. And black pudding for breakfast. And Greek mytholo She was so smart. Funny, too. And beautiful.'

Marla smiled. 'I see that. She seems like the kind of woman who wakes p with smudged eyeliner after two hours of sleep, throw n your shirt from last night and looks ready to be on the co of Vogue.'

'You're not wron ere.' Now he smiled, too. 'We met in the library at St. And vs. She was cool. Way too cool for me.'

He ran his hand through his hair. 'To this day, I still don't understand why she married me. But she wanted to. She proposed to me. And I wasn't even pregnant.'

Marla let out a short laugh. It was new and good that he would speak like this. Relieved, liberated. 'Silly lad. Were you happy? You certainly look like you were.'

'I think so, yes. At least I was.' He paused. 'If I'm honest, I'm not sure if she was ever truly happy here.'

'Why do you think that?' Marla asked.

'She missed France. Paris, her home. She never said so, but I could tell sometimes. Kilcranach wasn't the right place for her. Good people, but little going on. Too little. I think she stayed here because of me.'

She could see his eyes clouding now. 'I'm sorry, Niall. I am. Neither of you deserved that. Do you miss her?'

'Sometimes, yes. It's not as gruesome and all-consuming as it was during the first two years. But yeah. I'll always miss her. I'll always love her.'

'Come here.' Marla stepped towards him, took both his rough hands in hers, and pulled him up. 'That's okay, Niall. So very okay. I know how it feels. I know grief. It almost consumed me. I had given up, too.'

He gently squeezed her hands. 'Oh, love. Of course, you do.'

'Someone once said something helpful to me. "A loving relationship you had with someone for many years is not defined by their death, but by all the years that came before." It helped me. Perhaps it helps you, too.' Marla saw how he swallowed and tears filled his eyes.

'Thank you.'

Right there and then, her heart melted completely, instantly, and forever. A snowflake on a stove.

She stepped toward him, took his face in both hands, and kissed him like she would never let go. Because she wouldn't. Not this time. Not again.

His lips were shy t first. But then he wrapped his arms around her and kiss her, kissed with a need that took her breath away. Just w n Marla began to see sparkling little stars behind her clo eyelids, he released his mouth from hers and lifted her ch with his finger. 'Marla, my darlin'… I wasn't looking to fall love. What are we doing next? I don't know where to go om here,' he said, raw and a little breathless.

Her voice was de as she replied, 'I have an idea.' And then she led him thro h the bedroom door.

Chapter Twenty-Four

The curtains were closed, his bed was unmade, sheets and blankets in disarray. His tartan pyjama trousers and random band t-shirts lay scattered across the floor. An empty plate with toast crumbs stood on the side table, surrounded by three half-empty glasses. Niall should have been at least a little embarrassed by the state of it—the messy room of a miserable man—but felt nothing of the sort. Not with her here.

And it didn't matter, anyway. Because he wasn't that man, he wasn't miserable anymore.

On the contrary.

He was… happy?

Marla unbuttoned his flannel shirt until it hung open, revealing his chest. She ran her hands along his contours, as if she were trying to memorise every inch of him. He closed his eyes. Her fingertips prickled on his skin, like licking flames, as she stroked through the curls on his chest.

'Now that I'm looking at you… maybe you *are* a bear after all.' He noticed the teasing smile in her voice, and it made him giddy.

Marla's joyful sensuality amazed him as much as her

kindness. The way sl had made space for Nathalie as a part of his story, his life, nself. That she didn't shy away from saying her name, dic t look at him with pity. Marla made it all okay, taking awa he coiling grief and guilt. Being with her was like switchi on a light to make all the monsters disappear. Niall felt ure love for the woman. His heart expanded as though chest was about to explode, and that was all right with hir

'Tell me… what d ou want?' Marla whispered in his ear. His desire rose, came ive, stirring behind his navel. Untame-able need for her sur through him. Again. And not just for her body.

'You. All of you he replied, each word loaded with emotion, his heart nding against his ribs. He couldn't think, he couldn't re t. He didn't want to. Niall was aware that once those wor crossed over his lips, there was no going back. Not only him, but for Marla, too. 'If we do this now, this is it. With u There was a warning plea in his voice. 'You'll have to put with me. I'm not going anywhere. I mean it.'

'I hope so. Becau neither am I.' The hot wave of her breath brushed along is neck like a feather. 'That's why I'm doing *this*,' she adde easingly and slid her hands down his back, underneath th vaistband of his trousers and boxers, and pushed them bc down swiftly. He sucked in a breath as he was being s pped bare—exposed emotionally as much as physically- front of her. Her pupils were dark and huge as she re hed out to touch him. He couldn't believe how much h vanted her. And that she still wanted him, too.

'Oh, crap,' she sai Do you have protection?'

'Shite. Afraid not. iall's pulse palpitated in his veins.

Marla sighed, he disappointment echoing through the small room. His han ramed her chin. 'I don't exactly live a Mick Jagger lifestyle.

'And I'm out of pub-giveaways. Damn. I guess we'll have to wait then.'

'I mean there *are* other ways, you know. If you're into it.' His hand moved to her waist, pulling her body so close that there was no air between them. He grazed his mouth against hers, teasing her upper lip with the flicking tip of his tongue. A preview of what was to come.

Or rather, who.

Her mouth curved into a wry smile. 'So, is that what you're thinking?'

'Oh, aye. I might be rusty, but I remember how it's done.'

'Do you now? I think I shall be the judge of that,' she murmured against his lips.

He nuzzled her neck, eliciting a little sigh from her. She turned to the side, kicked her boots into the corner, and hurried to peel herself out of her jeans. Niall grinned.

Impossible woman!

But he couldn't blame her.

Because he, too, couldn't wait.

It had already been too long. Way too long.

He slid her striped t-shirt up and over her head. His fingertips passed over her neck and shoulders, down her back, her delicate hairs rising under his touch. His senses heightened with each moment, taking in the infatuating fragrance in the crook of her neck and the way her body reacted to his touch. He managed to unfasten her bra as if he had done nothing else for a single day in his entire life. *I guess it really is like playing guitar,* he thought with a sense of relief. She shivered as his hands cupped and caressed her breasts, so soft, so warm, so heavy in his palms. Her skin was smooth, a touch of sweat shimmered on her like a fine patina. Niall wanted to give her the pleasure she deserved. But he was determined to take his time, to relish every bit.

Anticipating what was going to happen next, she let herself fall backwards onto his unmade bed, into the pillows where he had spent endless sleepless nights. Thinking of her. Dreaming of this. Of her in his bedroom, wanting him, offering and demanding, sweet and irresistible. Niall leaned down towards Marla, smiling and nudging the tip of her nose with his. 'Can't wait, can you now?'

Smiling back at him, she shook her head. 'Stop talking.'

He covered her curves with kisses. Now that she was with him, they had plenty of time to get to know each other. All of each other. Every mole, every scar, every dimple, every wrinkle.

Niall felt Marla's nails digging into his shoulders as he moved lower, letting his tongue travel towards her navel, over her belly and further down. With tender intent, he painted invisible lines on the inside of her thighs, kissing the back of her knees. The tip of his tongue licked her skin and she let out a moan. Oh, that sound! He wanted to hear it again and again and again until the day he died.

Ever so slowly, he peeled her out of the last bit of fabric that was in his way. Inch by inch, prolonging the delicious agony.

And there she was, unabashed and uninhibited. A goddess. He marvelled at her unique and wonderful vulva. Delicate strands of glistening purple satin folded and curled between luscious labia. A dazzling forest of valleys and ridges that begged to be explored. He hadn't given himself enough time during their first encounter, when he had been swept away by his blind need—before he had even grasped what was going on.

Not now, though. Now he understood.

And he wanted to savour everything.

She was already visibly longing for him. Her captivating, earthy scent, a perfect symphony of pheromones, was driving him wild. It took all his strength to hold back, but he wanted to enjoy her joy. Maybe even make up for everything. And a part of him yearned to see how far he could push her. To experience the depths of her passion, which he had merely got a glimpse of.

His tongue moved slowly as he tasted her in gentle circles. Her tangy sweetness cascaded over his tongue, a blend of salty honey and musk that he couldn't get enough of. Marla gasped with delight, her fingers playing with his hair. He lifted his head. Seeing her unravel, trusting him… filled him with pride and gratitude.

'Do you want me to stop? I can if you want me to.'

'Don't you dare!'

He moved his tongue, humming and flicking, steering her pleasure, changing his rhythm. Alert to each sigh, to the tiniest of her movements. His hands rested on the insides of her thighs, her flesh warm beneath his palms. Hoarse moans poured from her lips as she rolled against him. Unrestrained, purely herself. Her reactions sent a searing thrill through his body. Giving her a moment to let the waves ebb away, just a little, he looked up at her again. 'I need to know you're mine,' he rasped, barely still master of his senses. 'Say you're mine.'

'I'm yours, Niall… Yes… always…' He could feel her surrender to his words. But he wanted more. He wanted—he needed—her to come undone completely. 'Touch yourself again,' he whispered, 'like you did before.' She moved her hand down and began to pet herself. The strokes of his tongue were in perfect synchrony with the rhythm of her fingers. She was getting closer now. He could tell from the way she was trembling, the way her breathing became faster and shorter, the way she moved her hips in minuscule circles. 'Let go, I got you,' he murmured. Her left hand was grabbing the back of his head, pushing him deeper, and he upped the pace and pressure. 'Oooh, yes, please… yes… Holy SHIT!' He didn't stop, not for a second, and she came powerfully as she released herself to him. His mouth was full of her, his breath caught in his throat. His hands held her hips steady while her whole body quivered against him and she let out a last deep, satisfied sigh.

Niall felt like the happiest and humblest man on earth. This was a wild woman, and she was with him.

Marla lay on his bed, exhaling gustily, spent and exhausted, her hand still on his neck, his head resting on her thigh. When she raised her upper body and looked at him, her hair a wild mess around her face and her silver eyes filled with tenderness, he knew he wasn't alone in the world anymore.

Then she tilted her head and said with a husky voice, 'Come up here. It's your turn.'

Eons later they lay entangled in the sheets, panting. After she had driven him to the verge of fainting again and again and he had cursed and prayed and yelled her name more desperately than he had ever thought possible, Marla now rested astride him. Both of them exhausted and content. Her long hair was weaving a cosy tent around him, capturing the sweaty heat of their settling bodies, skin on skin. These bodies that knew so much more than their minds, that could so effortlessly speak to each other before words were even formed. He wrapped his arms around her. She clung to him as he to her, their hearts beating in unison. Niall was at peace, safe. Something flowed out of his chest, filling the cocoon they were forming.

For the first time in ages, he was at home. Anchored.

Marla lowered her head for a kiss. She tasted like him, just as he tasted like her. That was what it was going to be like from now on. He laughed softly into her shoulder. 'You are sensational.'

'I agree,' she said. 'And, well, right back at ya.'

'Still cocky as ever, hm? Did I not make you tired, woman?'

'You did,' she said. 'And I think we should repeat that some time.'

'I was hoping you'd say that.' He grinned and then playfully bit her lower lip. 'What about later today? And tomorrow? And the day after tomorrow?' He flipped her around and gazed into her eyes as she lay on her back. 'And the day after that? Because I love you, Marla. I do,' he added in a lower tone. 'I still can't believe I found you in that tree. That you're here with me, despite everything. And I'm never going to give you up. Ever again.'

She beamed. 'As long as you also never let me down...'

'Well, what I can promise you,' he said and kissed her on the forehead, 'is that I'm never going to make you cry. Nor will I say goodbye. Let alone hurt you.'

Marla laughed so hard that she could scarcely breathe and let out an unbecoming grunt. This was *her* human, with no shadow of a doubt.

It wasn't that he set her whole body alight with a single touch, that he could make her come so fiercely and make her laugh so easily. That he was there when she needed him most. Be it an emotional breakdown in moments of doubt, a broken pipe, or a leaky castle roof. Nor that he challenged her or infuriated her all the time. Which he did.

That was a part, but not all of it. Not by a long shot.

Marla had thought that her heart was gone forever, shattered into a million pieces of dust. She had been certain it would never be mended. That it was dead, destroyed and obliterated by the pain of loss. Her mum, her dad, any boyfriend she'd ever had, her grandparents. Too much hurt for one person and one life. She thought that all was ash forever.

Yet she had never felt more alive, safe, and free than she did now. She could even breathe easier. To her, this was a miracle. She could be herself with him. Weak and strong. Sexy and silly. Vulnerable and invincible. All at the same time.

He was the right kind of weird and broken to match hers.

With him, she could conquer anything that life threw at her even better than alone. Bills, leaks, troubles… and yes, perhaps even more grief and loss.

Would it all be smooth sailing from here? Most certainly not. That would be an unrealistic expectation. They both had their wounds and baggage. But Marla saw now that the smooth part wasn't what mattered. Not even the sailing so much.

It was who you sailed with.

Without her having noticed it, Niall had become her solid wooden drawer with a cosy velvet lining.

She let out a happy, satisfied sigh. With both hands she stroked the thick, unruly strands of tousled chestnut hair from her Scot's brow and stared straight into his beautifully scarred soul, from one wounded heart to another. 'You're reasonably clever, so you might have guessed it. But to be crystal clear, I love you, too.'

Epilogue

The snow fell in flurries outside, like millions of tiny stars glittering against the dim morning sky. A small potted Christmas tree stood in the corner of Niall's cottage. Marla had aptly christened it 'Bambi II' and draped it in miniature twinkling lights. Crystals of ice frosted the windows, catching the light from the tree. But the crisp white blanket that covered Kilcranach in clean calmness wouldn't last.

Fortunately, the same could not be said of their love.

Almost one year.

Marla smiled and bliss spread through her body as she stood at the window next to Barclay, content in his holiday collar.

Not just because it was Christmas morning.

She had stayed in Scotland. And so had Niall. As a team, they had finished the work on the castle and fulfilled Marla's vision. Three months ago, Hazelbrae House had opened as a recovery centre for NHS personnel and a bed-and-breakfast. It was then that Marla had moved into the cottage. To separate work and life.

But also, to be with him. Every day and, almost as important, every night.

Like she had predicted, it hadn't always been easy. They had fights, they had misunderstandings, and now and then, one of their old wounds would get the better of them. But they worked through it instead of running away. Together. No matter how challenging, they always reached out to each other, held onto each other, through the depths of their emotional pain. It had made them stronger. Against all odds, they had found the wholeness of love. Joy, laughter, happiness. It wasn't that they were completing each other. Each of them was their own whole person. Yet together, they were more than two single souls.

Peace filled Marla's heart. An inner balance had settled within her. She was content and not afraid to jinx anything.

Right then, she felt a pair of strong arms wrap around her from behind. 'Good morrow,' he said and nuzzled her neck. 'Merry Christmas.'

She spun around to embrace him. 'Good morrow, sexy Grinch.'

The smile he slanted her was full of promise, with an undeniable trace of mischief. 'Hey, I'm simply wearing the pyjamas you wanted me to wear. I thought it was part of an elaborate role play.' He kissed the corner of her mouth. 'Me, the Grinch. You, the seductive Christmas elf who's determined to convince him otherwise…'

She laughed and kissed the tip of his nose. 'Daftie. It's part of the overall Christmas vibe.'

Niall had lit a fire which crackled and hissed, filling the room with a hint of smoke. It reminded Marla of the cosy fires at her grandparent's house. The thought of them was shrouded in profound gratitude and love, with only a drop of sadness.

They would have liked him.

'Marla, my hot little elf,' he said, positioning himself on

the bench with his guitar. 'I have a Christmas gift for you. I hope you don't find it too weird. Or cringeworthy.'

'I won't form a folk duo with you, if that's what you're after.'

His face was earnest. 'Trying to be brave here. Don't laugh. Promise?'

She grinned. 'Zero clue what's happening right now, but all right. I promise.'

He lowered his head and soon enough, the sound of his guitar and his voice filled the cottage.

I was fine before you
Came into my life
Cracking me open
Getting me hopin'
Twisting like a knife
In my broken heart

I was fine before you
Set my heart on fire
Breaking my walls down
Not letting my calls drown
Lifting my soul higher
Out of my misery

And I ran away
Didn't want you to stay
Didn't know what to say
Gave it all away
It was almost too late…

. . .

You were a force of life
    That I couldn't resist
    From the very first kiss
    This was everything
    We were everything

Because I wasn't fine before you
    Brought me back to life
    Mended my heart
    Right from the start
    I never felt so alive
    I really wasn't fine before you

When the last chord faded into silence, he chewed on his bottom lip, waiting for her response. Tears welled up in Marla's eyes. 'Oh, you absolute arse! That's the most beautiful gift anyone has ever given me,' she said. 'And all I have for you in return is my puffy snot monster face.' She wiped her eyes with both hands.

'I love you, my puffy snot monster. I will love you till your whisky-brown hair turns grey and all the years we have spent together show on your face.'

'Even though I put my icy feet between your legs every night?' she asked.

'Especially because of that.'

'A sign of true love. But I also *do* have an actual gift for you,' she added with a shy smile, and retrieved a tiny package with a red bow from behind one of the armchair cushions.

'It's heavier than it looks,' he said and furrowed his brow.

Marla clapped into her hands. 'Go on, open it!'

After slowly unfastening the bow and every single bit of Scotch tape, just to tease her, he saw what it was.

A small pocket knife with a red handle.

'It belonged to my grandda,' she said quietly. 'And I don't need it anymore. But you might, when you're in the forest.'

His complexion took on a rich pink, clashing with the russet of his short facial hair. 'I know what it is. Marla, I can't—'

'Shush,' she said. 'I want you to have it. It's a talisman and will protect you. From stoats and fairies and bears.'

'There are no bears in Scotland.'

'Oh, I know at least of one. A rather growly specimen.' Marla smiled. 'Plays the guitar and is really good in bed.'

She settled on his lap, and they held each other in silence, breathing in perfect synchronicity. She in her elf jammies, he in his Grinch pyjamas.

While all around them the cottage vibrated with holiday love, nearly enough to make the air twinkle, Marla gazed into his amber eyes. She saw their past, their present, and their future. It was all there.

Niall played with her tousled morning hair. 'Thank you.'

She kissed his forehead. 'Are you going to play with Jack and the band later?'

To everyone's astonishment, the Salmons of Knowledge had reunited for Hazelbrae's opening. Since then, they had been experiencing a revival, even becoming mildly popular with the locals.

'Aye, that's the plan. Small gig at the pub. For anyone who needs to get away from their family, before murder and mayhem ensue. Do you want to come?' He nibbled on her earlobe. 'Mmm… cause you're my favourite groupie.'

'Oh, groupies is it now! Are you adopting Mick Jagger's lifestyle, after all?' She chortled. 'But yeah, I will. After I check on the house.'

Hazelbrae was closed for the holidays, but Marla still felt the urge to look after the castle at least once a day.

Her castle.

It stood proudly on the hill, restored to its former grandeur. The thick sandstone walls were clean, the ivy tamed, there were new shutters and bright panes in its many mullioned windows. The once dilapidated grand house seemed vibrant, alive, and beloved. And it was. The weight of over two hundred years of legacy was not weighing it down anymore. It was supported by it, surrounded by it. Hazelbrae was magnificent again, and it appeared as if it was ready to take on anything that came its way.

So was Marla.

THE END

Would you like to listen to Niall's song for Marla? Sign up for updates on book 2 in the 'Escape to Scotland'-series and get the audio here: beatricebradshaw.com/nialls-song

Thank you so much for reading. If you enjoyed the story, it would be truly lovely if you could take a minute to leave an honest review on Amazon: tinyurl.com/winterhighlands

Don't worry, it doesn't have to be long! But it helps a lot, and I'd be eternally grateful. <3

Glossary

- awfy = awfully
- burn = a brook
- braw = great, beautiful
- Ceilidh = Scottish country dance in groups and pairs
- Cranachan = dessert
- daft = silly, foolish stupid
- dinna hing the lugs = don't be crestfallen, don't mope
- Ecclefechan = nut cake
- going for messages = running errands/ doing shopping
- gonnae = going to
- Haud yer wheesht = hold your tongue/ shut up and listen
- Mony words, muckle drouth = many words, large drought (in your mouth)
- Naw = no
- Nae = no/ not
- Hogmanay = New Year's Eve
- outwith = beyond

- a splorroch = the sound made by walking in water or mud, a squelching sound
- Whit's fur ye'll no go by ye = whatever is meant to happen, will happen

Resource: Dictionary of the Scottish Language https://dsl.ac.uk/

About the Author

Beatrice Bradshaw writes small-town contemporary romances set in Scotland with a bit of heat.

Scottish Historian and German journalist/ translator by day and romance author by night, she has escaped from Berlin to Scotland five years ago. And not looked back once.

Beatrice Bradshaw is the pen name/ pseudonym of Jessica Beatrice Wagener—chosen so as not to have German narrative non-fiction confused with her (English) romance books.

She enjoys sharing her love for her adopted home country with others, bringing a sprinkle of the real Scotland into her books. When she isn't glued to her desk in Glasgow, surrounded by baked goods and coffee, she can be found wandering around in Scottish castles and landscapes, finding peace and stories on cemeteries and in old buildings, or binge-watching romance series online.

Love in the Scottish Winter Highlands is her first romance novel, the second book is already in the making!

Connect with Beatrice here:

instagram.com/beatricebradshawauthor
facebook.com/beatricebradshawauthor
www.beatricebradshaw.com

Love in the Scottish Winter Highlands
By Beatrice Bradshaw

First published in the UK by Jessica B. Wagener under the pen name Beatrice Bradshaw 2023.

Suite 624
Claymore House
145-149 Kilmarnock Road
Glasgow, G41 3JA

Editing: Michelle Hazen

Cover design: Hellie Cory

Proofreading: Micki McNie

Print ISBN: 978-1-7395568-1-5
Ebook Edition © October 2023
ISBN: 978-1-7395568-0-8
Version: 2023-10-28

Printed in Great Britain
by Amazon

30903133R00137